SERIOUS TROUBLE

By
Alex McAnders

McAnders Books

*****

The characters and events in this book are fictitious. Any similarity to real persons, living or dead, is coincidental and not intended by the author. The person or people depicted on the cover are models and are in no way associated with the creation, content, or subject matter of this book.

All rights reserved. No part of this book may be reproduced in any form or by any electronic or mechanical means, including information storage and retrieval systems, without permission in writing from the publisher, except by a reviewer who may quote brief passages in a review. For information contact the publisher at: McAndersPublishing@gmail.com.

Copyright © 2021

Get 6 FREE ebooks and an audiobook by signing up for Alex Anders' mailing list at: AlexAndersBooks.com
Official Website: www.AlexAndersBooks.com
YouTube Channel: Bisexual Real Talk
Podcast: www.SoundsEroticPodcast.com
Visit Alex Anders at: Facebook.com/AlexAndersBooks & Instagram

Published by McAnders Publishing

Titles by Alex McAnders

MMF Bisexual Romance

Searing Heet: The Copier Room; Hurricane Laine; Book 2; Book 3; Book 4; Book 5; Book 6

*****

M/M Romance

Serious Trouble

*****

Titles by A. Anders

MMF Bisexual Erotica

While My Family Sleeps; Book 2; Book 3; Book 4; Book 1-4
Book 2
My Boyfriend's Twin; Book 2
My Boyfriend's Dominating Dad; Book 2

MMF Bisexual Romance

Until Your Toes Curl: Prequels; Book 2; Book 3; Until Your Toes Curl
The Muse: Prequel; The Muse
Rules For Spanking
Island Candy: Prequel & Audiobook; Island Candy & Audiobook; Book 2; Book 2
In The Moonlight: Prequel; In The Moonlight & Audiobook
Aladdin's First Time; Her Two Wishes & Audiobook; Book 2 & Audiobook
Her Two Beasts

Her Red Hood
Her Best Bad Decision
Bittersweet: Prequel; Bittersweet
Before He Was Famous: Prequel; Before He Was Famous
Beauty and Two Beasts
Bane: Prequel & Audiobook; Bane & Audiobook
Bad Boys Finish Last
Aladdin's Jasmine
20 Sizzling MMF Bisexual Romances

M/M Erotic Romance

Their First Time
Aladdin's First Time; Her Two Wishes & Audiobook; Book 2 & Audiobook

Bisexual-Friendly Suspense

The Last Choice; Dying for the Rose
It Runs

Romantic Suspense

Ford Stone: Prequel; Ford Stone

SERIOUS TROUBLE

Chapter 1

Quin

I can't believe Lou talked me into doing this. At one point he's talking about how my dick will fall off if I don't use it and the next thing I know I'm yelling at him about how that's not what college is supposed to be about. He then tells me that that is exactly what college was supposed to be about. And, what is even worse is that he was right, at least for me.

It took a long time for me to decide to go to college. It's not that I didn't believe in higher education. I'm all about it. It's that I didn't go to a traditional high school. At our school, we explored our interests, devoured it like a box of Oreos, and then hosted a class where we taught it to those who weren't as passionate about the topic.

Whenever I explain it to others, they can't wrap their head around it. But at my school, it worked. Mine was a special school for kids who caught on very quickly and I was their first graduate. By the time I was 18 I had the equivalent of advanced degrees in multiple subjects, so what would going to college get me?

After I graduated high school, I stuck around teaching classes and acted as an assistant principal. And the year after that, I traveled. I spent a couple of weeks in Africa and Asia and then finished off my trip backpacking through Europe.

The trip helped put things in perspective. Yeah, I had a lot of theoretical information on a lot of topics. But, at its peak enrollment, my high school had only 50 students. More than that, they were all like me. We all learned information quickly and we all came from the same New York penthouse background.

I was smart enough to figure out that there was more to life than that. Yes, the three months I spent traveling the world gave me some perspective. But the perspective was that I didn't know anything about the things that mattered and that I wasn't good at human stuff.

I had never been in love. I had never had sex. I hadn't even had a best friend. And, I didn't know how to talk to people to get any of those things.

So, instead of thinking I could reinvent the wheel, I did what everyone else my age did, I found a school as different from my high school as I could and enrolled. There isn't anywhere more different to New York than Tennessee. And to contrast with the 50-foot high-rises and concrete jungle, I chose East Tennessee University where your walk through campus was practically a nature hike.

I then filled out my roommate compatibility questionnaire and got Lou, the gayest guy I have ever met in my life. That guy is boy crazy. I grew up with two dads and a mom and not even I knew how many guys there were who were into other guys. Lou could scan a room full of boys with their girlfriends and have a date in 20 minutes.

I was far from that. I was open to dating either guys or girls, yet I hadn't gotten a single person's number in the month I had been here. Lou claimed that it was because I never left our room. I told him that he was just trying to get me out so that he could bring guys back to our place. He said, "Of course," and then threw what I told him about the reason I was here in my face.

"You can't meet new people locked up in this room. And, as much as I love you, Quin, you're not going to get what you want from me. Don't get me wrong, you're as hot as hell and any guy… or girl, I guess, would be happy to get all up in what you have to offer.

"But, I would prefer to have at least one person I can talk to without things getting awkward because we've made out. And you're my roommate, so congratulations, that's you. Which means that the one place you spend every waking minute of your life is the only place you shouldn't be."

"I go to class," I countered.

"Ugh! Whatever. Look, you wanna prove that you didn't just come here to observe the common folk until your father gives you a Wall Street job and the family yacht? Then, I want you to march out those doors and have some fun, young man," he said pointing.

"Ouch, Lou!"

"If it isn't true then go do it. Mingle with the people."

"Stop it!"

"Prove me wrong! Don't just talk about wanting to have a life. Get a life."

"I will!" I said furious.

"Good!"

"Good!"

"And I want proof. When I get back here tonight, I want to see a naked guy — or girl — in that bed and I want to see some shame, mister. Plenty of it."

"There will be! There will be plenty of shame, for you. Because of how wrong you were... and stuff."

"Good."

"Good."

"I mean it, Quin."

"Me too."

So now, here I am marching across campus to the only party that my last-minute research turned up. East Tennessee University's football team won against West Tennessee University their cross-state rivals earlier in the day and the football fraternity was throwing a party. Nothing about any of that sounded fun, but I'm going... because Lou tricked me into it. So much for me being the smart one.

Fine. I'll go. I'll get proof that I was there. Then I'll go to a coffee shop and read a book on my phone.

I know he mentioned that thing about finding someone naked in my bed, but there's no way that's going to happen. I couldn't lose my virginity in a pool full of dicks. Believe me, I've tried. I don't know what it is about me that no one wants to be with, but no one does.

Besides, I tend to have a thing for older guys, and I'm not going to find that on a college campus. Unless I consider professors, and I'm not going there. Nope. It looks like I'll just have to spend the rest of my life as a sad, lonely virgin.

Did I just bum myself out? I think I did. Now I'm really not in the mood for a party.

Rounding the corner, I could hear the music before the fraternity house came into view. It was intimidating. I had to tap into my anger at what Lou had said to keep me going.

Face-to-face with my impending doom, I almost froze. I'm just not good at this stuff. There is no way I was going to be able to mingle or cohort or whatever it was that people my age did.

New plan. I wasn't going in. I would get my proof that I was here, though. I was going to walk up to one of the half dozen people standing outside, ask to take a selfie with them and then get out of there as quickly as I could.

Looking around, I saw people smoking, people talking in a circle with red cups, and one guy standing by himself. That made the selection easy. All I had to do was walk up to him, ask to take a selfie, snap it, thank him and go. I could manage that. I wasn't a complete freak. I could talk to one person.

Tightening my lips, I hardened my resolve and charged over. I wasn't going to overthink it. I was just going to do it and be done.

"Excuse me, can I get a selfie with you?" I asked the guy with his back to me.

"You want a selfie with me? Why?" The guy said with an edge to his voice as he turned around.

Woah!

Do you know that feeling when you see something that takes your breath away? Warm prickles start at the back of your hands and shoot up your arms before settling in your face as the heat makes you lightheaded? That was what happened when our eyes met. The guy was beautiful.

His creamy skin contrasted with his jet black hair and pool-blue eyes. His jawline was carved out of marble. There were dimples, so many dimples, in his cheeks, underneath his bottom lip, on the tip of his chin. They were everywhere.

More than that, he was big. He was inches taller than me and twice as wide. That isn't saying much considering how slight I am. But his rippling muscles looked like they had muscles. God, was he gorgeous.

I couldn't speak and he was clearly waiting for me to. He had asked me a question. What was it? Oh yeah! It was why I wanted a selfie with him, and he seemed upset about it.

Had I made him angry? Was it weird to ask to take a selfie with a complete stranger? It probably was? Shit! What the hell was I thinking?

"Sorry," I sputtered before forcing my legs to move in the opposite direction.

I got two steps away before he spoke again.

"Wait! Don't go."

I stopped.

"I'm sorry. I didn't mean to be rude. If you want a selfie, I'll take one with you."

"No, that's okay," I said wanting to look at him again but scared that if I did I wouldn't be able to breathe.

"No really. It's fine. You can get one. I don't know why anyone would want one. But, it's fine. I'd be happy to take one with you."

That was when I looked at him again. I recognized what he was saying. He was talking like a guy who was used to people asking to take pictures with him. I knew a little about that. That was in part why I chose a university in the middle of nowhere. I wanted to be where I wouldn't be recognized as Quin Toro, the boy freak.

That was me, though. Why did people ask him for selfies? He was the most amazing-looking guy ever. Did random strangers approach him dazzled by his beauty? It wouldn't surprise me if they did.

"I, um, wasn't asking for a selfie because I know who you are. I don't recognize you. I don't know who you are," I explained.

The guy jutted his head back startled. As I stared, his fair skin turned pink.

"Oh! Okay. Then…" he shook his head as if trying to shake something loose. "I'm sorry, why do you want a selfie with me?"

"It wasn't you. It was anybody," I told him.

"You wanted to get a selfie with anybody? Why?"

I huffed as my predicament reentered my mind.

"It's my roommate. He told me that I needed to get out and have fun. He said he needed proof…"

"And the selfie was going to be the proof?"

"Yeah."

"So, after you took the selfie…, what? You were going to go?"

"Yeah."

The gorgeous guy looked at me like I was the freak that I am. A smile crept across his face. It would have made me feel bad about myself if it didn't make me want to melt into a puddle in the grass.

"This is going to sound crazy, but you're here. Why not go in and actually have fun?"

"I'm not good at this type of thing. You know, the social thing."

"Luckily, that's something I'm very good at. How about we make a deal? I'll give you your selfie as proof for your roommate, but you have to come in and actually try to have a good time. I'll introduce you to a couple of people. That way, when your roommate asks you about the night, you won't have to lie," he said his face exploding into dimples.

I stared at him. "Why would you do that?"

He looked at me twisting his head in confusion.

"Maybe I'm just being nice. Maybe I think you're a cool guy and that it would be cool to hang out. Maybe I'm flirting."

A chill shot through me upon hearing the word "flirting". What was going on? Did this guy like me? Was there something happening between us? Was there going to be a naked guy in my bed full of shame when Lou got home after all?

Wait, was I getting hard? I think I was. No, I definitely was.

"Um, okay," I said sure that I was turning beet-red.

"Cage, by the way?"

"What?"

"My name." He stared at me. "And your name is?"

"Oh. Quin."

"Cool. I like that name."

"Thanks. My parents gave it to me," I said losing control of my tongue.

Cage laughed.

"I mean, of course my parents gave it to me."

"Not of course. My parents didn't give me the name Cage."

"Who did? An uncle or somebody?"

"No, I did."

"So, what's your birth name?"

Cage looked at me with thoughts rushing through his head. "How about I take you inside and show you around?"

"So, I guess we're going to let that question go?"

Cage chuckled uncomfortably.

As he led me up the stairs, onto the porch, and then into the frat house, it was hard to take my eyes off of him. When I did I was surprised by what I saw. I didn't know what I was expecting, but it wasn't this. The large living room was sparsely furnished but full of people. Everyone had red cups in their hand and they spoke to each other like they were friends.

"It's still pretty early," Cage explained.

"What do you mean?" I said raising my voice over the country-pop music.

"There'll be more people later."

"More than this?" I asked looking around at what felt like a horde.

Cage chuckled. "Yeah."

"Damn. Okay."

"Cage!" A thick guy said throwing his arms around Cage spilling some of his drink onto Cage's shirt. "Oh, did I get you?"

"That's okay," Cage said casually. "Dan, this is Quin."

Dan turned to me and stared. "Quin!" he finally said removing the awkwardness. "Is he trying to recruit you?"

"What?" I asked confused.

"Is he trying to get you on the football team?"

I stared at him unsure what was happening. Was he being serious? I wasn't exactly built like a guy who ran full speed into 200-pound men.

"Football team?"

Dan turned to Cage confused.

"We play on the football team," Cage explained.

"You do?"

Dan threw his arms around Cage again. "Cage doesn't just play for the football team. He is the team."

I looked at Cage for an explanation.

He smiled with humility. "I'm the quarterback."

"This man isn't just the quarterback," Dan said mockingly. "He's the guy who is gonna lead us to a national championship, and then he's going pro."

"Ohhhh! Now I get it. The selfie. You thought I was asking for a selfie because you're a famous football player."

"I'm not a famous football player," he said quickly.

"Hell yeah, he's famous. There ain't anybody who doesn't know who he is," Dan said proudly.

I looked at Cage for his reaction. Cage looked back at me and chuckled uncomfortably.

"Not everyone knows who I am."

"Name me one person who doesn't," Dan challenged.

He gave me a knowing smile. "Quin, you want a drink? I think you need a drink. Follow me."

"Good meeting you, Quin," Dan said before wandering off.

"So, you're a quarterback?"

"Didn't you hear? I'm not just a quarterback, I'm the team," Cage said with self-deprecation.

I laughed. "I heard. Are you going to go pro? I have a couple of uncles who played in the NFL."

Cage looked back at me with surprise. "Do you?"

"Yeah. I mean, they're family friends. So, you know, "uncles"," I clarified.

"Did they like it?"

"Playing for the NFL?"

"Yeah."

"I guess so. You excited about getting drafted?"

"Sure," Cage said half-heartedly before turning to pump beer into two red cups.

"You don't sound excited."

"No. It's great. I can't wait for it. It's, ah, everything I've been working towards," he said handing me a cup and holding up his to cheers with mine. "To new friends."

I touched his cup and took a drink. "This beer is awful," I said looking down at my cup.

Cage laughed. "No, tell me what you really think."

"I mean that it's not very good," I explained.

Cage laughed louder. "You don't have much of a filter, do you?"

I froze. That wasn't the first time I had heard that. The previous time was with the last guy I fell for.

"I guess not. Is that bad?"

"Actually, it's kind of refreshing."

"Oh. Okay," I said falling for him more.

"You have a nice smile."

"I didn't realize I was smiling," I told him.

"You are," he said looking at me with a smile of his own.

"You too. It's very nice," I said feeling my heart thump and not knowing what to do about it.

Cage stopped laughing and looked into my eyes. God did I want to kiss him.

"I suppose if I ask you if you're having fun yet, you'll tell me the truth."

"I'm having fun," I said moving closer in case he did want to kiss me.

Cage watched me with a devilish look in his eyes. I could have sworn that he was about to move his lips towards mine when he said, "Why don't I introduce you to a few more people."

"More people? I've already met two. How many more people can a person meet in a night?"

"Haha. A few more than that," he said slipping his hand around my shoulders and leading me away.

Feeling his touch made every part of me tingle. I felt like such a little guy in his arms. He was so big and strong. I couldn't believe that I had met someone like him. I couldn't believe that he was acting like he was into me. Could a guy like him be into guys? The possibilities made my chest clench.

Cage led me around the party introducing me to one person after another. He wasn't kidding about being good at social stuff. Everyone he introduced me to hung on his every word. And, when it was my turn to speak, they hung on my every word, too.

I couldn't tell if they were all just being nice, or if being with Cage had turned me into a more interesting version of myself. Whatever it was, I loved the feeling. These types of interactions had always been so hard for me, but at Cage's side, I was a different person.

What was even better than that was how he took every opportunity to touch me. He touched my shoulder when he introduced me. His pointing finger lightly rested on my chest when he was emphasizing a point. And, standing shoulder to shoulder as if we were already a couple, he would bump his shoulder against mine when he laughed.

I was a helpless ball of putty by the time he was done with me and I couldn't stop thinking about the other thing Lou had suggested. What would Cage look like naked in my bed?

With one of his teammates waving his arms around telling a story, I couldn't take my eyes off of Cage. With his full attention on his friend, Cage subtly retrieved his phone from his pocket and peaked down. Slipping it away quickly, he waited for the arm waving to die down and then looked between his friend and me.

"Guys, I have to head out," he said wrapping his large hand around my bicep.

"Yes, me too," I said quickly.

"Yeah? Where you headed?" He asked enthusiastically.

"Back to my room."

"Where's that?"

"Plaza Hall?"

"Really? I'll go with you," he said squeezing my arm.

My heart stopped. He was coming with me? Was this it? I couldn't believe it might finally happen. I prayed no one looked down because there was no hiding my excitement.

I swallowed and forced myself to speak.

"Cool."

After saying a few goodbyes, the two of us exited into the night. I was giddy from terror and arousal. As the silence between us drew out, I wondered why he wasn't saying anything. Wasn't he the one who was supposed to be good at stuff like this? I was about to mumble something when he finally spoke.

"It's a clear night."

"What?"

"You can see all of the stars," he said turning to me. "You cold?"

"What?"

"You're shivering."

I was shaking. "I guess I'm nervous," I admitted.

"What are you nervous about?"

My face got hot. "I don't know."

Cage stared at me. "You're a good-looking guy. Do you know that?"

"So are you," I told him shaking even more.

"Thanks. Are you happy you came out tonight?"

"Yeah, definitely," I told him as my gaze fell to the ground.

"We're here," he said as we approached the door of my building.

"We're here," I repeated my heart pounding. "Do you want to come in?"

"Come in?" Cage asked caught off guard.

"Yes," I replied shyly.

"Ahhhh," he murmured before the door popped open and a girl came out.

"Cage!" She said before wrapping her arms around him and standing on her tiptoes to kiss his lips.

My mouth dropped open in shock. What was going on? What had just happened?

The petite, blonde with angular features turned towards me. "Who's this?"

"Ah, this is Quin. Quin this is Tasha."

Tasha looked at me suspiciously while Cage became uncomfortable.

"Tasha is my girlfriend."

"How do you know Cage?" Tasha asked me.

I was too shocked by everything to speak.

"Quin had asked me for a selfie."

Tasha turned to Cage surprised. "Oh. Did you give him one?"

"Not yet," Cage said with a smile.

"I can take it," Tasha volunteered. "Give me your phone," she said approaching me with her hand out.

Still speechless, I handed her my phone and stood next to Cage.

"Say cheese," she said.

"Cheese," Cage replied while I stared back stunned.

"Here you go," she said handing me back my phone. "Check it."

I looked down and saw my full humiliation on display. "Yes."

"Okay. Let's go. I'm hungry," Tasha said entwining her body with Cage's and pulling him away.

"It was nice meeting you, Quin," he said looking at me as he left.

"Yes. It was nice meeting… you," I mumbled sure that he could no longer hear me.

I watched as the perfectly suited couple walked off. Of course, he had a girlfriend. And, of course, she looked like that. My heart hurt watching them go.

I can't believe I thought he was interested in me. No one's ever interested in me. How could I have been so foolish? How could I think a guy like him could be interested in a guy like me?

Once the two had disappeared into the darkness, I entered the building. Ascending the stairs in a daze, I wanted to cry. Why didn't anyone ever like me back?

"Don't tell me that you went to a coffee shop and read a book," Lou said snapping me out of my haze.

"What are you doing here?" I asked not expecting to see him.

"Ugh! The date was a bust. But don't change the subject. I don't see a naked man on your arm. I don't see, sigh, a naked woman. I don't see any signs of shame."

I took out my phone, pulled up the picture of Cage and me, and handed it to Lou.

"Who's this?"

"Cage."

"Why do you look so heartbroken, Lamb Chop?"

"He has a girlfriend," I told him before looking into his eyes and crying.

"Ahhh," Lou said before wrapping his arms around me and holding me tight.

"What's wrong with me, Lou?" I asked before he guided me to my bed, climbed in beside me, and held me while I cried.

Chapter 2

Cage

Wow! I have never felt anything like that in my life. Looking at Quin I could barely contain myself. I couldn't keep my hands off of him. I could have stayed with him at the party all night. For the first time in a long time, I felt alive.

Returning to reality was a hard pill to swallow. When I got Tasha's text, it felt like the rug had been ripped from under me. I wanted to stay there with Quin. I wanted to see how far it would go. But, I had promised Tasha that I would take her to dinner whether or not we won the game. I always keep my obligations and I had made one to Tasha.

"So, I wanted to talk to you about something," Tasha said breaking the silence as we walked.

"What's that?"

Tasha looked at me excitedly and blushed. Seeing her display of emotion was an unusual sight. A dark cloud usually followed Tasha infecting everyone around her.

I had to assume she wasn't happy with her life. I was clearly a part of her dissatisfaction. But whenever I tried to talk to her about it, she accused me of trying to ruin the good thing we have going.

What good thing was that? She wasn't happy. I wasn't happy. And we never had sex.

"You know Vi, right?" Tasha asked bubbling.

"Your best friend Vi who you spend all of your time with. Yeah, I know her."

"You don't have to say it like that."

"You asked me if I knew the girl you always talk about."

"Why are you trying to start a fight? I'm trying to do something nice for you."

I caught myself and took a breath. I was feeling tense. I hadn't want to leave Quin, but I did because of Tasha. I couldn't even ask him for his number when we got back to his place. That was probably for the best, though. The way he made me feel could only lead to me making decisions I would regret.

I had larger things to consider. I had worked my whole life to play for the NFL. Being with a girl like Tasha helps sell the pack of me as the face of a franchise. At least, that's what my father says. And it had been his dream that I play professional football longer than it had been mine. I couldn't let him down.

"I'm sorry. I guess I'm still feeling beat up from the game. It's making me a little cranky."

Tasha smiled. "You're forgiven," she said wrapping her arms around mine. "And, I think I have something that will make you feel better."

"Okay," I said mustering a smile. "What is it?"

"Well, remember how we've been talking about spicing things up in… the bedroom?"

I looked at Tasha suspiciously. Spicing things up was something she had brought up and when she did, it felt like she had something very specific in mind that she wouldn't mention.

"I remember."

"So, I talked to Vi…"

"Okay," I said confused.

"I spoke to Vi and asked her if she would be interested in joining the two of us when we were… together. And she said yes," Tasha said crackling.

I stopped walking and stared at her. It took a second to wrap my head around what she was saying.

"You mean, like a threesome?"

"Yeah," she said turning bright red.

"Tasha, why would you do that?"

"What do you mean?"

"Why would you invite someone else into our bed… and without talking to me first?"

"I thought you would like it. Doesn't every guy want to be with two beautiful women at the same time?"

"Not every guy. And, if you would have asked me, I would have told you that I'm a one-guy, one-girl sort of man… if you would have asked me."

"I thought you would like it," she said heartbroken.

"Well, I don't. And, I don't know why you would even suggest it."

"Maybe it's because we never have sex anymore."

"And that's my fault? You're the one who spends all of her time with Vi."

"What are you saying?"

"I'm saying that I'm not the one who doesn't want to have sex."

"Well, you could have fooled me."

"Then, if you're so unhappy, maybe we shouldn't be together."

Tasha froze staring at me. "Why would you say that? Why would you say that?"

"Isn't that what's obvious?"

"No. We were meant to be together. I would make you the perfect wife. You know that. You're going to get drafted and become the starting quarterback for a big NFL team and I'll take care of the house and start a charity. We talked about this, Baby. Our futures are set."

She was right. We had talked about it and that was exactly what we had said. But now that I was in my senior year and I couldn't put off entering the draft any longer, I was starting to have my doubts. That wasn't her fault, though. And I shouldn't be taking it out on her.

"You're right. I'm sorry, Tasha. I'm just in a mood today. But, please, no more talking about threesomes, okay?"

As soon as I said it, I saw the light in Tasha's eyes blink out.

"Okay," she agreed before the two of us continued our walk to the restaurant in silence.

"I told you not to take that class, Rucker."

"Coach, it was something I was interested in," I tried to explain for the thousandth time.

"Intro to Childhood Education? What does a starting quarterback for the Dallas Cowboys or L.A. Rams need with a class on childhood education?" my coach asked more than a little pissed off.

"Look," I said finally losing my cool. "I took every class you told me to whether I wanted to or not. I attend every practice you schedule and I work hard enough to puke…"

"And look where you are because of it. A top prospect in a competitive draft class. You should be thanking me for how hard I've pushed you."

I caught myself and took a breath. "And I am. But Coach, I needed to take at least one class that was for me."

"But why that one?"

"It's what I'm interested in."

"Yet you haven't attended a single class since the beginning of the year?"

"That's because it starts 20 minutes after the end of practice. I thought I could just run over when I was done. But sometimes practice runs late, or I have to take an ice bath. Sometimes I'm just too tired."

"Well, you should have thought about that before you chose the class because this professor isn't as sympathetic to the challenges of student-athletes as the others are. This one thinks you should have to attend and take the tests to pass. And if you don't pass this class, you won't be allowed to play spring quarter. That means this team won't win and no one will scout you."

"I got it. I'll start going to class."

"Not just that. You're getting a tutor. I'll have one of my people find you someone. When's your next class?"

I looked up at the clock on the wall of Coach's office.

"Right now."

"Then get your ass over there."

"Coach, it's across campus. By the time I get there, there will only be five minutes left."

"I guess that means you'll have to run, doesn't it?"

"Coach, we just did 20 minutes of wind sprints."

"Don't talk back, just run. I mean it. Go, go, go!"

Backing out of the office, I did what I was told and ran. I had taken off my chest padding, but I was still in my cleats, compression shirt, and padded pants. The class was on the third floor of a building clear across campus. I didn't have time to change if I was going to make it.

I didn't know how I had gotten into this mess. Actually, I kinda did. It was my act of rebellion. Yeah, I knew that it would butt up against practice, but I thought it would give me an excuse to leave practice early. I was wrong. And now my entire future hung in the balance.

Entering the building and the stairwell, I was completely out of breath. Luckily no one could hear my panting over the thunderous noise of my metal cleats echoing off the concrete. There was no quietly sneaking into the back of the class. By the time I had opened the classroom door, everyone had already turned to look. There were 50 students and one angry professor all staring at me.

"Sorry. Please continue," I said between struggling breaths and plenty of humiliation.

Taking the first open seat, I rested my head on the desk to quietly catch my breath. I again felt like I wanted to throw up, but that wasn't happening here.

Gathering myself I sat up realizing that I hadn't grabbed my book bag from my locker. It wasn't like I had the notebook for this class in it or anything. I had given up on attending a long time ago. But it would have been nice to have something in front of me so I didn't look like an idiot.

Pulling out my phone, I did my best to seem like I was taking notes on it. I wasn't because I had no idea what the professor was talking about. It looked like everyone else did, though. They were all laser-focused on the woman standing in front of us. That is, everyone was paying attention except one person. And when I saw him, I couldn't breathe.

It was Quin, and he was looking up at me. Our eyes connected for a second but then he looked away. Everything inside of me tingled. I could immediately feel myself breathing harder.

Just seeing him did something to me. I had been given a second chance with him. I wasn't going to let him slip out of my life again.

"And, that's it. Next class will be a quiz on what we covered over the past two weeks. Be ready," the professor said before turning her attention to me. "Mr. Rucker, can I see you a moment?"

I wasn't expecting that. Worst still, Quin was seated on the opposite side of the room which had a different exit. He wasn't looking my way and he would be gone before I could ask him to wait for me.

"Mr. Rucker," the grey-haired, Asian woman called again.

"Coming," I told her keeping an eye on Quin as he approached the door.

Quickly swimming upstream past the flood of people, I approached the professor as she erased the board. She was taking her time with it and it was killing me. When Quin disappeared, my heart sank. He was gone again and I felt like crap.

"Coming in five minutes before the end of class isn't considered attending. At least not in my book."

"I know. And I'm really sorry about that. I ran over from practice. But I promise I won't be late again."

"I'm told you need to pass this class to remain eligible to play next season."

"That's correct, Ma'am."

"Then I would think you would take this class a little more seriously."

"And I promise, I will… moving forward."

"If you don't want to be here…"

"I do want to be here."

"Why?" She asked sincerely.

"Because it's a subject I'm really interested in. Teaching kids is something I've always wanted to do."

"What about football? I hear you have a promising professional career."

"Football is what I'm good at. It's a blessing. But it's not…"

I didn't finish the sentence. That was a box I didn't want to open right now.

"Well, if you are serious about this class, you're going to have a lot of catching up to do."

"I realize that, and I'm willing to work. I'm getting a tutor."

"Are you?"

"Yes, Ma'am. In fact…" I said suddenly getting an idea. "Could we pick this up next class? I promise I'll be on time for it."

"You better be. Remember, attendance is mandatory."

"I got it. I'm on it. I'll be here. Promise," I said clomping my cleats on the carpet as I trotted to the door.

As soon as I was in the hall, I scanned both directions looking for him. He wasn't there. Where had he gone so quickly?

Most of the students were entering the stairwell headed downstairs. I jogged over and joined them. Craning my neck over the crowd, I couldn't see him. I was about to hate myself for not leaving sooner when I saw the back of someone who could only be Quin exiting the stairwell onto the main floor.

"Excuse me. Excuse me," I said squeezing past everyone.

It only got me down a few seconds sooner and by the time I was there, he was again nowhere to be seen.

Looking into every classroom as I ran past them, I didn't see him. I was about to give up hope when I popped open the door to the building and spotted his sexy frame walking away. Warmth washed across me. It felt like a spot of sunshine on a cloudy day.

Jogging towards him, I slowed when I was a few feet away. I couldn't lose my cool just because I was about to talk to the best-looking guy I had ever seen. I had to at least pretend like kissing him wasn't the only thing I could think about since the moment we met.

"Quin?" I said trying to be as casual as I could.

He stopped and turned around. He did not look as happy to see me as I was to see him. It triggered a twinge in my chest but I pushed past it.

"I thought that was you. How have you been? Hit up any big parties since I saw you last?" I said with a smile.

When he didn't reply, I said, "Cage. Cage Rucker. We met at the Sigma Chi party."

"I remember," he said coldly. Ouch! There was that twinge of pain again. "How's Tasha? That was your girlfriend's name, right?"

"Tasha? Oh, yeah. She's good. She's fine. Ah, did I do something to piss you off? If I did, I'm sorry," I said desperately wanting to see him smile again.

Quin stared at me with a look of frustration and then relented.

"No. You didn't do anything wrong. Don't mind me. I'm just being stupid."

"You? Being stupid? I find that hard to believe," I said with a smile.

He stared at me again. This time he looked like he was searching my soul.

"Why would you say that?"

"I don't know. I guess you strike me as being someone really smart."

He softened the intensity of his gaze.

"I'm not smart about anything that matters," he said before continuing his walk.

I caught up to him.

"I don't think that's true. In fact, I'll bet you're pretty smart at Intro to Childhood Education. I bet you're at the top of the class."

Quin looked at me when I said that.

"You are, aren't you?"

Quin looked away.

"I'll be damned. Okay. Then that will make the next thing I say less awkward. It turns out that I need this class to stay eligible for football and ultimately, the NFL draft. And, since I haven't been attending classes, I'm a little behind. I kind of need a tutor. The football program is willing to pay you for your time."

"I can't tutor you," he said dismissively.

"Why not?"

"I just can't. Sorry."

"Okay. Then how about if I make the pot a little sweeter?"

"What do you mean?"

"When we were at the party you said that you weren't good at being social, which I don't understand because you seemed perfectly comfortable with it."

"I was only comfortable because…"

"Because of what?" I asked hoping he would say because of me.

"Nothing."

"Well, if you're willing to tutor me in what you're good at, I can tutor you on what I'm good at."

"You mean being a football star that everyone wants a piece of."

"First of all, ouch. Second of all, there's a little more to me than that."

"I know. I'm sorry. See, I'm not good at this," Quin exclaimed.

I took his hand as casually as I could. I tried to pretend like this was just something I did when I talked to people, but the truth was I had been dying to hold it.

"You are good at this. At least, you can be. Let me help you. I know I can help you with this. And once you're done, you'll be a star football player who everyone wants a piece of like I am," I said with a smirk.

Quin laughed. I tingled so much I thought my teeth would fall out.

"So, what do you say?"

Quin pulled his hand from mine. He wasn't subtle about it. I think he was trying to send a message about boundaries. Fair enough, I could respect that.

"Okay," Quin said with a smile.

"Okay?" I repeated melting in his eyes.

"Okay," he confirmed to my absolute joy.

"I hear there's a quiz in the next couple of days."

"It's in two days and it covers two weeks of material."

"That sounds like a lot."

"It is," he confirmed.

"It sounds like your tutoring should start right away," I suggested wanting to spend every waking moment with him.

"How about tonight? I'll set up a lesson plan and we'll go from there."

"A lesson plan? You don't play around."

"I don't. You can't either if you want to pass the quiz."

"I won't."

Quin hesitated. "And you don't have any plans with your girlfriend or anything, do you?"

Being reminded of Tasha was a bucket of cold water on my runaway excitement about spending the night with Quin. My smile diminished.

"Even if I had something, I would cancel it. Passing the class and playing football comes first. She would understand."

"Okay. Then I'll see you tonight."

"Should I get your number?" I asked him not missing the opportunity this time.

"Yes. Give me your phone."

I handed it to him and he typed it in. A second later I heard the phone in his pocket ring.

"You know where I live. I'll text you the time and my room number," Quin said professionally.

"So we'll be doing this at your place?"

"Unless you have somewhere better. I guess we could go to a library but I don't know how much talking they'll allow."

"No, your place is great. I look forward to it."

"You look forward to studying?" He asked reminding me that this wasn't a date.

"Of course. Intro to Childhood Education is what I live for. Ask anybody."

Quin laughed. It melted my heart.

"See you then, Dimples," he said with a smile before turning and walking off. Man, was I in trouble.

Chapter 3

Quin

'See you then, Dimples?' Did I actually say that? What was I thinking? What was I thinking agreeing to any of this?

There was no way I was going to be able to resist him. When he looked at me, he made me feel like I was the only person in the world. Time stopped when I spoke with him. How was I going to be alone with him long enough to help him pass his class?

I should have continued to refuse to help him. But, his offer had been pretty great. I had come to college for one thing, and it wasn't the formal education. It was to learn the things I hadn't and couldn't learn from books. It was all of the subtle back and forth that went on during conversations.

To me, life would be more efficient if everyone just said what they were thinking and got on with stuff. But, I get it, that wasn't the way things worked. There was a dance to it and I had to learn the steps.

I couldn't ask for a better dance teacher than Cage, though. What he offered was the one thing I had come to college to learn. How could I refuse his offer of help?

I just had to keep reminding myself that he had a girlfriend, and no matter what I thought was going on, it was only in my head. He would never love me back. Ours was a union of convenience. That was it. And once we got from each other what we wanted, we were going to go our separate ways.

A wave of pain washed through me thinking about it. This had clearly been a bad idea. There was no way I was going to survive this. But there was no backing out of it now. And, I had to admit, I couldn't wait to see him again.

"Lou, you can't be here tonight," I told him when I got back to my room.

"Lamb Chop, I told you, if you're going to be making out with some boy, just put a sock on the doorknob."

"What type of sock?"

Lou looked at me shocked. "Wait, what?"

"Like, is it supposed to be a gym sock or one of those ankle socks? Because the ankle sock would probably stay on the doorknob better."

"Wait. Wait! What are we talking about? Are you bringing a boy here tonight… [sigh], or a girl?"

"Cage is coming over."

Lou's mouth dropped open. "The boy from the mopey-Quin photo?"

"Yeah. But it's just to study. I'm tutoring him in a class."

"You have a class with him. How are you just telling me this now?"

"He didn't show up to the class until today. And he was wearing his football gear," I said with a smile creeping across my face.

"You mean the very tight ones that football players wear."

"Ah-uh," I said feeling my face heat up.

"Oh! He's not just coming over to study, is he?"

"No, he is," I said bringing things back down to earth. "He needs to pass the class to play football next semester, and he asked me to tutor him."

"So, you're holding his life in your completely irresistible hands?"

I looked down at my hands wondering how hands could be irresistible.

"I mean, not really. But, kind of."

"Oh my god, you two are so gonna make out."

"We're not. He still has a girlfriend. That hasn't changed."

"Maybe he wants you to join the two of them. You'd be into that, wouldn't you? I mean, you of all people with your parents and all."

"You know, to be honest, I don't think I would be. I see what my parents have, and it's great. I love all of them and they love each other. But, I'm not sure that's for me."

"So, we're going to have to break the two of them up?" Lou asked with a devilish look in his eyes.

"No! I'm not doing that either. If she is who he wants to be with, then… fine. I'm okay with that."

"How much did that hurt to say?"

"A lot. But, it will have to be true. I don't want to be with someone who doesn't want to be with me."

"You're a better man than I am," Lou said giving up.

"I don't know about better, but I am a lot more alone."

"Ahhh!" Lou said getting up and hugging me. With his arms still wrapped around me, he said, "This boy is going to devastate you, isn't he?"

"Probably."

"Don't worry, I'll be here to pick up the pieces, Lamb Chop. I'll always be."

"Unless you have a hot date?"

"Unless I have a hot date. But, other than that, I'll be right here," he said pulling away and giving me an irresistible smile.

Chapter 4

Cage

I can do this. I can spend a little time with Quin, not fall head over heels for him, and not blow up my entire life to be with him. I'm sure I can. Although, the closer our meeting time got, the clearer it became that I wasn't going to have a say in the matter.

How is it that every guy, or girl, or whoever he's interested in, didn't see everything I did in him and snap him up? I don't understand it. The guy is gorgeous and awkwardly adorable. I could push my fingers through his dark, wavy hair until I was lost in it.

Oh, and his eyes. Don't get me started on his eyes, those vulnerable, bedroom eyes. Just thinking about them makes me so hard. How is he able to do this to me?

It's like… what is that thing that animals release to attract a mate? Pheromones? It's like he's releasing pheromones and there is nothing I can do to resist it.

I really shouldn't have asked him to tutor me. He was probably the last person I should have asked. How will I be able to concentrate with him in arms reach of me? It was such a mistake. But, I can't wait. And time has never moved slower in my life.

I waited at The Common for our meeting time instead of driving home and driving back. Staying with Tasha might have also been an option considering she lived on the floor above his. But odds were that she was hanging out with Vi.

The two of them were inseparable. It was no wonder she suggested Vi join us for sex. They did everything else together. Why not that?

Once the painfully long wait for me to head over had passed, I hurried across the quad. Slipping into the building as someone exited, I ran up the stairs two at a time and knocked on his door. I heard some scrambling inside before an unfamiliar voice said, "I just want to see," and the door opened.

"Hello," I said to the puckish-looking guy standing in front of me.

"Lou, nice to meet you," he said neither offering me his hand nor inviting me in.

"Cage."

"The football star?" Lou said with a smile.

"I guess. Is Quin here?"

"He is. And what intentions do you have with my friend?"

"Lou!" Quin yelled from behind him. Pushing past Lou and placing his body between the two of us, Quin said, "I'm sorry about that. He was just leaving."

Quin's body was so close to mine.

"That's Okay. Lou, I would invite you to stay and hang out, but we have two weeks of classwork to go over… Unless Quin thinks we could do both?"

"We can't do both and Lou was just leaving. Bye, Lou."

"Toodles," Lou said pushing past me allowing Quin to invite me in.

"I'm sorry about that. Lou means well."

"It's always good to have a friend who'll look out for you."

"It is. So, welcome to my room."

I looked around. "Is this how the other half live?"

"What do you mean?"

"The Plaza dorms are pretty fancy."

"Doesn't your girlfriend live in here, too?"

"Yeah, but that doesn't make it any less impressive. Besides, she has two roommates and has to share a bedroom. Your place is better decorated than my house."

"You live at the fraternity?"

"No. I'm not a member. I know, a football player who doesn't belong to Sigma Chi, unthinkable. But, fraternity life was a little outside my price range."

"Where do you live?" Quin asked ushering me to the couch in their living room.

"At home with my dad."

"Not your mom?" Quin asked gathering books and sitting next to me.

"My mom died when I was born."

Quin froze. "I'm sorry to hear that."

"No need to be sorry. It happened a long time ago."

"So, it's always just been you and your dad."

"Yep. And sometimes just me."

"What do you mean?"

"Nothin'. We should get to studying. I have a feeling there's a lot we have to cover," I said changing the topic.

Although I never knew my mother, the topic was still a sore spot for me. Mostly because of my dad. He would never say it, but I think her loss hit him hard. At least, that was my guess.

Quin started by showing me the most organized flow chart I had ever seen in my life.

"Here's what we're going to have to cover by Thursday," he said getting right to business.

His assertiveness was almost enough to distract me from his knee hovering inches from mine as it supported the textbook. Or, the whiff I got when he leaned over to point out something on an opposite page.

His sweet musk kept making my dick hard. Bending forward was all I could do to hide it.

"You keep leaning forward, is your back okay?"

"My back? Yes. That's why I keep bending over, because of my back. I need to keep it stretched. You know because of practice."

"If you want, we can move to the dining room table? The chairs have a little more support," Quin suggested sweetly.

"Yeah, maybe that would be best."

I was about to get up when I realized I was still massively hard.

"Um, maybe in a second."

"Your back's really hurting, huh?"

"Yeah, it's *hurting* really bad."

"I'm so sorry. I wish you would have said something sooner. This might sound weird, but I can give you a massage if you'd like. I taught myself a few years back. I haven't had many opportunities to practice, but I think I'm still pretty good."

"Umm…"

"I'm sorry, is that weird? Offering to give you a massage is weird, isn't it?" Quin said wilting before my eyes.

"No, it's not weird at all. I'd love to have one. It would really help… my back."

"You sure?"

"You don't know how much," I said with a smile.

"Okay. Then…"

Quin looked around. "My bed would probably be more comfortable."

There was no way I was going to be able to get up now.

"I think the couch will be fine."

"Okay."

Quin got up and began stretching his fingers.

"Undress to your level of comfort and lie down."

Heat flashed across my cheeks. Did he just tell me to undress to my level of comfort? The idea of getting naked for him made me so hard my cock started twitching. Only God knew what would happen if I were to take off my pants. There was no way I could do that. But, I could take off my shirt.

Slowly pulling it off, I peeked up at Quin. The way he stared did all sorts of things to me. I was going to have to think of a lot of baseball if I wasn't going to cum in my shorts as soon as he touched me. It was worth the risk, though. I needed his hands on me. And when I lied down and he got on top of me, I was in heaven.

With him pulling and kneading my muscles, I lost myself. Jesus, did this feel good. It was better than sex, at least, any sex I had ever had. And it didn't take long before, I felt a familiar gnawing start at my balls and slowly climb.

Oh god, I was cumming.

"I need to go to the bathroom," I said tossing the smaller guy onto the couch.

Luckily I knew where it was and it was open. Throwing the door closed behind me, I could barely get my pants down fast enough before I exploded into orgasm.

I groaned fighting myself from screaming with pleasure. I managed to catch most of it in my palm instead of spraying it onto the ceiling. But with it came lightheadedness that tossed me to my ass. I hit the ground with a thud.

Chapter 5

Quin

"Are you alright in there?" I asked hearing what sounded like the towel rack break and then someone falling to the floor.

"I'm fine," Cage shouted back. "But, I think something broke. Sorry about that."

"Don't worry about it, whatever it is. Are you sure you're alright?"

"Yeah. I just need a second."

I freaked him out. I know I did. Sitting on top of him I was getting hard and he felt it somehow. That's why he threw me off of him and sprinted to the bathroom like his hair was on fire.

Why did I offer to give him a massage? How weird was that? I'm ruining everything.

But he said his back was hurting and it just slipped out. If someone says their back is hurting, you offer to give them a massage, don't you?

Agh! I don't know. I don't know anything. Why am I so bad at this?

"Are you sure you don't need any help in there?"

"I have everything in hand," Cage said before turning on the faucet and eventually coming out.

Damn, did he look good standing there with his shirt off. His muscular, bulging shoulders, his thick pecs, his abs. How did he have abs without flexing? He was just standing there. How?

Staring at me with the most heart-melting puppy dog eyes, he said, "Sorry about that?"

"No, I'm sorry," I told him feeling bad for crossing the line.

"Why should you feel sorry," he asked me as if he didn't know.

"You know, because…"

"…Because you were willing to tutor me in a subject I need to pass to have any sort of life, and I made things weird?"

"You made things weird? I'm the king of making things weird."

"You might be the king of something, but this is on me. Look, why don't we get back to studying."

"How's your back?"

"It's much better now, thank you," he said grabbing his shirt and putting it on. "That helped a lot. I can focus now. I'm also a little sleepy but, I can definitely focus."

Continuing from where we left off, we covered a lot of material by the time Lou came back.

"Still at it? You two can just keep going and going, can't you?" Lou said playfully.

Lou was clearly making Cage uncomfortable.

"Yeah, I should go."

"Don't let me stop you," Lou said. "You won't even know I'm here."

"Or, we could just go to my room," I suggested.

"No!" he said abruptly. "I mean, maybe we can pick it back up tomorrow. There are a lot of things swirling around up here and I need to process it all," he said circling his hands around his head.

"Oh, yeah. Sleeping helps you retain information. Tomorrow, then. If you want to start earlier, my last class ends at four."

"That sounds great. How about we meet at the study hall next time? That way we don't disturb Lou."

"Oh, you don't have to worry about me. You two can do it wherever you'd like," Lou added as he stood watching the two of us.

"Yes, we could study here," I confirmed.

Cage fumbled his words. "I think study hall would be better. I mean, if it's okay with you."

I was disappointed that I had screwed things up so badly that he didn't want to come back to my room, but I understood.

"No, that's fine. We'll be covering the rest of the material, so you might want to bring some snacks."

Lou added, "Knowing Quin, it will be a long, hard session. Very long… if you know what I mea…"

"…Alright, I'm gonna go. Text me," Cage said before escaping, glancing at Lou as he did.

"What was that all about? It's going to be a long, hard session?" I asked Lou pissed.

"Very long," he said with a smirk.

"What were you doing?"

"You said he has a girlfriend?"

"Yes. He has a girlfriend!"

"Very interesting," he said smirking at me like he knew everything and I knew nothing. "Very… interesting," he continued before slipping into his bedroom and not returning.

I didn't get much sleep that night. If I wasn't trying to figure out what Lou was seeing that I wasn't, I was thinking about how I had made things weird with Cage, or what it would be like to see his naked body again.

I was a complete mess. That man did things to me. And after only the third time seeing him, I couldn't get him out of my mind.

Why did he have to have a girlfriend? Why did he have to be so perfect? And, why did he have those dimples? Someone explain to me why he had to have so many adorable dimples.

The next day at study hall was less weird than the night before. For the most part, we stuck to the course material and only veered away when we took our dinner break.

"I brought an extra sandwich if you want one?" I told him pulling it from my bag.

"You brought an extra sandwich?" He asked more surprised than I could have guessed.

"Yes. Do you want it? I figured you would have a lot swirling around up there and might not remember to bring something."

"Wow! I'm not used to people being so thoughtful."

"What? Come on. You're a famous football player. You must have people doing things for you all of the time."

"It's not the same," he said taking the sandwich. "Thank you, by the way. Yeah, there's a difference between someone doing something for you because they're getting something from you, and someone doing something just to be nice."

"I get that. There are a lot of people who can see you as a stepping stone on their path to getting what they want. You're just an object to them. They forget that you have feelings too. And, maybe your desires don't line up with everyone's expectations for you."

"Wow! Exactly," he said staring at me and once again turning me into a heaping pile of boy-crush.

"What?" I asked when his gaze became too much.

"How would you know that feeling so perfectly?"

What was I supposed to say to that? I liked Cage. I liked him a lot, maybe more than I should. So, I didn't want to freak him out. At least not yet.

Besides, I chose a school in the middle of nowhere for a reason. Coming here was the best shot I had of fading into the background. I just wanted someone to see me as a normal guy for once. Was that wrong of me? I couldn't tell.

"My uncles played in the NFL. They told me."

"Oh. Yeah, they got it right," Cage confirmed leaning back and relaxing his gaze.

Finishing our sandwiches, we got back to work. By midnight, we had covered everything.

"So, that's all of it?" Cage asked.

"All that's going to be covered in the quiz tomorrow. Do you think you have it?"

"You're a very good tutor. If I've missed anything, it wouldn't be your fault. By the way, I spoke to my coach. He told me you have to contact his office to get paid."

"Oh. Don't worry about it," I told him.

"You put so much work into helping me. No one could have made everything clearer than you have. Not even the professor. You deserve to get paid for your hard work."

"Okay," I said relenting.

Cage looked at me strangely and I couldn't figure out why.

"Since you're not excited about getting paid, how about the other thing I promised you?"

"Oh right, 'How Not to be so Awkward' classes."

Cage laughed. "I don't know about all of that. I was just thinking that we could play some flag football at the park."

"On your time off from football, you play more football? You must really love playing."

Cage gave me a muted smile. "You would think."

"So tell me, Mr. Expert, how is playing flag football in the park supposed to help me not feel like a freak at a party?"

Cage became pensive. "I've been thinking about this. The reason why I feel so comfortable in social situations is because I know that, no matter what happens, I'll be able to handle it. Also, I know that if I do say something stupid, which I do… often, everything will be fine. The world's not going to implode. I'm not going to be sent into the desert to live alone. My life will most likely go on unchanged.

"And, the only way I got to that realization is because I have been put in many comfortable and uncomfortable social situations and have worked my way through them. You need to be in those situations. You need your own opportunities to work your way through it.

"Then, when you've gotten familiar with all of the most common situations that come up, and you've figured out what to do and say when they do," he held up his hands, "I'm done."

I stared at Cage with my mind blown.

"That's kind of genius. You're absolutely right. Social comfort is experientially based. Familiarity breeds comfort. So, the answer is being willing to be uncomfortable. I'm not sure I could have thought of that."

"I guess I'm good for something after all," Cage said proudly.

"Although, I'm not exactly a football player. So, I'm not sure being stampeded by jocks will fill me with the confidence you think it will."

"I guess you'll have to trust me on that," Cage said with a wink.

Why did he have to wink? Didn't he realize I was doing my best to see him as a friend? Why did he have to remind me how sexy he was?

Offering him a lingering goodbye which turned into an awkward hug, I headed back to my room and bed. Tucked away, I heard Lou enter the apartment and approach my door.

"I know you're not asleep," he said without knocking. "I know you're hiding in there because you don't want to tell me how it went. Or, is he in there with you. Are you guys doing it? Oh my god, you two are doing it!"

"Goodnight, Lou!" I told him needing the teasing to end.

"Night, Lamb Chop," he replied smiling as he left.

The idea of Cage and me naked together ran through my mind for the next three hours. I blame Lou for that. By the time I woke up, I was already late for class. Sprinting across campus and bursting through the auditorium doors, I learned how Cage had felt.

As everyone turned to look at me, the only one I cared about was Cage. Was he there? Had he made it?

When I saw him my heart fluttered. He was smiling at me. It was five cups of coffee all at once.

Professor Nakamura held up a handout and pointed me to an open spot. It was on the other side of the room from Cage. Maybe that was for the best. I wasn't sure I could look him in the eyes considering all of the things I made him do in my fantasies the night before.

With my brain moving slower due to the lack of sleep, I wasn't close to being done by the time the class ended. I figured I would keep answering questions until I was told to stop. Keeping one eye on the professor I didn't miss when Cage handed in his paper and said something to her. She looked at me immediately after and then Cage winked at me again as he headed out.

When I was the only one left, Professor Nakamura said, "Cage told me you were up late tutoring him, so I'll give you an additional 20 minutes."

"Thank you, Professor," I said gratefully.

The 20 minutes were barely enough. I did get it done, though, and it was thanks to Cage. The guy was doing something to me that I wasn't going to be able to come back from. I could barely wait for our flag football date to roll around so I could see him again. He was all I could think of until I did.

When I saw him park his truck and approach me at the entrance of the park, I couldn't help but smile. He was smiling too. God, did I love the way he smiled. It almost made up for the stress I felt about what was going to happen next.

"You ready for this?" Cage asked looking confident and gorgeous.

"No."

"Nervous?"

"Petrified might be more accurate."

"There's nothing to worry about. Be yourself. If you say something that feels awkward just push through it. Remember the world isn't going to end, and no one here will be any less awkward than you."

"I highly doubt that. And your teammates are going to demolish me. I don't know if you know this but I'm not a big guy."

"Everything's relative," Cage said with a smile.

"What do you mean?"

"Cage!" A voice said grabbing my attention. I turned and looked. It was a kid who said it. He was about ten years old and he was one of 15 kids the same age.

"You guys ready to play some football?" Cage yelled enthusiastically.

"Yeeeaaahhh!" They shouted back.

"We're playing with kids?" I asked him confused.

"I organize this event with the kids in the local peewee league. When neither of us has games, I spend some time with them sharpening their skills. Iron sharpens iron," he said with a smile.

"So, I'm supposed to practice being social with kids?" I asked confused.

"I didn't start too difficult for you, did I?"

I laughed. "No, I think I can handle this."

"There's the confidence I was hoping for," he said before jogging over to the group.

Cage was a natural with kids. He treated them like adults without forgetting their age.

"Whose team is the big guy on?" One of the kids asked referring to me.

"I don't know," Cage replied and looked at me. "Tell me, Quin, what team do you play for?"

"Do you mean, which team am I playing on?" I corrected unsure if he was asking what I thought he was.

"Isn't that what I asked?" Cage said with a knowing look on his face.

"No," a kid corrected. "You said, what team do you play for."

"Oh. My bad. Quin, which team are you going to play on?"

"Which team usually wins?" I asked.

Cage looked at the kids who were split up into red and blue shirts.

"Usually the red team."

"That's not true," a kid on the blue team protested. "We won the last time."

"But, was it luck?"

"No!" he protested.

"Then let's see if you can do it again. You have the big guy."

"Yes!" He said pumping his fist.

It was just a kid, but it felt good to be wanted for a team sport.

Thinking the whole thing would be a cinch, I was wrong. My being so much bigger than everyone else turned out to be a disadvantage. The object of the game was to pull the flag from the belt of the person with the ball. However, the waist of a ten-year-old is surprisingly close to the ground. The most I could do was block them from running while one of my teammates grabbed their flag.

Cage's role in the game was as the designated quarterback. No matter which team was receiving, he was the one throwing the ball. Not only was his throws pinpoint accurate, but the kids could catch.

"I see a few NFL stars in the making out there," Cage told me as the kids ate orange slices at halftime.

"You enjoy this, don't you?"

"I really do," he said with a smile.

"Hence taking 'Intro to Childhood Education'?"

He tightened his lips and nodded his head.

"You ever thought about teaching instead of going to the draft?"

"All of the time. But I can't. There are too many people counting on me."

"I understand that."

"Do you?"

"I do," I told him thinking of the world I left behind.

It was getting harder to think of him as just a guy I was crushing on or who I was tutoring. Cage was beginning to feel like a friend. I was sure he was someone I could share things with if they needed sharing. And, the things I was keeping from him about my life were starting to weigh on me.

"I get the feeling you're not much for revealing stuff about yourself," Cage said picking up on my hesitation.

"I don't know what I am."

"I know the feeling," he said with a sad smile.

"I know what you are."

"And, what's that?"

"You're a hot football player with a girlfriend, who is preparing to go pro."

"You think I'm hot?"

"Shit, did I say that?"

"You did," Cage said amused.

"I meant that you're popular. Like, you're trending. You're hot right now."

"I'm not sure that's what you meant," he said cockily.

The truth was that I wasn't sure either. The man was sexy as hell and there was no denying that.

"Well, it wouldn't matter even if it was what I meant. The other thing I said was that you had a girlfriend. I definitely said that."

Cage's smile dropped. "Yeah, there is that."

"And, how is Tasha, by the way," I asked not wanting to know but wanting him to keep her in mind before he flashed another of his irresistible smiles.

"She's good," he said soberly. "She's hanging out with her best friend this weekend. I think they're hiking trails or something."

"You didn't go with them?"

"No. I just feel like a third wheel when I'm around them. Hey, maybe the four of us could all hang out together?"

"That sounds like the worst idea I have ever heard," I told him honestly.

"Yeah, it probably is," he said searching his thoughts. "Did you want to, maybe, grab something to eat after we're done here?"

I looked at Cage settling in his kind, light eyes. I wanted to spend every moment of the rest of my life with him. Of course, I wanted to grab something to eat with him after this.

"I can't," I told him meaning that I shouldn't.

"Oh, okay. Are you doing something with Lou, later?"

"With Lou?"

"Yeah, you two seem close. It was almost like he was a little jealous when I came over."

"Jealous? Lou? No, he's just a little protective of me, I guess."

"Are you sure because it felt like a little more than that? And, I mean, he's a good-looking guy. I don't know if you're into guys are not, but…"

"I am," I told him wanting it to be clear.

He smiled before catching himself.

"Well then, I'm pretty sure he is too. Why wouldn't you…," he slowed choosing his words carefully. "Why wouldn't you try to make things happen with him?"

"Are you saying I should?"

"You're, like, an amazing guy. You deserve to be with someone who will make you happy. If Lou could do that, then why not?"

I looked at Cage as pain shot through my chest. He was trying to hand me off to someone else. I wanted him to want me. I wanted him to feel jealous that someone else would want to be with me.

But, he didn't. I was a fool to entertain the thought of the two of us together. He didn't like me like that, and it hurt.

Chapter 6

Cage

What was I saying? I didn't want Quin to be with Lou. I didn't want Quin to be with anyone. Hell, I didn't know what I wanted, whether it had to do with Quin, or football, or anything. I was the last person who should give someone relationship advice. All you had to do was spend two minutes with Tasha and me to know that.

"We should get back to the game," Quin told me looking a lot sadder than when we sat down.

I was ruining things with him. I thought this would be something fun we could do together, but I was turning it all wrong.

"Yeah. We should probably get back," I repeated willing to do anything to stop myself from talking.

Returning to the game, I made sure that the kids had a great time even if the person I most wanted to didn't.

"Are we playing again next weekend?" One of the kids asked me with her mother standing behind her.

"I have a game next weekend. I think you do too, don't you?" I asked looking up at her mother.

She shook her head.

"Oh yeah, I forgot," the little girl said with a smile.

"I'll let your coach know. It should be in a few weeks."

"Okay, thanks, Cage," she said waving bye.

Her mother mouthed 'Thank you,' and the two walked off.

"Is there anyone who doesn't love you?" Quin asked turning me around.

"All I care about is one," I said without thinking.

"Who's that?"

I had meant it to be something casual and flirty. Of course, Quin would call me on it.

"Anyone."

"Just anyone?"

"I meant, I would be happy as long as I had someone to love me."

"And, you have that don't you?"

"Do I?" I asked wondering who he was talking about.

"Yes. Tasha."

This had to stop. Every time Quin brought up Tasha, he made me say something about our relationship which wasn't necessarily the case. Yes, she and I were together and we were trying to make it work. But, trying to make it work, and succeeding at it, weren't the same thing.

"Tasha and I aren't what everyone sees us as."

"Oh," Quin said suddenly giving me his full attention.

"Yeah. I mean, we've been dating for a while and we've talked about our future together. But sometimes it feels like there's something missing. Actually, it feels like that a lot."

"What do you think is missing?"

"Her presence, for one. She's never around. And, that's fine when I'm in the heart of football season with twice-a-day practices. That might even work if I were to get drafted and spend a third of the year on the road. But, shouldn't she want to spend time with me more than she does? Shouldn't I want to spend more time with her?"

"You don't want to spend time with her?"

"It's not that don't want to spend time with her. It's that I don't care whether I do or not. It's harsh to say out loud, but it's true."

"If you don't want to spend time with her, then why are you with her?"

"It's not that I don't want to spend time with her."

"I get it. I get it. But, it would seem to me that if you two are talking about, um, spending a long time together, you should look forward to it."

"I can't argue with that," I told him.

"Then, why don't you?"

I stared at Quin not sure what to say. I wanted to say that it was because she wasn't him. But that felt unfair.

"Because she doesn't give me the tingles," I said meaning the same thing.

"That's important," Quin said suddenly in a better mood than moments before. "Have you ever felt the tingles from someone?"

"From one person," I told him hoping he wouldn't ask anymore.

"Who's that?" Quin asked hesitantly.

Staring into his beautiful eyes was too much. I couldn't do this, not to him, not to myself.

"Someone I shouldn't feel them for."

"Oh," Quin said deflating.

"So, change your mind about grabbing something to eat? I could always grab a bite. And Tasha wouldn't be back from hiking with Vi for a few hours."

"No. I should go," Quin said resigned.

"Okay. That's fair. Did you have fun?"

"It had its moments," he said with a smile.

"You still trust me to teach you how to be the life of the party?"

"First of all, I never trusted you to be a miracle worker."

I laughed.

"But, I'm willing to see what you have to offer," Quin said with a smile.

Man, did I love his smile.

"Fair enough. I think I passed the quiz, by the way."

"Good! I guess I'm not that bad of a tutor after all. Though, I would have hoped you did more than just pass."

"I'm sure I did. And you are a hell of a tutor. I can't wait to see what you have in store for me next."

"I guess you'll find out," Quin said with a devious smile.

Wait, was Quin flirting with me? However he meant it, it shot a tingle through my body and shook me to my core. When that guy did something, he did it right.

"I can't wait to find out," I told him before walking him back to campus and awkwardly returning to my truck.

I had never wanted to kiss someone so much in my life. I knew I couldn't and I wasn't even sure if Quin was interested in anything like that. At least I was able to establish that he was into guys. For the time being, that was enough. I could survive on that hope for a while.

When Tasha texted that there was traffic and that she wouldn't get back to campus until late, I drove home. It was probably for the best. After spending the day with Quin, my mind was elsewhere.

After a forty-minute drive, I turned onto the empty road that led to my house. My dad's truck was running in the driveway with its lights on.

"Oh no," I said knowing how the rest of the night would go.

Parking next to my father's truck, I got out and looked into its windows. He wasn't there. It was a worse sign that he had made it into the house. At least if he was passed out, his night would be over.

Opening the truck's door, I reached in and shut it off. With the keys in hand, I looked back at the cabin. The kitchen and living room lights poured onto the ground outside the windows. The TV was blasting. I took a long measured breath, gathered myself, and made the short walk to the front door.

Stepping inside, the place was a mess. This wasn't the way I had left it. The lamps shone from the floor where they had been tossed, the couch was overturned, the TV was sitting on its side, and things that used to be in the fridge were now scattered between the two rooms.

"I don't want to hear it," my father grumbled drawing my attention to the kitchen table.

The red-headed man looked his usual shade of ruddy pink. Like I suspected, he had a near-empty bottle of Lonehand Sour Mash Whiskey clutched in his grip. Tennessee's finest.

"Dad…"

"I don't wanna hear it. Do you know how much I sacrificed for you?"

"I know, Dad. You sacrificed everything," I recited from our script while looking around to see what I had to clean up first.

"That's right, everything! I God damn sacrificed everything. And for what?"

"So, I could become a big star," I said skipping a few pages ahead.

"Don't you fuckin' do it. Don't you talk to me like that," he bellowed. "I should just go. I should get in my fuckin' truck and never come back to this shit hole again."

This was always that part that hurt the most. You would think I would have gotten used to him talking about leaving, but I never could. Maybe it's because I knew his leaving was in my hands.

My father saw what I was capable of doing on the football field long before anyone else did. He saw that I would be a top NFL draft prospect and with it would come millions of dollars. He always made clear that he would stick around for that. There was no telling what he would do once he got his cut, but until then, I was pretty sure he wasn't going anywhere.

"This wouldn't be a shithole if you stopped wrecking the place."

"Fuck you!"

"Nice Dad. Way to talk to your son."

"You're not my son."

"Come on, Dad. Don't start this again."

This was a new subplot he had added to our script not too long ago. It went that I embarrassed him for not living up to my potential, so I couldn't be his son.

"You're not. You're just some baby I stole thinking I could make some money…"

"Enough, Dad! I can't take it anymore! You wanna leave so bad? Here!"

Pitching back my arm, I through his truck keys so hard it shattered the window and disappeared into the night.

"You wanna go? Take your fuckin' truck and go. If you wanna stick around and milk me of everything I got for eternity, then stay. I just don't give a shit anymore. You hear me? I can't take this anymore."

Bubbling with anger, I stormed to my room. The cabin shook as I slammed the door behind me. Staring back at it, I panted in fury. Tears rolled down my cheeks in rage. I wasn't crying because of the things he said, it was because I was trapped.

I had no mother or family. He was all I had. Without him, I was alone. But the only way I would ever get his horrid voice out of my head was if I let him go.

As hateful as he was, I knew I wouldn't be in the position I was if not for him. When sober, he reminded me of it every day. And, he was right.

Yeah, it was me on the field for 6 am practices and 7 pm sprints. But all he did for sixteen years was drive me from place to place and stand on the sidelines watching me play.

I knew what he was doing. He was keeping an eye on his investment. And, when I was 10-years-old and I would beg him in tears to do anything else but throw another football, he forced me to continue.

I truly wouldn't have anything without him. Not my scholarship. Not my football-loving girlfriend. And not my chance to play in the NFL. I don't know who I would be without everything he did. But, was the price I paid too high.

All of my swirling thoughts stopped when I heard a terrifying sound.

"No," I said sprinting back into the living room and finding my dad gone.

It was him starting up his truck. He was doing it. He was leaving. I didn't want him to go.

Running outside I saw him sway as he ground his gears looking for reverse. As drunk as he was, he was going to kill himself. I had to stop him.

"Dad!" I shouted running to the door of his truck and throwing it open.

"Get the fuck off me!" He yelled as I reached across him and again took the keys.

He didn't put up much resistance after that. We were both out of breath and dazed.

"You were really gonna go, weren't you?" I asked him staring into his eyes for the truth.

"You're not my son," was the only thing he replied.

Hurting me was so easy for him that he didn't even look evil when he said it. He stated it as if it were a fact.

"Ya know, sometimes I wish I wasn't. But I am. And you're my dad," I said resigned. "Come, let me get you to bed."

"I don't want to go to bed," he mumbled.

"Then I'll put you in front of the TV. You want that?"

His mouth puckered like he was trying to remember how to pout. "Yeah."

"Okay. Let me help you inside."

He leaned towards me and the door and I took his weight into my arms.

That was the beginning of a few very hard weeks. I'm not sure how different it was for my father. But, for me, it was when I realized that, if I didn't watch him every chance I got, he could be gone.

I still went to practices, games, and classes, but not much else. The only thing that brought my life any joy was the few hours a week I would spend with Quin. I was barely keeping up my end of our deal, but I told him

I was having a little trouble at home and he seemed to understand.

I think he saw how stressed I was. I definitely didn't feel like myself. The strange thing was that Tasha didn't even notice. She didn't notice that I wasn't around as much and that my life was crumbling around me. I was starting to wonder if this was what I should expect for the rest of our lives together.

With final exams and the end of the semester quickly approaching, Quin suggested that we increase our study time. Although I was on top of everything mentioned in class since I started attending, there were still a few weeks of material that Quin hadn't caught me up on.

"The final exam is going to cover all of that material," Quin said with the serious look he always got whenever we talked tutoring.

"As you keep reminding me," I said with a smile.

"You need to pass this class. It's not funny," he implored.

"I know."

"Then what are you laughing at?"

"You," I said teasingly.

"Oh, that's nice. Laugh at the guy trying to help you."

"Come on, it's not like that. It's just, you get this little crinkle in your forehead whenever you start worrying about me. And when you get it, I know I'm going to get a lecture about how important it is that I pass this class. At this point, I'm pretty sure you care more about it than I do and my entire future rests on it."

Quin looked at me for a second and then relaxed and laughed.

"Okay. I guess I've gotten a little intense about it," Quin admitted.

"A little?"

"Just a little," he insisted. "But it's that I want this for you. You've spent your life working towards this one thing. I can't be the one responsible for you not getting it."

I looked into Quin's worried eyes and stepped towards him. Gripping his shoulders in either hand, I squeezed.

"Quin, that is so sweet of you. I'm not sure anyone in my life cares about me more. But, you have to know, if I don't get what I've been working for, you won't be to blame. Everything I do and have done, has been my choice. You are simply the angel sitting on my shoulder whispering in my ear trying to get me to do the right thing. I thank you for that."

"I just want you to get everything you deserve. You're so close."

I let go of Quin and scanned the campus quad through the window of the study hall.

"I want it too, but I feel like I'm burning the candle on both ends. Between school and football, and watching over my dad, I can barely breathe."

"What's wrong with your dad?" Quin asked concerned.

"What's not wrong with him?" I said searching my mind for what I could tell him that could explain it. "He just needs me around a lot. That's all."

"If it helps, maybe we could meet at your place," Quin said hesitantly and with a hint of something else in his eyes.

When he looked at me like that, I usually lost all resistance. As much as I wanted to return our sessions to somewhere where we could be alone, I wasn't sure if I wanted to subject him to my life. He didn't talk much about it, but everything about him told me that he came from a stable home and money. My life was exactly the opposite.

I liked him thinking of me as the famous football player without a care in the world. I liked it when everyone did because the truth was so far from that fantasy. I didn't know if I was ready for Quin to see me for who I was.

"I'll think about it," I told him.

"Why not just say yes?" He asked softly.

It suddenly felt like this wasn't just a request to change our venue. This somehow felt like he was asking me to… I don't know, choose him, or something.

"I'll think about it. But, I'm here now. Maybe we should get to work?"

Quin's request haunted me for the rest of the night. Was I reading too much into it? I didn't think so. He had asked me why I didn't just say yes. It was a great question.

It was like two worlds were clawing at me. The first was the one I had known my whole life. It included my dad, Tasha, football fame, and a huge payday. The other included Quin, happiness, and a life I couldn't begin to imagine.

Would choosing a life with Quin mean I would have to give up playing in the NFL? It was hard to tell. I had heard of a few ex-players coming out as bisexual. But as far as I knew, there were no current players who had.

And, if I did come out, what was I supposed to come out as. At least gay was acceptable. Everyone cheers for the gay guy who pushes against societal pressure and overcomes. Who cheers when someone comes out as bisexual? No one. And, that's what I would be, wouldn't I?

I'm not foolish enough to believe that because Quin makes me tingle unlike anyone has before, that all of the feelings I had for girls growing up meant nothing. Sure, I've been drawn to guys before Quin, but that didn't change what I thought about Tasha when we first met.

The reason I'm questioning my future with her isn't because I'm questioning my interest in women. It's because I'm questioning if Tasha and I work together. She clearly wants to spend more time with her best friend than she does me. And, now that Quin has shown me how it feels to be cared about, I'm wondering if what Tasha is offering me is enough.

Who's going to champion that struggle. What organization is going to offer me an award for having the courage to acknowledge that? And, without society pushing back on the NFL, what team is going to invite a person like me into their showers?

So, choosing the world with Quin in it does feel like giving up on football which also means giving up on having a father. Because, I can't be sure how the NFL would react to an openly bisexual player. But I can be sure how my father would react to a son who doesn't make it to the NFL.

At the same time, though, I might be falling in love with Quin. I've never felt like this for anyone. I can't stop thinking about him. I fantasize about touching him. I can't wait to see him.

I thought I loved Tasha. I really did. But it was because I didn't know what love was or how it felt. This feeling is what people write songs about. I get it now. And, I get all of those movies that implied that love came at a cost.

My cost would be everything I have. I could have fame, family, and financial stability for the first time in my life. Or, I could have love. That was the choice I had to make.

Chapter 7

Quin

"You know you're eventually going to have to make a move on him, right?" Lou said with his elbows on the table and cut of stripped steak gangling from the end of his fork.

"I do not know that," I protested.

"You don't expect him to do it, do you?"

"I'm not expecting anyone to do it. I'm not expecting anything."

"Ahh, Lamb Chop, sometimes you make me so sad."

"There's nothing to feel sad about. Nothing's going on between us."

"That's what makes me so sad. On one side there's you, an obliviously scrumptious love nugget who can't seem to lose of his virginity…"

"You're a virgin, too," I quickly reminded him.

He put his hand on his chest and gave me a sad look.

"But for me, it's by choice. I'm saving myself for the right man. You? You want to get rid of yours like it's the plague. Yet you're hooked on a guy who is clearly in love with you but can't see past the sham relationship he's in. Tragic!"

When I didn't respond, Lou said, "Not going to say anything?"

"No. I think you said it all. And I am kinda sad."

"Wait, I didn't say *you* were sad. You're great. You're hot and smart, and you come from a good family…"

"What does my family have to do with this?"

"You're marriage material! Some guy needs to put a ring on that."

"Wow, that progressed quickly."

"That's my point. You're moving too slow. Get on that man, preferably with him on his back and you riding him like a cowboy. Or, are you a top? I can't tell with you. What is your preference? You like it Lone Ranger or side-saddle?"

"Which one's which?" I asked confused.

"Doesn't matter. You like it going or coming?"

"I don't know. Both, maybe."

"So, you're vers? I've seen you in the shower. That makes sense."

"When did you see me in the shower?"

"When haven't I seen you in the shower? That's not the point."

"Then what is the point?"

"The point is that you're vers and that man, Cage, is a definite top."

"You think so?"

"I know these things," he said confidently.

"But you've never had sex?"

"You don't have to have had sex to feel the energy. That boy has serious top energy. He's a quarterback for crying out loud. He's used to being in control… holding onto people's butts. It's quarterback stuff."

"I see."

"And, usually he would be the one to make the first move. But, in this case, you're going to have to find your big dick energy and sack up."

"Seriously, though, when did you see me in the shower?"

"This is you trying to change the topic so you don't have to think about moving things forward."

"No, this is me wondering if I need to start locking the bathroom door."

Lou put his hand on his chest. "I have so little. Do you really want to take that away from me, too?"

I stared at Lou wondering if this was him teasing me again. It wasn't that I was shy about my body. Clothes were considered optional in my household growing up.

But, there were times when I thought about Cage in the shower. The thought of bending over and hiking that quarterback the ball usually made me have to take things into my own hands… And then again once I was back in my room.

God, did that man make me feel things. Mostly, what he made me feel was thirsty — the human body only had so much fluid in it — and… sore.

My phone rang stopping me from exploring the shower situation with Lou any further. Pulling out my phone, I was surprised to see Cage's name.

I held up my finger asking Lou to give me a moment.

"Cage, what's going on? You never call me."

Lou reacted with childish delight. I ignored him.

"Do you think we could do our study session at my place tonight?" Cage asked sounding distressed. "If the final exam wasn't tomorrow, I wouldn't ask. But…"

"No. Of course. Is there something going on with your father?"

"Um, yeah. He's having one of his bad days and I don't think I should leave him alone."

"I'm sorry to hear that. Yeah, I can come by. Just tell me when."

The phone fell silent.

"Cage?"

"I'm here. Um, before you come, there's probably something you should know."

"Okay."

"We don't have much."

"What do you mean?"

"I mean, I attend school on a scholarship and my father isn't working right now. He hasn't worked in a while."

"Should I bring snacks, or… something?"

"I mean, if you want. But, that's not what I'm trying to say. I just don't think you should expect much. I'm not… Just don't expect much."

"Will you be there?" I asked clarifying.

"Yeah, of course."

"Then, your place will have everything I need."

Cage was again silent.

"Cage?"

"I'm here. I'll text you my address. I would offer to pick you up, but…"

"Don't worry about it. I'll do rideshare or something."

"It's kind of far. If you ever turn in your timecard for all of the tutoring you're doing, I'm sure the football program will reimburse you for it."

"Unless you're commuting every day from Florida, I'm sure I can handle it."

"Okay. I'll see you then."

"See you."

I ended the call and stared at my phone.

"Ouuuuu!" Lou said excitedly. "Quin and Cage sitting in a tree. K I S S I N G."

"Shut up."

Lou stuck out his tongue miming a French kiss.

"You're disgusting," I said with a smile.

"I'm just proud my Lamp Chop is gonna be gettin' some fixin's."

"You're ridiculous," I said still staring down at my phone.

"Okay, what's wrong?"

"Cage is embarrassed about me seeing his place."

"I get that."

I looked up at Lou surprised.

"Why should he be embarrassed? He shouldn't be embarrassed. Whatever he has has made him who he is and I like him… a lot."

"Says the guy whose family is worth, like, a billion dollars. And, have you shared that fact with him."

"I didn't want to make it an issue. Besides, that's not my money, it's my parent's money."

"No. You just have access to as much of it as you want whenever you want."

Lou's words stung. He wasn't wrong. And, as much as I would like to believe that it didn't shape me, it did. Just like how Cage grew up had shaped him.

"More important than your family's ungodly amount of wealth, have you told Cage about the other thing? Because to me, that feels a slight bit more important than being able to charge an airplane to your credit card."

"It hasn't come up yet," I admitted knowing Lou was right.

"Then, maybe you should get on that. Because, he needs to know who he is getting involved with… you know, if he ever grows a pair and asks you out. Or, you ask him out. You know that's an option, right?"

"He has a girlfriend."

"From what you've told me, I need to ask, does he?"

"He does."

Lou leaned back and crossed his arms. "Okay."

"But, you're right. He might need to know."

"That's my Lamp Chop," Lou said with a sober smile.

Cage wasn't exaggerating when he said he lived far away. For him to make a 7 am practice he would have to leave his house at 6 am and get up at 5:30 at the latest. The amount of devotion it would take to do that every day for years, if not his entire life, was impressive.

And, the closer I got to his place, the more nervous I got. Whatever it was that he was embarrassed about, I was sure I would be able to accept. But, what I had to tell him could easily be too much for him.

Telling him might be the end of what we have going on… whatever that is. Tonight could be the last night that he looked at me like I was the only person in the world. That would hurt.

By the time the car pulled up in front of Cage's place, I was nearing a panic attack. Everything surrounding me was too much to ask someone to be around. Cage had his whole life ahead of him. He was going to be a famous football player with millions of fans. I would be an anchor around his neck.

It wouldn't even be fair to ask him to deal with my stuff. He had his own stuff going on. Add that to whatever he was dealing with with his dad, and my stuff was starting to feel like something best kept to myself.

Cage stepped out the front door before I could call him letting him know I was here. Adding a healthy tip for the driver, I got out and approached him. He wore a plaid shirt, shorts, and he was barefoot. I had never seen his feet before.

I didn't have a foot fetish, but his were wide and strong looking. It made me think of other parts of him that I did have a thing for. But I quickly pushed aside the thought knowing that I didn't want to meet his father for the first time with a huge bulge in my pants.

"You made it," Cage said uncomfortably. "Did you have any problems finding the place?"

"No, it was pretty easy."

"It was far, right?"

"You don't live close to campus. Did you grow up out here?" I asked looking around at the thick woods surrounding the cabin.

"From as early as I remember. You said you grew up in New York, right?"

"Manhattan," I clarified.

"Right. So this place must be…"

"Where Bigfoot lives? Pretty much."

Cage laughed, seeming relaxed for the first time.

"Well, Bigfoot actually lives a few miles from here so you're not far off. Great guy, by the way. You don't even notice the fur once you've talked to him for a while."

I laughed, and like that we were both comfortable.

"Let's go inside. We have a lot of stuff to cover," Cage said leading me in.

With the door closed, I looked around at the space. I didn't know what to expect after Cage's warning. It was certainly nicer than I was picturing.

As a kid, I had spent a lot of time in the Bahamas. Both of my dads had places there and we often ate at neighbor's homes. This cabin was much nicer than many of them.

Of course, I couldn't tell Cage that his place was nicer than the places in the Bahamas where we had our winter homes. I didn't think he would take that how I would intend it. So, instead, I said, "It must have been cool growing up here."

"It was okay. If not a little isolating."

"I know what you mean. One of my dads owns an island with only the house on it. So, replace the trees surrounding this place with water and the birds for sharks, and you have every one of my summers since I was three," I said with a smile.

"Did you say that your father owns an island?"

I froze realizing what I had said. Not only was Cage looking at me like I was a freak, someone on the couch in front of us turned around and stared at me. Cage followed my gaze.

"Dad, this is Quin. He's my…"

Cage paused making me more than anxious to hear how he was going to describe me.

"He's my good friend. He's helping me pass the class I was telling you about."

"It's good to meet you, Sir," I said to the red-headed man.

Cage's father looked me over, grunted, and then returned to watching TV.

"We should go to my room," Cage told me.

"It was good meeting you, Sir," I said getting nothing in reply.

Entering Cage's bedroom, he closed the door behind us.

"You have to excuse my Dad. He's having an off day."

"He seemed fine to me."

"Well, fine is relative. We can sit on the bed."

I took off my shoes, emptied the contents of my backpack into the center of the bed, and sat cross-legged. Cage joined me searching my eyes.

"What?"

"Are you expecting me to forget that you just said that your father owns an island?"

"Oh, that."

"Yeah, that."

"It's small. Everyone in the Bahamas owns an island."

"Everyone in the Bahamas owns an island?" Cage asked shocked.

"Okay, that's not true. I don't know why I said that. Actually, that's not true either. I do know why I said it, it was because I don't want you to think we're that different."

"We are that different," Cage said matter-of-factly. "But that's okay. I like your differences. I just hope you aren't too disappointed by mine."

"I literally don't know what you're talking about. You are the most normal person I know. Of course, the only other person I know here is Lou, so that's not saying much."

Cage laughed. "So it's a low bar."

"You just have to be able to deal with me and you've surpassed 99% of the population."

Cage laughed. "Come on you're not that bad. Maybe 95% of the population," he teased.

"You're right. Thinking about it now, it's 95%. I stand corrected."

Cage laughed again. God, did I love hearing him laugh.

"You know, you do that a lot," Cage said with a smile.

"What?"

"Put yourself down."

"Do I?"

"Yeah."

"I didn't realize I was doing it."

"You do. You should be nicer to my friend. He's a great guy," Cage said playfully.

"Great is a relative term."

"There you go again. Take the compliment."

"It's easier said than done. What if I said you were the most amazing guy I've ever met and that every time I was with you I wished the time would never end?"

Cage froze.

"Not so easy to take a compliment now, is it?"

"Do you really feel like that?"

"Oh, that was kind of a lot wasn't it?"

"No, seriously do you feel like that?"

"Does it matter? You have a girlfriend."

"What does it matter if I have a girlfriend?"

"It matters because if I did think that, it would be because I wanted more to happen between us than was possible."

"What if it was possible?"

"What do you mean?"

"I mean, what if I didn't have a girlfriend?"

I looked into Cage's beautiful, soul-crackling eyes. He was serious. He was considering breaking up with his girlfriend for me.

"There are things about me you don't know," I said unable to stop myself.

"What? That you're more adorable than I already think you are?"

"No, stop. There are things I need to tell you before you do or say anything that we won't be able to come back from."

"Oh, you're serious."

"I am."

Cage shifted uncomfortably. "Okay. What's up?"

My heart pounded.

"Where do I begin? Okay. I mentioned my father has an island."

"I remember something about that, yes."

"It was ten minutes ago. I hope you do."

Cage chuckled. "Yes, I remember."

"Well, he owns an island because he is very rich."

"Like how rich."

"Like, he owns an island, rich."

Cage laughed. "Got it. And you grew up very rich?"

"Yes."

"I figured. Is that what you were scared to tell me? That you grew up with your own island?"

"Not even close."

Cage leaned back startled. "Okay."

I touched my brow wondering if I was sweating. I was starting to.

"Here's the thing. I grew up with two dads."

"So, your parents are gay? Big deal."

"Actually they're not. And neither is my Mom."

"Oh, so your family is polyamorous."

"Yes, and my dads are bisexual."

"That's cool!"

"Is it?" I asked surprised.

"Yeah. Are you polyamorous?"

"I don't think so. I think I'm looking for one person."

"I feel that way too. I mean, if the person I cared about needed that, I would consider it. But if I had a choice, I would choose to be with one person," he said with a smile.

"Okay. That's great. But…"

"There's a but?"

I searched for the words.

"I'm… kind of… the poster child for a polyamorous relationship, specifically one with two men and a woman."

"How are you the poster child for that?"

"Because, do you know how they discovered a way for two men to have a baby with a woman?"

"I mean, I heard something about that, but I assumed it wasn't real," Cage explained.

"You thought it wasn't real?" I asked stunned.

"Yeah. Why? Is it?"

I stared at Cage shocked. He had heard about it and had dismissed it as being made up. That meant we could have gone for a long time without having to talk about it. Caught in the storm that was my life, I had never imagined that there were people who simply didn't believe it.

"Wait, are you saying that science has figure out how two men could have a baby together?"

"A woman is necessary for the procedure, but yeah, they know how."

"How do you know this?"

I touched my brow with my heart slamming against my chest.

"Because my family knows the doctor who created the procedure."

"Your family knows the doctor?"

"Yeah."

"That's amazing. How does your family know the doctor?"

"Because…" I swallowed. "They met him when he performed the procedure on my parents."

"Wait… You?"

"Yeah. I was… the first."

"You were the first child ever born from two men having a baby?"

"A woman is a part of the procedure, but yes. And, I'm kind of famous for it. My face has been on the cover of pretty much every magazine that exists. I came to East Tennessee because I was hoping that the paparazzi wouldn't be able to find me here. So far it's worked, but it's just a matter of time before my whereabouts get out."

"That's unbelievable."

"If you find that hard to believe, buckle up because there's more."

"Okay," he said with his mouth now permanently hanging open.

"The procedure has a side effect."

"Oh!" He said looking concerned.

"It's not necessarily bad," I quickly told him. "Though it can be sometimes."

"What's the side effect?"

"The kids that come from the procedure are all really smart."

"How smart?"

"Really smart."

"How smart are we talkin'? We talkin' build a time machine smart?"

"No. But, I guess one of the kids is building a quantum tunneling device which is technically a time machine, but you have to be the size of a quantum particle to ride in it," I joked.

Cage didn't laugh.

"But that's her. And, quantum physics isn't my specialty."

"Then what is?"

"I can make connections that other people might miss."

"What do you mean?"

"I mean, I can make observations."

"Like what?" Cage asked skeptically. He wasn't believing me.

"Like, I know you're adopted."

"What?" Cage said stunned.

I had him.

"Yeah. And it wasn't the red hair, either. Red-headed parents have children with black hair all of the time. It's the dimples."

"What do you mean?" Cage asked captivated.

"Dimples are a genetic trait, meaning that it has to be passed down from your parents. But they aren't a collective group. Meaning, having a chin dimple doesn't make you more likely to have a cheek dimple. That means that you would have had to inherit each dimple separately. And the ones you have on either side of your bottom lip are called 'fovea inferior anguli oris' and are very rare.

"The odds of you inheriting all of your dimples from one parent is very low. I'm talking extremely low. For your dad not to have any dimples at all and for you to have so many, every member of his family would have had to have dimples going back for generations. And since that is even less likely, the obvious answer is most likely the correct one, that is that you're adopted."

I could not have been more proud of myself for making these observations. Would anyone else have noticed something so easy to miss? Even if they noticed, would they be able to put everything together like I had? I don't think so.

For me to be able to do it on demand for Cage, had to have impressed him. I wanted so badly to impress Cage. I wanted him to think I was special in a good way. I desperately wanted him to see that my difference could be useful and something he would want in his life. I would do anything for him not to see me like the freak everyone else did.

As I stared at Cage a lot changed on his face. The look of amazement he appeared to have as I explained my theory, morphed into something else. He wasn't happy. It looked like he was battling with something, and before the words left his mouth, I knew I had made a mistake.

"I'm not adopted," Cage said firmly.

He didn't know. Shit!

"You're right."

"What?" He asked confused.

"I'm mistaken."

"What do you mean, you're mistaken."

"I was thinking of, um, what was it again?"

My mind swirled trying to come up with something he would believe and that wouldn't make me seem like a complete asshole.

"Butt dimples."

"What?"

"I was thinking about butt dimples. You know, the indent people sometimes have in the butt cheek. That requires both parents to have it."

Cage looked at me confused.

"So, you said all of that, and what you meant was butt dimples."

"Yes," I said wanting him to believe me.

"I don't have butt dimples."

"Oh, then I guess none of what I said applies."

"Is anything you just told me true? I mean, about you being the first child born that way and the whole genius thing?"

As relieved as I was that he seemed willing to let my adoption theory go, I again felt the weight of having revealed myself to him.

"You can look it up," I confirmed.

Cage looked at me not knowing what to think. Slowly pulling out his phone, he typed in my name.

"What's your last name?"

"Toro. Quin Toro," I said feeling a sharp pain in my chest.

Cage's face shifted as the search results came up. He was overwhelmed by it all. He silently searched page after page scanning articles before going to the next one.

"It's true. You're a genius."

"And a freak," I added.

"No. You're amazing," Cage said looking up at me in awe.

A warm wave washed through me. I could have cried. It took everything in me not to. I came with so much baggage. Yet, he didn't seem to care. More than that, he saw them as something positive. I never felt more in love with someone in my life.

"Why didn't you mention any of this before? If I had what you have, it would be the first thing I told people."

"It wouldn't be."

"Oh, I think it would be," he said offering me his first smile in what felt like forever. I was getting addicted to them.

"It wouldn't be," I said unable to hide my sadness on the topic. "But thank you for saying that. Maybe we should get to work?"

"Oh right. We have an exam tomorrow."

Cage paused staring at me.

"Do you have the entire textbook memorized?"

"That's not the way it works. At least, not for me. I have to study like you do. It just comes easier."

"Oh. Okay," Cage said turning his attention to the books in the bed between us.

Filling him in on the last of what he missed before he joined the class, I found it hard to stay focused. Every so often he would look up at me. When he did, he would give me a smile that would melt my heart.

I pushed through because Cage needed to understand the material for the exam. But, it was hard not to melt in his gaze. I never wanted to be apart from him again. Knowing I couldn't have that ripped my heart out.

"That's all of it. I think you have it," I told him when he repeated the last of it back to me without having to refer to the textbook.

"I think I do," he said proudly. "That took a while."

"Did it?" I asked pulling out my phone. "It's 1:30?"

"Time flies when you're having fun," he said looking as charming as sin.

"Do rideshares still run at this hour?"

"They do in the city. But, you're not going to be able to get one to come out here."

"A taxi maybe."

"You could stay over. I have practice before class tomorrow. I could get you back early."

"Stay over?" I said feeling my heart race. "I guess I could sleep on the couch."

"You're not gonna sleep on the couch. Besides, my dad probably fell asleep out there."

"Then, the floor?"

"I'm not letting you sleep on the floor! You're only here this late because you were helping me pass my class. If anything, that's where I'm sleeping."

"I can't let you sleep on the floor. It wouldn't be good for your back. How is your back, by the way?" I asked remembering him having an issue with it the night I started tutoring him.

"My back?"

"Yeah. Remember at my room?"

"Oh, yeah! No, it's, um, a little stiff but not as bad as it was. It was probably just all of the tension that night."

"You were nervous about not being able to play next semester?"

"Something like that."

"So, if neither of us is going to sleep on the floor, where are we going to sleep?" I asked hoping I knew what he was going to say.

"We could share the bed."

"Are you sure that's a good idea?"

"Why wouldn't it be? We're just going to be sleeping."

Or, not sleeping considering how hard my heart was beating just thinking about it.

"I guess. Okay."

"Okay," he said confidently.

We cleared off the bed and stared at each other.

"Would you like something to change into? You probably don't want to sleep in your jeans."

"I'm fine," I told him nervous as all hell.

"You sure, because I'm gonna get comfortable," he said before taking off his shirt. "See."

I definitely saw. The man was a god. His muscular arms, his rippling chest, everything about him sent tingles through me that landed between my legs.

"Come on. You can get comfortable," he said with a smile.

I badly wanted to get naked with him. It was the beginning of every one of my fantasies. I didn't know if I should, but I couldn't resist anymore.

"Okay," I said slowly pulling off my shirt.

"Woah!" Cage said once my shirt was in my hand.

"What?"

"You are in surprisingly good shape."

"Genetics," I admitted feeling self-conscious.

"Nice. So, are you going to sleep in your jeans?"

"Are you?"

"No," he said not making a move to take his pants off.

I stared at him waiting. Was he actually going to do it? If he did, maybe I would too. What was he waiting for?

When he finally reached for the button on his pants, my dick grew hard. Without a shirt, there was nothing to hide my bulge. What was I supposed to do?

He wasn't looking at me as he pulled down his pants. As he stepped out of them and pushed them aside, he didn't look up. I wondered why until I saw the outline of his large dick stretched across his boxer briefs. Cage was hard. Very hard. At least I hoped he was because he was already humongous.

I couldn't believe what was happening. Were we just getting comfortable for bed, or was something else going on? I drank in all of him making my hard cock flinch. When he finally met my gaze without looking down, he said,

"What about you?"

My cock flinched again. There was no way I was going to be able to hide my arousal even if I wanted to. Did I want to hide it?

I don't think I did. I wanted him to see all of me. I wanted to see all of him. And with his eyes still locked on mine, I lowered my pants standing in front of him in just my underwear.

Cage did nothing but stare into my eyes until for a brief moment, he blinked down to see me. It made him smile.

"Should we get into bed?" He asked me.

"Okay," I told him unsure what was going to happen next.

The two of us climbed into bed and under the sheets. We both laid on our backs staring at the ceiling.

"I should get the lights," Cage said to me.

"I guess," I told him barely able to hear him over the sound of my heartbeats.

Cage got out of bed again, flicked the light switch next to the door, and returned to bed in the dark.

It took a while for my eyes to adjust to the darkness, but it was a moonlit night. Still not sure what was happening, I stayed on my back not looking at him. At no point did he move. Had he already fallen asleep? Could anyone fall asleep so quickly?

With the deafening silence enveloping us, I couldn't take it anymore. Cage was so close that it was torture not to touch him. I had to at least see the beautiful body whose heat consumed me. So, moving like it was the most natural thing in the world, I rolled over settling on my side.

Buried in the shadows, I opened my eyes. He was facing me. His eyes were closed. Maybe he was asleep. If he was, it meant that I could look at him unhindered. I could examine every contour of his angular, masculine face.

Cage was the most gorgeous man I had ever seen. His wavy hair that lay gently across his forehead, his broad shoulders that sat uncovered, his lightly hairy chest, I desperately wanted to touch him. To feel the heat of his skin next to mine would be enough to live the rest of my life on.

Needing to be closer to him, I moved my hand onto the bed between us. I was less than a foot away from his sleeping body and didn't dare to get any closer. I wanted to. God did I want to, but I knew I couldn't… until, as if sensing me there, Cage moved his hand between us an inch away from mine.

I could feel the heat of him on me. I could barely breathe. Parting my lips as my heart thumped, I couldn't stand it. I needed to be closer. Being apart from him hurt too much.

Moving my fingers slowly, I stretched them out. They weren't long enough. He was right there. I could practically feel them. I would need to move my entire hand if I wanted his touch. Could I do that, though? Should I do it?

My debate didn't matter because as if he needed it too, his strong hand crossed to mine and moved on top of it. It was him who had done it. It could have been the reflex actions of someone asleep, but I didn't think it was. He wanted to hold my hand and I wanted to hold his.

So, moving delicately, I allowed his fingers to fall between mine. When they did, I slowly intertwined them. It was everything I had hoped it would be. I tried to breathe without making a sound but it was the most erotic moment of my life. His touch was a swirling wind that encircled my warm, naked body.

I was in love with Cage. I could no longer deny it. And, touching him in the moonlight, there was nowhere else in the world I would rather be. I wanted this moment to last forever. It lasted for hours, but eventually, my exhausted heart slowed down and I fell asleep.

Chapter 8

Cage

I'm falling in love with Quin. I can't deny it. Even as I lie in the morning light not getting nearly enough sleep, all I could think about was how I could touch him like I did last night.

When I heard him place his hand on the bed between us, I sent out my hand in search of his. I didn't know if I should or if he would want me to, but I couldn't stop myself. I need Quin. I ache to be with him. I feel like I would go crazy without him. And to be so close without being able to wrap my arms around him was torture.

I was about to relieve myself of the painful agony when I shifted and something buzzed. When it did, I realized I was still half asleep because it woke me up. I knew the sound. It was my alarm clock. I had forgotten to turn it off.

It was probably more accurate to say that I wasn't foolish enough to turn it off. Ever since I had met Quin, getting eight hours were impossible. Even if I was in bed in time to do it, alone in the darkness was when I thought about him the most. So to have him here now was like a dream come true.

The alarm buzzed again. Oh right, the alarm. I didn't want it to wake up Quin.

Instead of letting it ring like I usually had to, I popped open my eyes and figured out where I was. I was on the right side of the bed. The alarm clock was on the left. I had to reach over Quin to get it.

Not thinking about it, I straddled the guy beneath me and hit the switch. With it off, I realized where I was. Although our bodies weren't touching, I was hovering above him. I froze and looked down. He was on his back facing up.

My God, did I want to bend down and kiss him. I was right there. He was so close. And then he opened his eyes.

I stared at him, caught. He smiled, or was it a blush?

"Good morning," he said in a raspy morning voice.

Looking at him, I relaxed.

"Morning," I said getting one more good look at him and then rolling back to my side of the bed. "Sorry about that," I told him.

"No, I liked it," he said smiling ear to ear.

"You liked the alarm?"

"Oh, I thought you meant…" He blushed again. "It was fine. Does that mean we have to get up? It's so early."

"I have to get to practice. It's a long drive."

"Okay," he said squirming his body adorably.

Watching him settle, I was about to get up when I noticed something. I had a serious morning wood situation going on. Sure, I was only too happy to show him my hard dick last night. But, I was so turned on by being with him that I had lost all inhibition.

After a night's sleep, as short as it was, I wasn't so bold. Yeah, I was still as turned on as all get out. But, we weren't getting into bed. We were leaving it. That made a difference.

"We could sleep a little while longer, right?" Quin asked facing me, his gorgeous eyes begging for me to hold him.

"You can, but I have to get up. The bowl game's on Saturday. This is our last full practice before it. I can't be late."

"Fine," Quin said disappointed.

Staring into his eyes I tried to think of the next time I could get him back here.

"Do you want to come to the game? Have you ever been?"

"You want me to come to your game?" He asked with a smile.

"Yeah. Why wouldn't I?"

"I don't know. I thought it might be your manly space or something."

"Manly space?"

"You know, a place for your girlfriend and all of your football friends to meet and do football things."

"First of all, the stadium seats 20,000 people. There's room for everyone. Second of all, Tasha hasn't been to one of my games in I don't know how long. You should come. That way you can see what all the fuss is about."

"I can see what all of the fuss is about from here," he said making my heart melt.

"I mean, why it's so important for me to pass the class we stayed up all night studying for."

"Oh, yeah. Okay."

"I can get you a couple of tickets. You can bring Lou."

"I don't know how much he's into football."

"Is he into football players?" I asked with a smile.

"He's into anyone with a dick."

"Then tell him that everyone on the field is guaranteed to have a dick," I said with a smile.

Quin chuckled. I loved hearing him laugh.

"I'll see."

"Cool."

"Will you win?"

"For you? Anything. I wouldn't have been able to pass the class without you."

"You haven't passed it yet," he reminded me.

"But I will. I'm confident. You're a good teacher. Thank you."

"Does that mean my tutoring time with you is done?"

I looked at Quin realizing it for the first time.

"I guess it does."

The thought of not having an excuse to be with him broke my heart.

"You definitely have to come to the game. I mean it. Promise me you will even if Lou doesn't."

Quin looked me in the eyes and smiled.

"I will. I promise."

"Good. Now, I guess I have to get up."

I flinched my dick finding that it was now only partially hard. That meant that I could look impressive for Quin without making things incredibly awkward for our 40-minute drive back to campus.

Getting out of bed, I was sure to stand profile for him as I readjusted my shorts. I gave it enough time for him to get a good look at me, before turning and heading for the bathroom. There was only one in the house and it was outside my door. Leaving Quin, I closed the bedroom door behind me and I did what I had to to prepare for the day.

When I got back to the room, Quin was dressed. As he took care of morning business, I made a breakfast smoothie and packed my bag getting ready to go.

Our ride back to town consisted mostly of him drilling me on what we had gone over the night before. With his help, I really did feel ready. I couldn't imagine anyone else preparing me as well as he did. I really wanted to do well on the exam for him.

It turns out that he was a literal genius. I was nowhere near that. But I wanted to at least show him that I wasn't a dumb jock. I wanted to be someone worthy of being with someone like him even if I couldn't be with him right now.

When I had floated the idea of breaking up with Tasha, I didn't get the response I was hoping for. I guess I was looking for something a little more enthusiastic from him. If I was going to dismantle my world to be with him, I wanted to feel like it wouldn't be for nothing.

His response was positive, but not motivating. That left things still entirely up to me. It was a lot to think about. But, before I got there, I had practice, an exam, and what was probably the biggest game of my life.

If you are a legitimate NFL prospect, NFL teams might request film on you at the beginning of the school year. After sifting through the hundreds of hours they get from around the country, teams select where they will send their scouts.

Bowl games were where scouts came to see you in person. College bowls were highly attended, televised games during winter break. They allowed scouts to see how we played under pressure. At the end of bowl season, most teams knew who to put on their draft board. Bowl games were what allowed players to go pro.

As a senior, it would be the last bowl game of my life. It had to go well or else everything everyone sacrificed to get me here would have been for nothing. But, it wasn't like my relationship with my father hung in the balance and the weight of it was an elephant on my chest. Nope, it wasn't like that at all.

"Good luck at practice!" Quin wished me when I dropped him off at his dorm.

"Thanks."

"See you in class. And don't worry, you won't need luck for that one. You got it," he said with a smile.

"Thanks… for everything," I said hopelessly taken by him.

I watched him walk away. God, did his ass look good. He looked back a final time before disappearing into his building.

As I sat there, what I wanted became clear. I could no longer imagine a future without Quin in it. He had quickly become everything to me. What the hell was I supposed to do now?

Fortunately, I didn't have time to think about it. If I didn't get my ass to practice immediately, I was going to be late. Whatever I decided to do, it would probably affect my NFL prospects and I was going to need Coach's help. So, the last thing I wanted was to be on his bad side.

"You're late!"

"I'm sorry, Coach. I was up all night studying," I said as I ran past him on my way to the locker to change.

He followed a step behind.

"Studying, huh? It's funny how you're doing it without a tutor. You better not be bullshitting me, Rucker. If you don't pass that class, you'll be suspended from the team. There won't be anything I'll be able to do about it."

"I promise, I have a tutor. I keep telling him to register with you guys, but I don't think he needs the money. I'll pass the class, though. He's pretty incredible. He has me ready."

"You better be."

"Coach. I'm ready."

"Huh," he huffed looking at me suspiciously.

I couldn't tell what Coach was thinking or what it would mean, so I put it out of my mind by giving it all I had in practice. I was on the verge of puking by the end.

"I gotta go, Coach. I gotta take my exam," I told him staring at the giant clock at the far end of the stadium.

"Take it and get back here! We have more plays to go over."

"Got it, Coach."

I took off my helmet and upper pads before running across campus. Unlike the first time I did it, I was there at the beginning of class. There were no open seats left near Quin so I took one up front.

"Good luck, Mr. Rucker," the professor said as she handed me the exam.

"Thanks," I said before looking back for the only encouragement I cared about.

Quin smiled at me and mouthed, "You have this."

I mouthed, "Thanks," back.

It turned out that Quin had been right. I had never taken an easier exam in my life. I didn't pretend it had to do with anything other than Quin's preparation. It was like he knew what was going to be on the exam. The guy was incredible.

It did worry me a little that I was the first person to turn in my paper. I handed mine in before Quin did. There was no way that could be right. I probably hadn't gone over my answers enough times. But that couldn't be helped. I had to get back to practice.

Handing it in, the professor gave me a surprised look. I wasn't about to do anything that would indicate that I found it easy. I knew that would be tempting fate.

But I did make eye contact with Quin on the way out. I gave him a cocky look telling him it had been a breeze. He stopped himself from chuckling and then returned to his exam.

Leaving the room, I considered waiting for him. He couldn't be too far behind me. But, I had told Coach that I would head back as soon as I was done. Also, I didn't want to be the douchebag hanging out in the hallway in his football gear and cleats.

Running back across campus I got there in time for the film section. There was a lot to go over. From there, the team had another walk-through of plays. Coach was preparing us like Quin had prepared me for the exam. So, by the time I got back to the locker room, I was exhausted. All I wanted to do was go home.

Turning on my phone, I found a message from Quin.

'How was it?'

'So easy,' I wrote back. 'It's a good thing you stole the exam. I could never have passed without it.'

I thought it was funny, but Quin didn't reply.

'You'll be there on Saturday, right?'

'Wouldn't miss it,' he immediately wrote back.

'I'll put the tickets at 'Will Call'.'

'Okay. Thanks.'

'No. Thank you!' I said not knowing how else to express how grateful I was to him.

I knew that I didn't deserve to have someone like Quin in my life. My life was a mess. I had a girlfriend I didn't love. I didn't want to leave my house in fear that when I returned my father would be gone. And my career was set to take me away from him.

Quin was an incredibly amazing guy who deserved so much more than someone like me. He was someone who would literally go down in history. On top of that, he was sweet, and thoughtful, and brilliant. Who was I compared to all of that?

"You'll be at the game on Saturday, right Dad?" I asked him when I found him drinking in front of the TV.

"Yea," he said without looking at me.

I didn't stop staring at him. As much as I tried to ignore it when Quin said it, his words had stuck. Without knowing about my dad's drunken tirades about me not being his son, Quin had said that I was adopted.

That couldn't be a coincidence. Quin was an extremely smart guy. He knew all of that stuff about dimples. There was no way he had mixed it up with butt dimples. There was no way.

And, beyond dimples, there were a few more things that weren't quite as obscure. My father was a real redhead who went from pale to freckled pink. Quin had said that redheads had dark-haired kids all of the time. And that was what I had told myself growing up.

But, on top of that, my dad was left-handed while I was right-handed. He liked foods I found disgusting. He was super hairy while at 22, I still struggled to grow facial hair. And, I was pretty sure he was colorblind. Either that or he severely rejected societal pressure to match his socks.

None of those things meant anything on their own. But add them all together? It had always made me think. Now add that to my dad's rants and what Quin said about dimples and I couldn't ignore it anymore.

"What?" My father said having felt me stare.

Did I ask him about it while he was still somewhat sober? Would my asking him be the thing that finally made him leave? I couldn't deal with this. Not now, at least.

"What?" He asked again, this time a little pissed off.

"Your ticket will be at 'Will Call'," I told him looking away and heading to my room.

He grunted in reply.

"Boy?"

"You know I don't like it when you call me that," I told him.

"You know scouts will be there on Saturday, right?"

"I know."

"You prepared?"

"Coach has us ready."

"Good. Who was that boy you brought around last night?"

I stopped my exit as soon as he brought up Quin. If I was going to have a life with Quin, at some point I was going to have to talk to him about it.

"I told you. He's my tutor."

"He didn't leave last night."

"We were up late preparing for the exam I took today."

He grunted not taking his eyes off of me.

"By the way, I know you like her, but I don't think it's working out between Tasha and me."

"Make it work. She's good for you. Teams will like her."

"I can't be with someone because some team might like the way we look together. There's more to life than that."

"Do you know how much I sacrificed to get you where you are? You couldn't even begin to guess."

"And I appreciate that, Dad. But I don't see what that has to do with who I date."

"Don't you go ruining this now, Boy."

"I'm not ruining anything. I'm just telling you that she might not be the one."

"And, who is?"

"I don't know. But there are a lot of people out there."

"And none of them would do what she can do for you."

"You mean stand beside me on draft day and look pretty? I can't base my life on one moment that will have more to do with how I play on Saturday than who I stick my dick in."

"Don't you ruin this, Boy."

"I told you, don't call me that."

"I'll call you whatever I God damn want, Boy."

"Okay, I'm done," I told him seeing where the conversation was headed.

"Don't you walk away from me," he said after I exited to my room and shut the door behind me.

"Don't you fuck this up. Don't you go fuckin' this up, Boy. This is the best thing that will ever happen to you. Don't you give it all up for some piece of ass."

He had heard me. He knew what I was hinting at with Quin and it was clear that he didn't approve. But, it didn't matter. I was falling in love with him and there was nothing my dad could do to change that.

If Quin let me, I was going to make him mine. To others, it might seem like a choice, but it wasn't. I didn't think I could stand to be away from him if I tried. He had me and nothing that happened was going to change that. Not my father. Not what some scout would say. Nothing.

'Did you get the tickets?' I texted Quin as I sat in the locker room waiting to go out for the game.

"Put your phone away, Rucker. Get your head in the game," Coach said forcing me to return it to my bag before I got a reply from Quin.

Holding out as long as I could, I stared at the screen until the phone was out of sight. Still nothing. I had texted him yesterday and he had told me he and Lou would be here. I told him that I would make sure to win the game so that he enjoyed himself. He had just told me that he was looking forward to it, but nothing else.

I was expecting more from him. The truth was that I was having a hard time interacting with him since our class ended. Our class had been our excuse to spend time together. Without it, the only thing remaining was my intense feelings for him. But I didn't feel right expressing how I felt as long as I was still in a relationship with Tasha.

Tasha, on the other hand, was nowhere to be seen. I had put tickets for her at 'Will Call' like I always did, but I hadn't spoken to her in days. I would say our relationship was over except even when she disappeared like this, she would reappear and remind me of the dream we had had where I traveled the country playing for the NFL and she got involved with some charity.

I don't know what it was about that dream that always got me to excuse the shittiness of our relationship, but it did. It had to stop, though. I wasn't sure what I wanted my life to be, but I was feeling more confident that it wasn't that.

How did I break that to her? How did I break that to my dad?

Taking the field, I looked around at the stands. The place was jammed packed. I knew where Quin's seats were but there was no way to see them from here. Past the row closest to the field, the stadium became a blur of cheering, colorful dots. Usually, that was how I preferred it. Today, there was one person I wished I could pick out.

Was Quin here or not? Whatever the case, I was going to play like I was only playing for him. I wanted him to be proud of me. I wanted him to think that I was worthy of someone as great as him.

Our offensive team took the field to start the game. As quarterback, I surveyed the defensive line looking for all of the weaknesses Coach had been training us to spot. I didn't see anything until my tight end shifted indicating that he thought he could make a hole for our running back.

We had run this play in dozens of games. The other team knew that. That meant that the opposition would be looking to adjust to it as soon as we committed to the play. So, if I called the play and waited for the defense to commit…

"Orange, 52, summer, hike," I said telling my guys my plan.

As expected, our tight end opened a hole in their defensive line. As soon as he did, our running back charged from behind me looking for a hand-off. Wrapping his arms around nothing, he charged the line causing the defense to collapse on his position. The right safety moved into place to stop our running back if he got through. And the man who was defending our wide receiver favored his right to back up the charging safety.

That was when our wide receiver broke loose and sprinted down the field. This was it. He was open. I just had to stay on my feet long enough for him to reach the ten-yard line.

The grunts of 300-pound men echoed in my ears. They were coming. My heart pounded.

'Stay calm. Wait for it,' I told myself.

When our guys couldn't hold back their line any longer, their linebacker cut through like a bullet through metal. He was going to get me. I had to throw. Whipping my arm back, I let go. The second the ball left my fingertips, a freight train hit me leaving me on the ground for dead.

Lying there, I heard the collective awe of the crowd. They were watching something. It was my pass. I had gotten it off in time. It was spiraling forty yards through the air. It took a while to get there. When it did, the screams of the crowd were deafening.

"Touch down!" The announcer yelled.

20,000 people shot to their feet. Celebration. Agony. The rush of it all was amazing. Dan ran over to me and helped me up.

"Fuck yeah!" He yelled slapping me on my back.

Jogging off the field watching everyone go wild, there was only one person who I hoped had seen it. I looked toward his section again. There were too many people and it was too far away. I didn't see him. It broke my heart to think he might not have been there.

I played like a man on fire for the rest of the first half. I had never thrown a more perfect game in my life. I had my offensive line to thank for it, of course. And, it didn't matter how well I threw if my receivers didn't catch it. But, there was one name the crowd chatted as we jogged off the field for halftime, mine.

Hurrying back to the locker, the only thing I cared about was checking my messages. I would have given anything to see Quin's name pop up. Ripping my glove off to unlock the phone, I tossed it aside and illuminated the screen.

There were two messages from him. One said, 'Got the tickets. Heading up now!' And the other one said, 'WOW!!!!' That was it and it was enough.

I was so happy I felt drunk. He had seen me do what I did best. I couldn't feel better if I tried.

I entered the field for the second half beside myself. I felt like I was glowing. I felt intoxicated. It was a good thing we started the second half playing defense. It gave me a few extra minutes to pull myself together.

As much as I tried to focus, I couldn't help but search the crowd for him. He was out there somewhere. I could now feel his gaze on me. I wanted to show off for him. So with my helmet in hand headed back onto the field, I called a series of plays that would guarantee we would win the game.

It started with a few passes that got us closer to the end zone. I just needed to be within thirty yards. That was it.

When my final pass got us there, I gathered the guys into a huddle and called the big one. They looked at me questioningly but I was their quarterback. They listened.

In the line, I called for the hike. With the ball in hand, I pulled back my arm ready to launch it. After a continuous parade of passes, the defensive line stepped back. That's when I lowered the ball tucking it under my arm and charged.

Caught by surprise, the other team was late to react. It opened a gap down the sideline. Ahead of me, I could see the end zone. I wanted this touchdown. I wanted Quin to see me do this.

Rifling towards me was the free safety. He was going to get to me before I got to the goal. I had two options. I could run out of bounds, or I could risk my life and charge through.

I wanted this. I wanted it bad. Picking up speed I made my decision. Nothing was going to stop me.

An arm's length away, the safety lunged. That was when I leaped into the air. I was going to jump over him. I had seen it in movies and the most spectacular games. I could do it.

Leaving the ground, I watched as the safety cut under me. I wasn't high enough. I would have to step on him to clear him. But when my foot reached down for his body, I felt his hand.

It was hard to tell what happened after that. What I know is that I heard a crack. It was as my body hit the ground.

There was nothing, and then there was a roar of fire. The pain consuming me was unlike anything I had ever felt. It was my left leg. Something in it had shattered.

I was told that athletes know the moment a career-ending injury has occurred. I used to wonder what that felt like. I didn't have to wonder anymore. Because in that moment, I knew this was the end.

Chapter 9

Quin

"Oh my God! What just happened? Why isn't he getting up? Lou, what's going on? Lou?" I asked turning to him.

With his face painted in the school colors, Lou stared at the field with his mouth hanging open. Like everyone else, he was speechless.

I turned back to see medics running onto the field. Cage flopped around in so much pain they could barely get to him. I couldn't believe what I was seeing. This was a nightmare.

In a few moments a paramedic was pushing a stretcher to Cage. It took two men to get him onto it. Tears rolled down my cheeks watching it. I was in shock. I didn't know what I could do to help, but I had to do something.

"I need to go to him," I told Lou.

"Yeah. Of course. Where do we go?"

"I don't know. The locker room?"

"Lead the way," he said ushering me on.

As I headed to the stairs I realized there was one problem, I had no idea where I was going. Not only was this my first time at the university's stadium, this was the first stadium I had ever visited. I could barely navigate us to the bathroom.

Despite that, we descended the stairs from the upper deck and wandered around the concession stands.

"Excuse me, how do I get to the locker rooms," I asked one of the security guards.

"It's off-limits to visitors," the burly man replied.

"But, my friend's injured. I need to go see him."

"Off limits," he repeated before looking away.

It took almost an hour to circle the stadium and realize where the entrance to the lower levels was. We got there in time to see an ambulance pull away with its lights flashing.

"You think that was Cage?" I asked Lou.

"I would guess," he said sympathetically.

"They're probably taking him to the closest hospital, right?"

"That would make sense."

"We need to get a ride to the hospital."

"I'm on it," Lou said whipping out his phone and arranging a ride.

Between the congestion around the stadium and the traffic, it took another hour before we got to the emergency room. I was going insane with worry by then.

Dropped off at the main doors, I rushed in with Lou in tow.

"I'm looking for Cage Rucker's room. He was just brought in. He was probably wearing football clothes," I told the stout woman behind the desk.

"I saw him come in. I think they took him for an MRI."

"Great. Where do I find that?"

"It's going to take a while before he's assigned a room."

"So, where do I wait for that?"

The woman held out her hand gesturing towards the seats in front of her desk.

"Okay. When do I check back?"

"Give it an hour."

I was disappointed everything was going to take so long, but I knew it couldn't be helped. The most important thing was that Cage was being taken care of. I was willing to wait here all night as long as that was happening.

I hadn't needed this to realize how much I cared for him. The pain I felt thinking about what Cage had gone through was unbearable. All I wanted to do was wrap my arms around him and never let him go.

Lou and I took a seat and waited as I was told. In an hour we checked back. Cage had been moved into a room on the third floor. She wasn't sure I would be able to see him yet, but she allowed us to go up and check.

Getting off the elevator I saw a few familiar faces. Hovering in the hallway was Tasha and Cage's father. Both turned and saw us. I wasn't sure what I was supposed to do.

I continued towards them. As I got closer, Cage's father headed towards me. There was something about the look on his face that confused me. He didn't look like a person overcome by concern like I thought he would be. There was instead a look in his eyes that made my heart clench.

"You're Cage's friend, right? The tutor?" He said with his eyes locked on me.

"Yes, sir," I told him getting a chill down my spine.

"Come here," he told me gesturing for me to leave Lou.

I swallowed not liking where this was going. The ruddy, grizzly man was terrifying to look at. And when I finally approached him, he put his arms around my shoulder, gripped it like a vice, and pushed me into an empty room.

Before I knew what was happening, the man's hefty body had pinned me against the wall. He was manhandling me. I couldn't get away. With his hot, alcohol-laden breath flooding my ear, he said,

"I know what you are. I can tell. If you contact my boy again…" Cage's father paused, pulled something out of his belt, and pushed its sharp point into my stomach. "…I'll gut you like a hog. You hear me? You contact him, you text him, you reach out to him in any way, I'll kill you, then I'll kill your boyfriend out there. Then I'll find your family and kill them too. You hear what I'm tellin' you?"

I was in shock. I couldn't move. When I didn't respond, he pushed the blade harder into my stomach. It was cutting into me.

"I hear you," I said terrified out of my mind.

"Good. Don't let me see your face again. Get the fuck out of here," he ordered before letting me go.

As soon as his grip loosened, I escaped his grasp and the room.

"What?" Lou said seeing me approach him with terror in my eyes.

"Let's go!" I demanded grabbing his arm and pulling him to the elevator.

"What are you doing? We just got here."

"Let's go!" I insisted not daring to look back.

As soon as the elevator doors opened, I was on it. Lou followed confused. I hit the lobby button continuously until the doors closed. Still not feeling safe, I leaned against the wall watching the floor's numbers descend.

"Quin, you're bleeding," Lou said grabbing my attention.

He was pointing at a growing red spot on my shirt where Cage's father had stabbed me. It didn't hurt until I pulled up my shirt and saw it.

"It's nothing. I'm alright."

"What did he do to you?" Lou asked horrified.

"He didn't do anything. Let's just go."

"Quin?"

"Let's just go!" I yelled.

Lou didn't say anything else.

I couldn't get out of the hospital fast enough. Back in our dorm room, I locked the door behind us and left Lou for my bedroom.

"Quin, are you okay?"

I didn't answer. Instead, I locked my bedroom door and sat in the furthest corner of the room.

I was going to give Cage's dad what he wanted. I was never going to contact Cage again. If he reached out, I wouldn't text him back.

I didn't doubt that he would kill me. The look in his eyes told me he was capable of murdering everyone around me. Cage's father was insane. I might have been falling in love with Cage, but was I willing to die to be with him?

Chapter 10

Cage

"The good news, Mr. Rucker, is that you're young. With time to heal and rehab, you'll be able to play football again," the doctor said in a soothing tone.

"That's good," my father said happier than I was.

"The bad news is, the recovery time will be long. You are certainly out for the season."

"This is his senior year. He wouldn't have any more time before a draft to prove himself. No, he has to come back before the end of this season. I don't care what you have to do."

"Healing doesn't work like that," the doctor explained to my father. "It takes time. He couldn't come back before the end of the season if he wanted to."

"He can play. He'll just be in a little pain, right? My boy has played through pain before. He's tough."

The doctor looked at my father with sympathy.

"I understand your passion for your son's career. But, if he were to play before he's ready, his return would be short and he could do damage that wouldn't only threaten his long-term prospects, but could hamper his mobility for the rest of his life."

"I don't care. Fix him. Get him on that field."

"Dad!"

"You need to get to that draft. I've sacrificed too much to have you not make it now."

"He's talking about me not being able to walk," I clarified.

"I knew you should have entered the draft last year," he said looking at me with hate. "I told you. You didn't listen. Now, look at you. Crippled. Useless. A big sack of nothing."

"Mr. Rucker, I would like to remind you that your son should be able to play football again. He can make a full recovery."

"And, who's gonna care?" My father spit back.

The doctor was getting a taste of what I had been dealing with my whole life. It was comforting to see the horror on the doctor's face. It told me I had been justified in hating my father in the moments that I did.

"Don't worry, Boy. You're a fast healer. You've always been. You'll play before the end of the season. Trust me."

"I'm not," I said before I realized what I was saying.

"Yeah, you are."

"I'm telling you that I'm not. I don't care if there's no pain. I don't care if I can dance for hours on it. I'm not playing again this year. I might never play again."

"You will play again," my father insisted.

"Have you ever asked me if I wanted to play football?"

"It doesn't matter because you're good at it."

"It does matter, Dad. It matters what I think of it."

"I saw you throwing those passes today. No quarterback leaves the pocket to run the ball for a touchdown if they don't love what they do."

"Well, I guess you're wrong because there's a part of me that's relieved that I'll never have to play again."

"You'll play again. I'll guarantee you that," my father said with his eyes narrowing on me.

"No, Dad. I won't," I said taking the first stand of my life. "I'm done. You forced me to do it my whole life, but you heard the doctor. I'm done."

"That man doesn't know who you are. I do."

"You don't, Dad. You've never known. I'm not doing it again. It's over."

After twenty-two years, I wasn't sure what had given me the courage to say that to him. Maybe it was meeting Quin and realizing I could have a life outside of football. Before him, all of my friends and everyone I dated was there for Cage Rucker, the football star and NFL prospect. Quin was the most thoughtful, wonderful guy I had ever met and he couldn't care less about who I was. Besides, he was famous enough for the both of us.

As painful as it was, maybe my injury was a blessing. It was my way out. The doctor was very clear. My season was over. Coach and my teammates would understand that. And although it will be the talk of sports media for a while, they'll quickly forget about me.

After that, I could have the freedom to do what I really want to do. I wasn't sure what that was yet. But I was sure it included Quin.

My father left my hospital room without another word. There was no question that he was leaving to get drunk. He would be back, though. I knew my father. He wouldn't give up on his cash cow just like that. I might have made my decision about it, but what I wanted never mattered to him. He wouldn't give up on getting what he wanted.

"I'm sorry about that," the doctor said sympathetically.

"Injuries happen," I told him hiding the relief I felt that my football career might finally be over.

"I meant, about your father."

"Oh. Yeah," I said finally numb to his constant heartbreak. "Thanks."

"Do you have any other questions?"

"Yeah. Has anyone else come to see me? Maybe there was a guy, 5'9", shaggy dark hair, cute as all get out?"

"I can check. But your visitations haven't been restricted. So, if he came, you would have seen him."

"Okay. Thanks," I said disappointed.

I understood, though. Yes, something was developing between us. But we weren't at the 'rush to the other's hospital bed' level yet.

There was no question that I wanted to see him. He was the only person I cared about coming. Everyone else was great and I appreciated them for it. But staring into his beautiful eyes always made my day. Doing that now would make me feel like everything was going to be alright.

When the game was over, there was an endless parade of teammates and coaches in and out of my room. They all looked at me like I was dying. It was obvious that I was out for the season. They could figure out what that did to my NFL prospects.

I played along as if I was devastated. But each time someone knocked on my door, I had to hide my excitement that it would be Quin and the two of us would begin our new life together.

After I didn't hear from Quin the first day, I was sure that I would the day after. I didn't. In fact, I didn't hear from a lot of the people I thought I would. I knew that part of the reason was that winter break had begun and the majority of the school had headed home.

Dan couldn't afford to fly home for winter break so he visited a couple of times. So did Tasha who grew up an hour away. My father never came back after that first day. And confusingly, Quin never showed up.

I tried not to feel heartbroken. He was a good guy. If he didn't come to visit, there had to be a good reason.

For the life of me, I couldn't figure out what it was. The best I could come up with was that he had booked a flight home for immediately after the game. If that was the case, he wouldn't have had the time. But, why wouldn't he have at least texted?

When I realized that he wasn't going to, I decided to text him.

'Didn't I promise you a helluva game?' I wrote.

I stared at my phone waiting for a response. A day passed and nothing came. I was about to text something else when Tasha arrived to drive me home.

I would have asked my father to do it but he wasn't texting me back either. I didn't want to think about what that meant. He couldn't be that pissed at me, could he?

He had to have heard what the doctor had said. If I tried to come back this season it could cause permanent damage. If not for that, I probably would have played in the NFL for ten years, not because I wanted to, but because he wanted me to.

I was a good son. That had to be enough. How could that not be enough for him?

"You ready?" Tasha asked in a somber tone.

It felt like something was up with her.

"Yeah. Thanks for doing this. I don't know what's up with my dad."

"Of course," she said grabbing my bag as I maneuvered my way onto my crutches.

The drive back to my place was a long, quiet one. I wasn't sure what I was supposed to say to her. My playing football was at the heart of the dream that held us together.

She hadn't been in my room when I told my dad what I had. She did know that my season was over, though. And, she was smart enough to guess it meant that my easy path to the NFL was gone.

What did we have left together? I had to bring our relationship to an end. I couldn't do it now because she was in the middle of doing me a favor. But, I was going to have to do it whether or not I heard from Quin again.

Pulling into my driveway, my father's truck wasn't there. I felt a burn in the pit of my stomach. I dismissed it by telling myself that he was at a bar getting drunk.

I was about to get out of the car when Tasha stopped me.

"Can we talk?"

"Sure. What's up?"

"I feel like it's kind of shitty to do this now, but whatever. I think we should break up."

I didn't know if I was more relieved or rattled. Certainly, our relationship was going to end and her saying it meant that I didn't have to. But, with everything in my life changing and Quin being M.I.A., I was hoping we could have waited at least a few more days to have this talk.

"I agree," I told her.

"You agree?" She asked like she had said it as a test.

"Of course. You were with me because you wanted to be a football wife. You didn't care about me. If you did you didn't act like it."

"You think I didn't care about you?"

"If you had to choose between me and Vi, who would you choose?"

"Vi is my best friend."

"Exactly. I feel like I should have been your best friend. Or, let me rephrase that. I feel like the person I spend the rest of my life with should be my best friend. And, I should be theirs. You have your best friend and it's not me."

"So, you're blaming me for this?"

"I'm not blaming anyone. There were probably things I could have done to be a better boyfriend."

"Yes, there were. So many things!"

"That's fair. And, I don't know how much of a difference doing those things would have made. I think you've just found someone you love more than me, and… I've found someone I love more than you."

"You're interested in someone else?"

"Yeah, I am. But, so are you."

"You think I want to date Vi?"

"I think you're in love with her. And, I'm happy for you. I think you two might be really happy together."

"Are you saying I'm a lesbian? Fuck you, Cage!" she said refusing to entertain the idea.

I shifted to get out and then stopped.

"Look. I know how hard it is to escape the box that we put our lives in. When we're kids we think we know what we want and we keep going after it even when we realize that it's not. But there is a liberation that comes when you don't allow everyone else's dreams define you… even when the other person won't text you back," I said solemnly.

"Goodbye, Cage," Tasha said not giving me an inch.

"Goodbye, Tasha. Thank you for the ride," I said throwing my bag across my shoulder and exiting on my crutches.

Tasha didn't wait for me to reach the door to pull off. I didn't blame her. She probably wasn't ready to accept how she felt about her best friend and I had forced her to look at it. If the situation was reversed and she was saying that about Quin, I would probably be pissed too.

But, there was no doubt that she was in love with Vi. I hadn't realized it until I said it, but it all made perfect sense.

The girl was practically heartbroken when I said that I didn't want to have a threesome with her. I didn't know if she was lesbian, or bisexual, but Tasha had unresolved feelings and she needed us to break up as much as I did.

The only problem was that the person I was in love with might not feel the same way about me. It had been days since the game and Quin was gone. Why? I didn't understand. What had changed?

The only thing I could think of was that he was no longer my tutor. Could that be it? Was everything I thought that was happening between us just in my head? Was I just a stray puppy to him, and once he found me a home he was done?

I didn't want to think about that now. I had more pressing things to deal with like how I was going to smooth things over with my father. He was clearly pissed. The man hadn't checked up on his only son as I lay in the hospital. I would have been upset if I hadn't come to accept it. The bar for him was so low that all he had to do was come home and that would be enough.

Balancing on my good foot, I retrieved my keys and let myself in. What I found surprised me. I was expecting to find the entire place a mess. It wasn't. It almost looked cleaner than the last time I saw it. That was weird because my father hadn't cleaned anything in years.

Crossing through the kitchen to the living room, I realized that the place hadn't been cleaned. Things were missing. The liquor bottles that sat on the glass table next to the couch were gone. So was my father's coffee mug and favorite drinking glass.

Dread filled me as I slowly realized what was going on. Dropping my bag I quickly made my way to my father's bedroom. A long time ago he had put a lock on the door. He was sure to lock it whenever he left. I didn't know what he kept in there and I didn't want to know. But, when I turned the knob this time, it opened.

The room was a mess. There were papers and house decorations everywhere. What was he doing with all of this stuff? And why would he keep house decorations in his room?

Pushing past the crap, I navigated to what I really wanted to see.

"It's empty," I said staring into the closet. "All of his clothes are gone."

Quickly I turned to his bed. Part of the reason he had put a lock on the door was that he realized I had found his hiding spot under it. It was a metal box under loose wooden planks. In it, he had more cash than an unemployed man should have had. And sitting on the cash was a gun.

Tossing my crutches aside, I fell to the ground and made my way past the junk and under his bed. If his cash and gun were gone, so was he. My heart pounded as I inched closer. Was this it? Had he done what he had threatened to do?

Peeling back the planks, I found the metal box. There it was. I didn't want to open it but I had to. I prayed to God that it was all still there. But, opening the lid, it wasn't. The gun and cash were gone. The only thing left was an I.D. with my father's picture on it.

He left me. He really was gone. I pulled myself from under his bed and retrieved my phone. My first thought was to call Quin. I desperately wanted to talk to him. I needed to talk to him.

'I'm not sure why I haven't heard from you, but would love to talk,' I texted hoping beyond hope that I would get a text back.

I didn't. Not that day or the next. I was alone in the world. I had no one and nothing.

Heartbreak overwhelmed me plunging me into darkness. Days earlier I had everything and a guy I loved. I had lost it all and now I was barely holding onto my sanity.

I probably would have wallowed in despair forever if it wasn't for one thing, hunger. I had no money to buy anything so the only thing I could eat was what was in the cupboards. That lasted me a week and a half before it ran out.

Luckily spring semester was about to start. I couldn't lose my scholarship in the middle of a school year even with an injury. And with my scholarship came meal stipends.

I would be fine as long as I attended classes and found a job. Both things meant that I would need to reengage in life. I wasn't ready to do that, but what I was ready for didn't matter. This was about survival.

"Dan, could you give me a ride? I need to get back to campus to pick up my truck," I said calling him instead of sending a text.

"Of course, man. Anything you need. Just let me know."

It was good to hear someone else's voice. I was going crazy living in the woods alone. I had been hesitant to do it, but talking to Dan reminded me that I still had friends.

"Did you register for class yet?" He asked me on the long ride to campus.

"Not yet."

"You gotta get on that."

"I know. Which reminds me, do you know of any campus jobs I could get? I'm a little short on cash."

"Of course. There's an opening where I work. I could get you a job there no problem. And you don't even have to stand up to do it."

As hesitant as I was to call Dan, I left his car with a new lease on life. Transferring over to my truck, I reminded myself how lucky I was that I had broken my left leg instead of my right. Driving wouldn't be fun, but at least it was possible.

From the stadium parking lot, I followed Dan to the student activity center. There we met with his boss. There was an opening for a job behind the front desk like Dan had said. Being a fan of football, the manager gave me the job on the spot.

"When would you like to start?" He asked me.

"Is tomorrow too soon?"

"No. That would be perfect."

"How quickly can I get paid? I'm going to need gas money to get here."

"I'll rush the first paycheck through. It will be every two weeks after that."

"Thank you!" I said overwhelmed with relief. "You don't know how much this means to me."

I was there the next day for training and the job was even easier than Dan had said. All I had to do was watch as people slid their student I.D.s into the scanner and then compare the picture on my monitor to the person entering. It was a mind-numbing job, but I didn't know where I would be without it.

With not everyone back from break yet, barely anyone came in. Once the semester started, it was a different story. School began for me too. I had signed up for more education classes. It was too late for me to switch my major from athletics to education, but taking the requirements would open up a few more doors.

Entering the classrooms for the first time, I always looked around for Quin. He had taken a class on childhood education, he might have taken another. If he did, it wasn't any that I had signed up for. And with a campus of 30,000 students, the odds were very slim that I would ever see him.

Did he even want to see me again? I had to guess that he didn't. If he did, he would have replied to any of the now numerous texts that I had sent him. It was hard for me to believe that it had ended like that. Quin was the one person I thought wouldn't care that I couldn't play football. Yet, he had vanished the same moment everyone else had.

Doing everything I could to push him out of my mind, I focused on class. But every time I did, I would remember that Quin had helped me overhaul the way I took notes and studied. I would remember how into it he was and how it would make me laugh. I would then spiral off into a million other things about him that I missed. The only thing that would snap me out of it would be hunger or the beep of the scanner at work.

Lost in a spiral of thoughts about Quin, it was a beep that brought me out of it this time. Remembering where I was, I looked at the monitor doing my job. The image that came up was for someone named Louis Armoury. It made me think of Quin's friend Lou.

Not bothering to look, a second name quickly appeared, Quinton Toro. My heart stopped. My face immediately got hot and my eyes flicked up.

It was him. I couldn't breathe. He and Lou were ten feet in front of me and neither of them was looking my way.

I froze not knowing what to do. He hadn't died or dropped out of school. There he was. Even if he had lost his phone, he could have found a way to contact me. I had been injured. It was his job as a friend to reach out.

Do I speak to him now?

As they passed, Lou seemed his usual energetic self. As he spoke, his arms bounced around wildly. Quin, on the other hand, looked like he had the weight of the world on his shoulders. He looked achingly sad. My chest clenched feeling his pain. Why was my Quin so sad?

"Quin!" I said unable to stop myself.

Both guys turned and stared at me. Quin had a look of shock that melted into elation that quickly dissolved into distress and then finally panic. He backed away as if he had seen a ghost and then ran. What was going on with him?

"Stay away from him!" Lou told me as if I had ruined his life.

I was in shock. What was I supposed to say to that?

"Wait! I don't understand. What did I do?"

"Just stay away," Lou said before retreating down the hallway and into the facility.

I sat frozen and dumbfounded. What could I have done that would elicit that reaction from Quin? Was he traumatized by watching me break my leg? That was ridiculous, but it was the only thing I could think of.

With everything that had happened between us, I knew I couldn't let things end with him running away from me like that. I at least needed an explanation. If I had done something, I needed to know what it was.

Leaving the desk unattended, I grabbed my crutches and rushed after them. The hallway spilled out into the multi-purpose room. There was a juice bar on the right, an area with weights in the middle, and a rock-climbing wall on the left. I couldn't be away from my desk for long so I chose a direction and took a shot.

Heading to the rock climbing wall, my gaze bounced onto everyone in the area. I thought I had chosen wrong until I saw my guy sitting on the mat with his face in his hands and Lou comforting him. I needed to know what was making Quin so upset. I needed to save him from it.

"Quin!"

Quin looked up in a panic about to flee.

"Please don't go. I can't move that fast and I can't stay that long. But, I need to know. What did I do? Why do you hate me so much?

"I thought we had a good thing going. But then I got hurt and you disappeared. Now you're running from me like you're scared for your life?

"None of it makes sense. You used to be the one thing in my life that made sense. Help me understand what changed. You owe me that much. Please!"

Both Quin and Lou stared at me as if I had three heads. Why wasn't anyone saying anything?

"It's your father," Quin spat.

I jolted shocked. Of all the things he could have said, that was the last thing I would have guessed.

"What about my father?"

Quin didn't reply.

"He threatened to gut Quin like a pig if he contacted you again. He said he would kill Quin, then he would kill me, and then he would go after Quin's family."

The words hit me like a punch in the face. I had to force myself to speak.

"He what? When?"

"At the hospital," Quin said gathering himself and standing up.

"You came to the hospital. I didn't think you did."

"Of course I came."

Lou added, "We waited in the waiting room for two hours to see you."

"So, what happened?" I said looking between the two.

"Your father pulled me into a room, stuck what I think was a hunting knife against my stomach, and said that he knew what I was."

"I can't believe this!" I said with my mind swirling.

"You can't tell him we spoke to you. He said if he found out, he would kill us," Quin explained.

"My father's gone."

Quin stared at me confused. "What do you mean "gone"?"

"I mean, when I came home from the hospital, all of his stuff was missing. He had been threatening to leave me for years. He finally did it. I don't think he's coming back. I don't think you have to worry about him anymore."

"Cage!" A voice called from behind me.

I turned. It was my boss.

"You can't leave the desk unattended."

"I'm sorry. I'll be right there."

I turned back to Quin.

"I don't know what to say about what happened to you, to both of you. All I can tell you is that I'm sorry. I never meant to put you in a spot like that. If you don't want to ever speak to me again, I get it. But, I wish you would. Maybe we could just get together and talk?"

"Cage!"

"Coming! Please, Quin. Please," I said not wanting to leave his soft, vulnerable eyes but knowing I had to.

Chapter 11

Quin

"You know that if you go talk to him and his father finds out, you're putting everyone you know at risk, right? Including me," Lou asked.

Lou was right and that was the reason I never replied to any of Cage's texts. I wanted to. When they appeared on my phone it would tear me apart. I wanted to be with him. I wanted to take care of him and relax in his arms. But I couldn't.

Cage's father stuck a knife into my stomach in a hospital. He broke skin. It was still bleeding when I got home. I didn't doubt that he was capable of pushing a little harder and slicing me open. And even though I was willing to risk my life to be with Cage, I wasn't willing to risk Lou's life or my parents'.

"He said his father was gone," I reminded Lou.

"But, what does that mean? Gone for the weekend? Gone for a vacation? Will he be back in a week or a month?"

"If you don't want me to talk to him, I won't. I'm not going to put you in danger. Tell me not to and we'll leave through the back door right now."

I tried not to look desperate to get his approval but I couldn't help it. Everything in me pleaded for him to say it was okay. I needed to talk to Cage. The pain of being away from him kept me from eating and sleeping. Lou had suggested coming to the activity center because all I had the strength to do was lie in bed and he was worried about me.

"Lamb Chop, you can't not see him because of me. You know I can't do that to you."

"How about this? I could talk to him and find out if his father is really gone. If I get the sense that he could be back at any minute, or if he's coming back at all, I'll walk away. In that case, it wouldn't be because of you. It will be because I can't trust him. And, if I can't trust him, then what would be the point of being with him?"

Lou smiled. "Well, there's a little more to being with someone than that. But I appreciate what you're saying."

He closed his eyes and sighed with resignation.

"I trust you, Lamb Chop. Go talk to him. I know you wouldn't put me or anyone you cared about in danger. And, for what it's worth, I don't think Cage would put you in that situation either."

"You sure, Lou. Because I don't have to."

Lou chuckled. "You have to. Don't pretend that you don't. Go. I'll just be here climbing this wall on my own."

Lou looked around and spotted a cute, dark-skinned guy putting on climbing shoes.

"Unless I can get that scrumptious bit of man meat to tie me up."

"Isn't the phrase, 'Tie you in'?"

"You heard what I said. Go. I have some rope work to do."

I watched as Lou walked over to the guy and struck up a conversation with him. That was immediately followed by Lou stretching in front of him. The guy was interested.

It amazed me how easy it was for Lou to talk to guys. He didn't know if they would be into other guys or not. He just did what he wanted to do and somehow it always worked out. It was like he had some sort of device that could tell him which guys were open to being with guys. It was like a built-in radar or something.

As smart as I was supposed to be, I could never tell what anyone else was thinking. That's what made parties so uncomfortable for me. If I could predict peoples' behaviors, I could relax.

But, for me, people were a series of random events. They rarely did what they said they wanted to do making it hard for me to tell when they were joking.

Why couldn't they just say what they were thinking and do the things they say they want to do?

That was one of the reasons I liked being around Cage. Yeah, he was the hottest guy ever. But, more than that, he was easy. He did what he said he was going to do.

Cage shared things about himself that told me who he was. He was exactly the man he presented himself as. He was the type of guy I could shut off my brain and relax with. I always felt safe when I was around him. So, why would I question whether he would keep me safe now?

Realizing that there wasn't a reason, I turned to the hallway to the front desk and headed back to Cage. As he came into view, our eyes met. He made me melt. The tingles were back.

"You came," Cage said telling me how much he wanted me here.

"Before you say anything, I need to know for certain. Will your father be coming back."

Cage opened his mouth to speak and then lowered his head instead.

"I don't know."

"I thought you said he was gone?"

"I did. And, he is. But, he's my father. I don't want him to be."

"Do you know where he went?"

"No. I don't know anywhere he goes when he leaves our house. I learned early that I shouldn't ask. I know there's a bar that he drinks at. But beyond that…" Cage shrugged his shoulders.

"So, how do I know that he won't show up one day, see us together and then go Colonel Kurtz on me?"

"What?"

"Apocalypse Now?"

Cage stared at me confused. "Are you calling for the apocalypse?"

I didn't laugh but I wanted to. "No. It's a movie I watched with my parents. It wasn't age-appropriate."

"Okay. To answer your question, I don't know. But, I think I know why he threatened you."

"Why?"

"He thought that you would get in the way of me becoming a rich football player."

"How would I get in the way of that?"

"I think he saw how much I liked you. I think he thought that NFL teams wouldn't want to draft me if I was with a guy."

"Oh. Isn't that true?" I asked remembering the way the sports world treated my uncle after they found out that was in a relationship with a guy.

My uncle had been the MVP of multiple Super Bowls. He had turned that into a billion-dollar business. But after things with him and his family went public, my parents told me that everything changed.

"It might be true," Cage admitted. "But it doesn't matter anymore because," he gestured towards his leg, "this."

I stared at the cast.

"I never got a chance to tell you how sorry I was that that happened to you."

"That's okay. I'm not that sad about it. I mean, I'm sad you didn't get the chance to tell me. But I'm not sad I got hurt."

"But, I heard you were out for the season and you can't enter the draft. What about your dreams."

"They were never my dreams. I was living everyone else's dreams for me, and the injury allowed me to come up with my own."

"Oh? What are your dreams?"

Cage chuckled. "I'm still working on that. Right now I'm focused on figuring out how to survive without football, and my Dad… and Tasha."

A sharp pain flashed in my chest hearing his girlfriend's name.

"What happened to Tasha?"

"We broke up."

I felt another flash of pain but this time it was as the wave of hope overwhelmed me.

"I'm so sorry."

"You shouldn't be. It was long overdue. I think she was in love with her best friend."

"Really?"

"Yeah. It took me a while to figure it out and she still hasn't accepted it, but she is."

"Wow! Okay."

"There is one thing about my dream that I have figured out, though," Cage said with a smile.

"What's that?"

"You. Because, when I dream, I dream of you."

I froze staring at him. I was speechless but my body reacted to his words yearning for more.

"I'm sorry, that was too much," he said looking down.

"No, that was the perfect amount."

I knew I should have said more or told him how much he meant to me too, but I didn't. I don't know why.

Cage looked away. "There's something I need to ask you."

"What is it?"

"It involves my dad."

"Oh. Okay. Ask away."

"I know you said you were joking — or whatever — after you said it. But, is what you said true?"

"About him not being your biological father?"

"Yeah," he said still not looking at me.

"I think it is. There's always an outside chance that your genetics formed themselves in exactly the right way. But most of the time, the simplest explanation is the correct one."

Cage looked at me with sadness. "Then, if he isn't my father, who is? And, what happened to my mother. Did she die when I was born? Or, could she still be alive?"

I looked at Cage not knowing how to respond.

"I'm sorry, I don't know why I'm asking you this stuff."

"We could find out."

"What?"

"I told you there are certain things that I'm good at. I could help you find out."

"Are you serious?"

"Yeah. But, I can't do anything that puts the people I care about in danger."

"You're talking about my father, or whoever he was?"

"Yeah."

"I'll protect you. I'll keep you safe. There's no way I would let him or anyone else do anything to you," he said making my heart pound.

"I believe you."

"Where do we begin?"

"At the scene of the crime."

As much as I wanted to be around him, I needed time to process everything. So, instead of talking anymore about it across a desk at his place of work, we made arrangements for me to meet him at his place the following day. It would be a Saturday and I could head up early.

He had ended the conversation by saying, "It's a date." Was it a date? Or, was he using it colloquially? I wanted it to be a date. I wanted every moment I spent with him to be a step that brought us closer together.

The location made for a strange first date, though. And, figuring out who his father was and if his mother was still alive made for a strange first date activity. Most people went for ice cream.

"I brought ice cream," I told him when I arrived at his place the next day.

"You brought ice cream?"

"And a few other things. Milk, juice, a couple of frozen pizzas, a couple of TV dinners… and ice cream."

"So, you brought groceries?"

"You said your father was gone. I didn't know who did the shopping. And I was already at the grocery store…"

"Getting ice cream…"

"Yeah. So, I figured why not pick up a few things. You could always just stick them in your freezer if you don't want them."

Cage chuckled. "Thank you. You're gonna make it really hard for me to stop dreaming about you."

"Who says I want you to?" I asked feeling my cheeks flush.

"Good point," he said looking at me like he wanted to kiss me.

I didn't know what to do. I wanted to kiss him too. But, how did a guy on crutches kiss a guy carrying two heavy grocery bags?

Instead of kissing me like I was desperate for him to, he led me inside.

"I'll put these away," I told him heading to the kitchen.

"You called it the scene of the crime, so I didn't clean up. I wanted to, but I didn't want to move something that Detective Quin might need to crack the case," he said teasingly.

"No. That was good."

"Where do we begin?"

"At the beginning. What do you know about your mother?"

"Nothing."

"Do you have a picture of her or her name?" I asked joining him in the dated living room.

"No. Nothing."

"What about a birth certificate?"

"I do have one of those. Let me get it."

When he met me at the door he was using one crutch. But inside, he shed it and hobbled around instead.

When he reentered the room with a piece of paper in his hand I asked him, "How's your leg?"

"Better with you around," he said with a smile.

"It doesn't hurt."

"Not as much. I think I'm good."

I looked at him questioningly but let it go. I took the paper from him and looked at it.

"This is fake," I told him without thinking.

"What?"

"This isn't your birth certificate. Where did you get it?"

"My father said that he got it from the hospital where I was born. Why do you think it's fake?"

"When you have two biological fathers, what goes on a birth certificate is an issue. Birth certificates become something you pay attention to. I've never seen any that looks like yours."

"What are you referring to?"

"Everything. Your mother's name is Jane Doe and your father's name is Joe Rucker?"

"Yeah. They didn't know my mother's name so they put Jane Doe."

"They didn't know your mother's name, but they knew your father's? How would that work? Was he there for your birth, but he didn't know your mother's name?"

"I never asked."

"You never asked?" I asked skeptically.

"My father wasn't a fan of questions."

I looked back at the certificate.

"It says here that your birth name is 'Boy'."

"Yeah, my father said he never bothered to name me," Cage said lowering his head.

"Cage, you have a name."

"I made up Cage."

"That's not what I mean. I mean, someone gave you a name. You have a name. So does your mother."

"Of course she had a name. I just don't know what it was."

"That's not what I mean. I mean that something tells me she's not dead. This certificate is fake."

"If she's not dead, who is she? Where is she? How did I end up here?" Cage asked desperately.

I thought about his questions and surveyed the messy room filled with worn furniture.

"What did your father do for a living?"

"I don't know. He wasn't a fan of questions."

"You never asked what your father did every day?"

"I'm thinking we had different childhoods. What my father did every day was drink. I guess it wasn't every day. He did teach me a lot about football. At least when I was younger. But, when he wasn't M.I.A., he usually did what you saw him doing when you were here."

I thought back to the cold, red-headed man I saw looking over his shoulder at me from the couch. The TV had been on and there was something about him that told me he was drunk.

"I'm sorry you had to grow up like that," I said as my heart broke for Cage.

"It's what I knew," he said casually. "You know what? I can show you this," he said leading me to the door opposite his bedroom. "I didn't touch this room either."

I walked into the cluttered space where household valuables surrounded a queen-sized bed. More accurately, it was filled with things that looked like they could have been valuable but aren't.

"Your father broke into houses," I said as it hit me.

I looked back at Cage who had again lowered his head.

"You knew?" I asked surprised.

"I suspected. It's why I didn't ask. As a kid, I found a stack of cash and a gun. Something told me he hadn't earned the money legally."

"Where did you find it?"

"There's a metal box hidden in the floor under the bed."

I turned on the flashlight on my phone and crawled under the bed.

"It's empty. I checked when I got back from the hospital. That's how I knew he wasn't coming back."

There was a lot of stuff under the bed with me. Mostly it was more of what was surrounding it. But there was a path cleared to curling planks of wood. I removed them getting a lung full of dust. Finding the metal box, I opened it. It wasn't empty. There was an I.D. card in it?

"What's this?"

"Oh, right. The I.D. Yeah, I saw that. I don't know. I just figured it was somewhere he worked when he was younger."

I stared at the picture. He looked twenty years younger than he did when he was stabbing me with his hunter's knife. I crawled from under the bed and showed it to Cage.

"He worked in a hospital."

"So?"

"It's where people generally have babies."

"What are you saying?"

"I'm saying that I think I know the hospital you were born in."

Chapter 12

Cage

My heart sank. After less than an hour of investigation, Quin had figured out where I was born. I didn't know what to think. On one hand, my skin prickled at the thought of what we would find if we dug deeper. On the other, Quin said that my mother might still be alive. What if she was?

"What do you think happened? How do you think I ended up living here with…," I took the I.D. from Quin. "With this man?"

"It's possible that your mother showed up to the hospital without I.D. and died giving birth," Quin said.

"But, you don't believe that," I confirmed.

"Your father broke into houses and stole things of value. It would follow that he stole you too."

"Why would he do that?"

"He saw you as something having value? I don't know."

"But, why me?"

"Cause you were the only one available, maybe. Perhaps he saw something in you and knew who you would turn out to be?"

"You think he saw that he could turn me into his NFL cash cow?"

"Maybe."

"That's ridiculous. I was a baby. How could he know that?"

"Maybe you weren't a baby when he took you. Maybe you were older but too young to remember another life. I'm really just guessing here," Quin admitted embarrassed.

"Then, how do we find out for sure?" I said pushing him to figure out more about where I came from.

Quin thought for a second and then turned back to me with a light in his eyes.

"There are a few things. The first is, we need to check to see if any children matching your age and description ever went missing."

"What's the second thing?"

"We need to find that hospital," Quin said with an intensity that I had never seen him express.

The man I was watching put clues together was different than the insecure guy I dragged into the party the night we met, or the one playing flag football with ten-year-olds. He was attractive before, but now he was off the charts hot. God, was I in love with him. If I didn't think that it would distract him from uncovering the secrets of my past, I would kiss him so hard.

Watching his incredible brain focus on me was a level of affection that made me feel seen in a way that throwing a pass never could. How would I ever be able to let him go? I didn't even know if I could stand to watch him drive away from me for a night. I was head over heels for this guy and I never wanted to be apart from him again.

"My phone service is really bad here. Do you have a computer I can hop onto?"

"No."

"You don't have a computer?"

"I always just used the one at school. The university has computer labs and so did my high school."

Quin looked at me stunned.

"My father preferred to stay off the grid."

"Considering what he did, I can understand why."

"You can use my phone if you need to look something up. It's slow but it gets online."

"Okay. There are a couple of missing-kids databases that I can check."

"How do you know about missing-kids databases?" I asked a little worried.

"My parents are ungodly rich and I was a first-off-the-line Frankenstein creation. When you grow up knowing that, you wonder what a missing-kids database looks like," he said with a painful smile.

"Jesus! So, you lived your life in fear of being kidnapped."

"And possibly murdered. Yeah. There are a lot of people who believe that I shouldn't exist. I was always afraid that someone would figure out a way to correct that error," he said dropping his smile.

"The error of you being born?"

"Yes."

"Wow! I'm so sorry you grew up like that," I said feeling my heart break for him.

"It's all I knew," he said sounding familiar.

Realizing he had repeated what I had said on purpose, it broke the tension. I chuckled.

"Well, let's check if I lived your nightmare," I said handing him my phone.

"Not my entire nightmare."

"Right. Because I wasn't murdered."

"I was talking about showing up to class and realizing I'm naked. But I guess that too," he said with a smile.

"I guess it's true what they say, one man's nightmare is another man's fantasy. Because you showing up at class naked would be the start of a very good day for me."

Quin looked up from my phone and blushed. God was he adorable.

"I'm distracting you. I'm sorry. Let me let you get to work. I'll warm up one of the pizzas for lunch. Are you hungry?"

"There are things I wouldn't mind getting into my mouth, but I don't know if it's pizza," Quin immediately regretted what he said. "I'm sorry, I'm not very good at flirting. I guess I like you so much that I forget how to use words sometimes."

"Did you just say you liked me?" I said feeling it swirl around my insides like warm caramel.

"Of course I like you. I've liked you from the moment I saw you at the party. The night we met I was hoping you were going to take me home and do things to me. I could barely breathe the weeks I was away from you. I…"

And that was when I kissed him.

His lips were a soft peach pressed against mine. Tense at first, they slowly loosened. As they did, I slid my hand around the nape of his neck pushing my fingers through his curly dark hair. His head fell into my grasp.

Gently parting my lips, he followed. Tilting my head, my tongue entered his mouth in search of his. They touched with a spark.

Curving the tip of my tongue inviting his, our tongues danced with one another. Tingles raced up and down my body holding him. My cock grew hard as I lost myself.

Not knowing if Quin wanted this, I loosened my grip about to let go. That was when Quin pushed his hands up my side and onto my back. He pulled my chest onto his removing the space between us. When he did, my hard cock pressed onto him.

The blood that rushed to my head made me lightheaded. I wanted to be with him so badly that I ached for him. And when I felt his hard cock push against my thigh, I nearly lost it.

I pulled my lips away from his burying my cheek into his mess of hair.

"Don't stop," he whispered making it even harder for me to let him go.

"I shouldn't distract you. This is important to me," I told him not sure if it was more important than kissing him.

Quin didn't reply, nor did he move. We both kept holding each other with our hard dicks pressed against one another. With him in my arms, I wondered what his soft lips would feel like around my cock. I flinched thinking about it. Quin felt it and his cock flinched in reply.

Jesus, I wanted him. I wanted everything about him. But, I wanted the first time we were together to be somewhere special and meaningful. I didn't want it to be an intermission from searching through records of kidnapped kids. And I didn't want it to be at the scene of a crime.

"I really care about you," I whispered, my lips right above his ear.

"I care about you too," Quin told me before slowly loosening his grip.

Our release was gradual and painful. It took everything in me to peel off of him.

"If your mother's still alive, we'll find her. I promise," he told me.

I believed him. If there was anyone in the world who could figure it out, it had to be him.

"Thank you," I said struggling to take my eyes off of him. "I'll warm up that pizza."

"Thanks. I'll get back to the search."

We were both quiet for a while after that. I was quiet because my mind was spinning. I wasn't sure why he was. But occasionally he would look at me and catch me staring at him. I didn't know why I couldn't hold his gaze.

I was a nervous teenager when I was around him. What was he doing to me? Whatever it was, I didn't want him to stop.

I placed the sliced pizza on the table where he sat locked in on my phone. Smelling it, he looked up.

"You're not in any of these," he said disappointed.

"How could you be sure?"

"I can't be completely. But you do have one distinguishing characteristic that should have been obvious even as an infant."

"What could that be?"

"Your dimples," Quin said with a smile. "You might not have had all of them. But chin dimples are pretty consistent throughout a person's life."

"You sure know a lot about dimples," I said teasing him.

"I have a weakness," he replied.

"Dimples?"

"No. You," he said making my legs quiver.

"I don't think you give yourself enough credit for your flirting skills."

"I guess I needed the inspiration," he said saying exactly the right thing to make me want to kiss him again.

"What do we do now?" I asked open to anything.

"I would suggest that we go to the hospital, but there's a problem."

"What's that?"

"The hospital doesn't exist."

I looked at him confused. "So my father's I.D. is fake?"

"I don't think it is because the place used to exist. I can find records of it online. It just isn't there anymore. I've checked maps. It doesn't appear on any of them."

"Can you find the address?"

"Yeah."

"Then we should go. If nothing else, at least I'll see where I was born. Is it close?"

"Is an hour and a half away, close?"

I looked at the kitchen clock. "We would get there around 4 p.m."

"We should get going if we are. Are we going to do this?"

"There's no reason to stop now."

"Do you think there's a chance we could run into your father along the way?" Quin asked hesitantly.

"Honestly, I don't think I'll ever see that man again, whoever he was."

"How do you feel about that?" Quin asked intensely staring at me. "I mean, I know he wasn't your biological father. But he still raised you."

"But, did he steal me away from someone who would have loved me like he couldn't… or didn't want to?"

Quin didn't reply.

"What I know is if it comes down to him or you, Quin, I choose you."

It was hard to hear me say that. Quin was right. He still raised me. And up until he finally left, my greatest nightmare was that he would take off.

But then he did it and Quin confirmed all of the things about him that I had suspected for a long time. I didn't know who the man who had pretended to be my father was, and allowing it to swirl around in my head, I had to wonder if he had ever loved me.

On the other hand, I couldn't be sure about how Quin felt about me either, but I was pretty sure I loved him. What was more, I needed him. Quin was the man I couldn't live without, not the one who made me feel like I was worthless.

Finishing off the pizza, the two of us got into my truck and headed out.

"How can you not know how to drive?" I asked giving him a hard time.

"I grew up in Manhattan. Who needs a car there?"

"Didn't you say you spent your summers in the Bahamas on an island?"

"I did. And if this was a golf cart, I would be all over it. But since you probably want to survive the trip, you should drive. If you're flexible on that point, I could certainly take over."

"No, no. Surviving a car ride is always something I look forward to."

"There you go. But don't say I didn't offer," he said looking at me with one of his adorable smiles.

During the hour and a half drive there, I asked a lot of the questions I didn't think I could ask before.

"Have you ever had a boyfriend?"

"No. Have you?"

"No. Girlfriend?"

"No. What about you? Anyone before Tasha?'

"A few. There was a girl I dated my freshman year. That didn't last long. There were a couple of girls in high school, but none of those were very serious."

"Have you ever been in love before?" Quin asked pulling out the big guns.

"I thought I was in love with Tasha. I mean, we could have been at one point. It's hard to tell now. I certainly had feelings for her. But, now I'm wondering if what I felt for her qualifies."

"Qualifies as love?"

"Yeah. I mean, it was definitely something, just not… Let's just say I've been given reasons to rethink things."

"I see," Quin asked not asking any more.

"What about you? Have you ever been in love?"

"I thought I was."

"Really?" I asked surprised.

"He was a real prince."

"He was a nice guy, huh?"

"No. I mean he was an actual prince. I don't think he saw me that way, though. And he was a lot older than me."

"How much older?" I asked not expecting to hear that.

"I don't know."

"No, tell me. Was he like, ten years older or something?"

"Probably closer to 15. But, he was a great guy. I thought we had a lot in common."

"You thought you had a lot in common with a prince?"

"A few things."

That was when I dropped the topic. If Quin thought he had a lot in common with a real-life prince, what did that say about the two of us? I was as far away from being a prince as you could get.

I grew up in a small cabin in the middle of nowhere raised by someone who probably kidnapped me and now I could barely afford to buy food. What type of shot did the two of us have to be together? I was starting to think that it wasn't much of one.

"We're getting close," Quin said staring at the trees as they whipped by the window.

"How can you tell? Is that one of your superpowers?"

"No. The mile markers correspond with the addresses."

"I didn't know that."

"Not every state does it and not everywhere in the state is consistent."

"There doesn't seem to be much out here," I said scanning the tree-lined empty road ahead.

"It's close. Wait, turn there," Quin said pointing at a path through the trees which could barely be considered a road.

I turned onto it and it wasn't long until a two-story decaying facility came into view. It was off-white and looked like a school with its alternatingly protruding exterior. The many windows were boarded up and much of them were graffitied.

"Falls County Hospital," Quin said reading the sign above the main entrance. "This is where he worked."

"And, this might be where I was born."

"It's a possibility."

"So, why are we here detective?"

"I don't know. I figured if we were standing in front of it, we'd know what to do next."

Quin and I got out of the truck and stared at the building.

"You don't suppose there are any records still inside, do you?" I asked.

"No. Health records are sensitive information. They would have moved them first."

"Then I don't know what we're going to find here," I told him.

"Neither do I. But, let's say that you were born here. The chances are that this was your mother's closest hospital, right?"

"She might have been traveling at the time and had simply stumbled on this place after going into labor. That could be why they didn't know her name."

"That's a possibility. But most women late in their third trimester aren't much up for long road trips. I think the most likely scenario is that this was the closest hospital to where she lived."

"Okay. So, what does that mean?"

"It means that she came from one of the surrounding communities."

"You saw the map. There's nothing out here but long roads and trees."

Quin looked at me. "We should take a drive."

"Okay," I said not wanting to disagree with him.

Quin's eyes darted around like his brain was in overdrive. We got back into the truck and circled through the driveway towards the empty road.

"Which way?" I asked him.

"We saw what was back that way on the drive here. Let's keep going on this road," Quin said completely engaged.

Before now, I didn't realize how interesting it could be to watch somebody think. Looking over as much as I could, I watched his eyes scan every tree and every bend in the road for evidence. This was my guy doing this. I knew that I couldn't officially claim him as my guy, but it still turned me on to think it.

When we approached a road to the left, he stared at it intensely.

"What's up?"

"Where do you think that goes? Why would a county put it there? It's not large enough to be a through road to a highway. Yet the county had to pay for it which means there had to be someone who convinced the members of the budget committee. Make a turn," he decided.

I did what I was told. For a long stretch, the new road was identical to the one we had turned off of. The elevation was increasing, though. And pretty soon, we were both wishing we brought our jackets.

When we saw snow on the ground we knew we had entered the Great Smoky Mountains.

"It's beautiful," I said awestruck by how the setting sun cast shadows behind the snow-tipped trees that extended like waves into the distance.

"What? Oh, yeah," Quin said momentarily seeing the forest instead of the trees.

"Could you imagine seeing this view every day? How incredible would that be?" I said thinking I was saying it to Quin but ended up saying it to myself.

"There! Look!"

"Welcome to Snow Tip Falls? Talk about being off the map. This place is actually missing from the map. Do you think people still live here?"

"There's only one way to find out," Quin said with a smile.

Continuing for another half mile, we approached what appeared to be deteriorating walls on either side of the road.

"Is that a wall? Do you think it's private property?"

"There's a chance this used to be. But if it still is, they're doing a horrible job of maintaining security. The walls only run for ten feet."

"It looks like they used to be longer."

"With the overgrowth on the rubble, it doesn't look like anyone has tried to repair it in a decade."

"Do you think we should keep going?" I asked second-guessing our decision.

"If they didn't want us to be here, why would they put a welcome sign?"

"Good point," I said speeding up and very quickly seeing our first buildings.

It really was a functioning town. And there were more signs of life than I would have guessed. Although the town was sparse, there was a gas station, a restaurant, and what looked like a mom-and-pop grocery shop.

"What do we do?" I asked the detective who was scanning the town as intensely as everything else.

"Let's go in and say hi?"

"You want to be social? You? The guy I had to force to go to a party?" I said tickled.

"Somewhere here could be answers to your past. I don't want to set up unreal expectations. But, your mother could have lived here. It's possible that she still does."

Pain gripped my chest hearing Quin's words. He was right. If my father did work at the hospital and that hospital was the closest one, this might have been where she lived. My heart pounded at the possibility.

"Where do we go?"

"Should we see if the general store has jackets?"

I parked the truck in front of the quaint wooden building and took a breath.

"Are you okay?" Quin asked watching me stare at the building.

"It's a little overwhelming."

"I don't want you to get your hopes up. This could just be another town in the middle of nowhere."

"Right. Or, it could be where I find out the thing I've been wondering about my whole life."

"It could be that too. But, we can't expect it to be."

"You're right. I need to reign it in. Okay, I'm good."

The two of us left the comfort of our heated truck and were hit by the biting cold evening air. I had a bit of bulk to me to keep me warm, but I could see the cold air cut through Quin like a knife. It was only a few feet to the door, but I quickly wrapped my arms around him to keep him warm. This was the first time I had held him like this. It aroused me immediately.

Scrambling into the general store, I wasn't quick to let him go. A bell sounded when we entered. Still holding Quin, a portly, dark-skinned man with a friendly face approached.

"Can I help you two?" He said in a way that immediately made me wonder if he was gay.

"Yes. Do you sell jackets?" I said forgetting that Quin was still in my arms and that there was anything unusual about it.

"We sell a few. They're right over here," he said leading us to the far side of the small store. "You two here to check out the falls?"

"The falls?" Quin asked as he held onto my waist not allowing me to let go.

"Sure. There are a group of falls a few miles away. They make for incredible viewing this time of year."

"I bet they do," I replied. "Quin, that sounds amazing."

"You should check them out. Unfortunately, it's getting dark so you probably wouldn't want to go tonight."

"That does sound amazing. But we're just driving through. And we have a long drive back," Quin said as if he had a plan.

"Stay over. There's a bed and breakfast close by."

"Maybe we'll check it out. But, we're actually wondering about the town's history. How long has this place been here?" Quin asked casually.

"The town? Since the 1920s. It started as a hub for moonshine running."

"Really?" I asked intrigued.

"Yes, it's all very interesting. But the person who could tell you more about it is Sonya. She's the one who runs the B&B. She's kind of the town's unofficial historian. My husband also knows quite a bit, but Sonya is the one who enjoys talking about it. Tom can be a bit of a grump sometimes. You two married?"

It was only then that I let go of Quin. I don't know why I did. It wasn't like the idea of marriage scared me. And, it wasn't like I wouldn't consider spending my life with Quin. I guess I wasn't ready to be asked something like that considering Quin and I were still just figuring things out.

"No," I volunteered so Quin wouldn't have to. "Just friends."

"Good friends," Quin added making me feel tingly.

"How did you two meet?"

"We attend East Tennessee University. He was a brilliant tutor. I was the dumb jock," I said with a chuckle.

"Yep, my Tom is the brilliant one between us. He's a doctor. I think it's important to find someone out of your league," he said giving me a wink.

I laughed. "Well, Quin here is definitely out of my league."

"That's not true," Quin objected. "You're out of my league. The star quarterback?"

"Not anymore," I told our new friend as I pointed at my cast.

"Oh!" He said looking down at it. "I think we also have some crutches around here somewhere. If you need to use them, I'll get them for you. You can just return them before you leave."

"Wow! Thanks. I guess it is starting to hurt a little."

"I'll go get them," he said quickly heading to the back of the store.

"He's so friendly," I told Quin.

"He really is. Do you think we should stay over?"

"I thought you were saying that we should get back."

"I was just seeing what information he would volunteer. He is clearly trying to get us to stay."

"Isn't it cool that he thought we were together and he was still being so friendly?" I asked.

"I noticed that too. I didn't expect to feel so welcomed in Tennessee."

"Hold on there. There are a lot of welcoming people in Tennessee. You met me in Tennessee."

"You know what I mean. East Tennessee isn't exactly New York City."

"You mean because the whiskey is so much better?"

"Yes, that was exactly what I meant."

I looked at Quin surprised. "Is that sarcasm I detect?"

Quin looked at me as if I had caught him doing something wrong.

"No. Sarcasm works on you. It gives you a bit of an edge," I said with a smile.

"So, you like bad boys?"

"I like whatever you are," I told him meaning it.

Quin stared into my eyes melting my heart.

"Sorry about that. It took me a while to find them back there," the man said returning to us.

"No problem," I said tearing myself away from the guy I could look at for hours.

"We'll take these jackets," Quin said handing them to our friend.

"Oh! I don't think I can…"

Quin cut me off. "I got it."

"You sure?"

"Of course. Don't worry about it. Maybe you can think of some way of paying me back for it," he said with a smile.

"Maybe," I replied.

Yeah, he was getting good at flirting. I had to stick my hand in my pockets to hide how good he was getting at it.

"I'm sorry, what was your name?" Quin asked as he approached the cash register.

"Glen."

"Glen from the general store. Got it."

"And you are?" Glen asked.

"I'm Quin and this is Cage."

"Nice to meet you two."

"We actually believe that Cage has family near these parts."

"Really? Which area?"

"We're not sure," Quin replied.

"It's a great area to be from," Glen said with a smile.

"Are there any Ruckers that live in town?"

"Ruckers? Not that I know of. Is that a married name?"

"It's his father's last name. His adopted father. We think Cage was born at Fall County Hospital."

"Yeah. That place closed about ten years ago. It was a real shame. Tom is now the only doctor in fifty miles."

"Wow! I can't imagine that," Quin said genuinely.

"It does keep him busy. So, did you want directions to the bed and breakfast?"

Quin looked back at me as if he was still thinking about it. I knew it wasn't up to me. I couldn't afford to pay for it if I wanted to.

"Sure, why not," Quin said with a smile.

"Excellent. The place is run by Sonya. She likes it when you call her Dr. Sonya probably because Tom hates it. "She's not a medical doctor," he says. I keep telling him, you don't have to be a medical doctor to be called a doctor. But he's just a grump," Glen said with a smile.

Slipping on our jackets, we returned to the truck feeling really good about the town. Glen made a great first impression.

The bed and breakfast was a half-mile away. It was easy to imagine the walk into town being a relaxing experience. It was now dark, but even in shadows, the place looked like a postcard.

The bed and breakfast had to be the highlight. It was a converted farmhouse and looked expensive. There was a large veranda surrounding the mocha, shingled, exterior, and a short flight of stairs that led up to it.

Standing outside the main door was a petite woman in her early 60s who wasn't wearing a jacket. She had to be freezing as she hugged herself for warmth.

"Welcome!" The woman said with an engaging smile.

"Hello," I said waiting for Quin and putting my arm around him as we approached. If people were going to mistake us for a couple and Quin was going to play along, I was going to make the most of it.

"Glen told me you would be heading over. Come in, come in. It's cold out here."

Stepping inside, the interior didn't disappoint. It was quaint but clean and very well put together. The floors throughout and the walls of the entrance were dark honey wood. The living room furniture was beige with floral print and comfortable looking. And the small tables that lined the room were dark wood and elegant.

"We can't afford to stay here," I whispered to Quin before remembering that he summered on a private island. "I mean, I can't afford to stay here."

"Don't worry about it," Quin said sincerely. "This is the upside of having to worry about being kidnapped every day. Let me share it with you," he said with a smile.

I felt uneasy watching him pay for our room without me being able to help. But I knew the only alternatives would be driving the two hours back or sleeping in my truck. I wasn't about to make Quin suffer to satisfy my pride.

"Okay," I told him knowing the only issues were in my head.

"Glen said you're in town to see the falls," the energetic woman said in a faint Jamaican accent.

"Quin?" I said not sure what he was going to say.

"We're actually in town doing some family research for Cage."

"Really? Do you have family in the area?" She said focusing her green eyes on me.

"We don't know. We're hoping but your guess is as good as ours."

"Well, you know this town used to be a pirate bay."

"Pirates?" I asked.

"Not the kind who sailed on water. The kind that ran on land. One man started the town and then invited his moonshine friends to take up residence to lower the cost of distribution. It was quite successful."

"Really? Wow!" I said fascinated.

"Did you see the wall on the way in?"

"Yes, we saw that," I volunteered.

"It used to surround the entire town. The school was the old distillery and warehouse. Glen's general store was the financial offices. I could have Titus give you a tour in the morning if you want."

"Titus?" Quin asked.

"He's someone about your age. He's a great guy. You'll love him. I'll let him know."

It was then that someone descended the stairs. He had Dr. Sonya's shiny dark hair and smaller build. He looked about 17 but could have been younger. And he didn't have anywhere near Dr. Sonya's rapid-fire energy.

"Mom, do you know where my sneakers are? I can't find them," he said intently staring at the two of us.

"If you put it back in the same place when you take them off, you wouldn't have to go searching for them every other day," Sonya said with the exhaustion of a mother.

"Mom!" He said embarrassed.

"I'll help you look for them later. Why don't you prepare room two for our guests. I'm sorry, what're your names?"

"I'm Cage and this is Quin."

"You know me. And this is my son, Cali."

"Hi," he said with a shy smile. The kid stared at us fascinated. I didn't think he meant it to be rude. But, considering I was new to showing affection for another guy, it made me self-conscious.

"Cali? Now," his mother said sending him back upstairs.

Sonya rolled her eyes as if to say, "Kids."

"Everyone's so friendly here," I told her finally letting go of Quin.

"It's a very friendly town. And you two will find yourselves very comfortable here. Glen and Tom are our resident gay couple but don't think they are the only ones. I used to teach at the school. Believe me, I know," she said with a smile.

"Have you lived here long?" Quin asked again turning into the detective.

"I moved here three years before Cali was born. I was just fascinated by the history.

"So, about 20 years?"

"This June," Sonya said with a smile. "Time flies doesn't it?"

"You wouldn't happen to know of any mothers dying during childbirth or any babies going missing about 21 or 22 years ago, would you?"

"Oh, goodness no. That was before my time but it's a small town. Gossip lingers. I haven't heard anything like that, though. Is that what you two are researching?"

"It's a working theory," Quin said clinically.

"A working theory? So, this is a mystery you're trying to solve," Sonya said excitedly.

"Hoping to," Quin added.

"How exciting! That isn't the type of thing that you go around asking people, but I'll see what I can find out."

"Could you? That would be wonderful. We think that she gave birth at Falls County Hospital."

"I'll keep my ear to the ground," she said delighted.

"It's ready," Cali said reappearing on the stairs.

"Cali will show you to your room. I don't know if you two have eaten yet, but the diner next to Glen's place is open until 9."

"Thank you. We'll check it out," I told her feeling very at home.

Approaching the foot of the stairs, I paused.

"I just realized I forgot the crutches in the truck."

"Do you want me to go get them?" Quin offered.

"I think I'm good," I said offering one hand to Quin while holding the railing with the other.

Cali waited for us at the top of the stairs. As soon as we got there he asked,

"Where are you guys from?"

"East Tennessee University," I told him.

"I was considering applying."

"You should. Are you a junior? Senior?"

"Junior," he said looking back at us puckishly.

"It's a good school," I told him trying to shake his gaze that had locked onto us. "Is this the room?"

"Yeah. If you need anything let me know," he said awkwardly.

"I think Titus is going to give us a tour tomorrow," I told him.

"Oh," he said immediately looking disappointed.

"Is there anything in particular that we should see?"

"The falls are cool," he said smiling again.

"We'll check them out."

Cali didn't leave.

"Anyway. Thanks for showing us to our room."

"Yeah. I'm down the hall if you need anything."

"Got it," I said with a smile.

When he walked away, we entered and closed the door behind us.

"I think someone has a crush," I said to Quin who looked at me amused.

"Yeah, he couldn't stop looking at you."

"Jealous?"

"Should I be?" Quin asked with a smile.

"You never have to worry about me wanting to be with anyone other than you," I told him.

Quin smiled.

"Besides, I meant, I think he had a crush on you."

"What?" Quin asked caught off guard.

"You didn't see that? He was looking at me because every time he looked at you, he would blush."

"Seriously?"

"Quin, how could you not see it? You're the most observant person I've ever met."

"I guess I don't pick up on stuff like that," he said as if realizing it for the first time.

"So, what do you think? Is it possible that my mother was from here?"

"I can't tell yet. It's possible."

Falling into silence, we both turned our attention to the one queen-sized bed.

"Everyone keeps assuming we're a couple," I said breaking the awkwardness.

"Are we a couple?"

I stared at Quin. "Do you want to be?"

"I told you how I felt about you," Quin said bashfully.

"And I was the one who kissed you," I reminded him.

"So, are we?" He asked again.

"I want to be."

I didn't add that I wanted to be for the rest of our lives.

"I want to be too."

I smiled hearing his words.

"Then, I guess we are."

"I guess we are," Quin said giving me a smile that made me feel fantastic. "What do we do?"

"Should we get something to eat? It's been a while since that pizza."

"Sure. And then, what are we going to do after that?" Quin asked with a faint blush.

"What do you want to do after that?"

"I don't know. Whatever you wanna do," Quin said making me hard all over again.

I knew what I wanted to do. I just wasn't sure if he was ready for it.

"We'll play it by ear," I told him feeling drunk with excitement.

"Okay," he said now glowing red.

Leaving our bedroom, we headed to the truck and drove to the diner. I was shaking I was so turned on by what the two of us might do once we got back.

Parking in front of it, we stared into the large windows as we approached. It was like any other in a small town. The space was aging, yet clean. The décor hinted that it had been around since the sixties. And there were no other customers inside.

"Sit anywhere. I'll be out in a second," a stout man yelled from the kitchen when we entered.

"I guess we can sit anywhere," I repeated taking Quin's hand and leading him to a booth against the wall perpendicular to the windows.

"I never asked, do you eat everything? It feels like something a boyfriend should know," I said loving the sound of it.

"I try to eat healthily, but I did stock your freezer with frozen pizzas and ice cream. And, most of that was really for me. So…"

I laughed. "Got it."

Quin had his arms relaxed on the table in front of us as he leaned towards me. I leaned forward wrapping my hands around his. I loved holding his soft hands. They were quite a bit smaller than mine.

My mind flashed on what of his I might hold later. I was about to tell him what I was thinking when the stout man from the kitchen appeared in front of us and handed us menus. I let go of Quin's hands and took the laminated sheet of paper from him.

"We're out of everything but the fried chicken, burgers, and sandwiches. We might be out of sliced ham, but I'd have to check," he said sticking around for questions.

"Well, I know what I want if you do. I'm starved."

"Burger and fries, please," Quin said handing the menu back to the stout man with the four-day stubble.

"The same," I told him handing back the menu and looking to pick up where I left off. "So, have you done anything with a guy before?" I asked feeling my hard cock pulse.

"Nothing," Quin replied glowing.

"At all?"

"No. Are you disappointed?"

"Why would I be disappointed?"

"I don't know. Because things might be easier if I had."

"Well, I haven't done anything with a guy either if that makes you feel better."

"I don't know if it does."

"I've thought about it, though. And I've thought about doing it with you."

"What have you thought about?"

I took his hands again.

"Let me see. I've thought about kissing you."

"I've thought about that," he said with a smile."

"I've thought about slowly undressing you and kissing you… there," I said suggestively.

"Where?"

"You know where. I've thought about sliding my hand down your body and taking hold of you," I said leaning in. "I've thought about taking you into my mouth. I've thought about running my tongue along the rim of your cock and seeing if I could make you squirm."

"Me too."

I stared into Quin's eyes. I never wanted to look anywhere else again. When I couldn't resist him any longer, I leaned further across the table and kissed him. Our lips lingered on one another's sending a chill down my spine. The kiss continued until the sound of someone grunting in disgust ruined the mood.

Hearing it, I lowered to my seat unsure how to feel. Still staring at Quin, he knew what I was thinking before I said anything.

"Let it go," Quin pleaded. "You know nowhere can be perfect."

Sure, I knew Quin was right. But I didn't like him having to experience that. And as long as I was around him, no one would ever disrespect Quin or our relationship.

I slowly turned searching the room for who had made the sound. Our waiter was back in the kitchen making our burgers. We probably wouldn't have been able to hear it over the sizzling if it had been him. And the only other person in the place was a young guy dressed as a busboy.

I eyed the busboy wondering how long it would take me to beat the crap out of him. The kid couldn't be more than 20 and clearly had a chip on his shoulder. His tussled, dark blonde hair highlighted his incredibly squared jaw. His angular features spoke to how lean and muscular he was. And, more than anything, he seemed like he was looking for a fight. Looks like he found one.

"You have a problem with something," I said getting him to lift his head and look at me.

"What?" He said using it as an excuse to bring his tray a little closer.

"I said, you got a problem with something?" I repeated sliding out of the booth and showing him who he was talking to.

By any comparison, I was a big guy. The only guys bigger were the 300-pound ones who hurled themselves at me on the field. This kid couldn't be more than 170 soaking wet. Yet, he kept coming like he had something to prove.

"Yeah, I got a problem with something. I got a problem with you two. Are you going to do something about that?"

"Cage, don't."

"Yeah, *Cage*, don't," he mocked sending my blood boiling. "You two come in here thinking you could do whatever? This ain't that type of town. We don't accept your type here."

This was it. I just needed to hear him say it and I was going to make it the worse day of his life.

"And what type are we?" I asked slowly readying to pounce.

"What type? The fa…"

"Nero!" The cook shouted cutting him off. "Come here!"

The guy shut up but didn't look away.

"I said get your ass back here. Now!"

I was ready to kick the snot out of him. But instead of him taking that final step, he looked to the ground and headed to the kitchen. I remained standing as I watched.

"What are you doing talking to my customers like that? I said what are you doing talking to people like that? Speak!"

"I don't know," he said avoiding the cook's eyes.

"You don't know, huh? Then get your ass out of here and don't come back until you figure it out. Go! And I'm docking you a day's pay for what you said."

"I didn't say anything!" The guy pleaded.

"You said enough. Now go before I change my mind and fire you instead."

The guy slithered out of the restaurant staring me down as he left. I was willing to finish my meal with Quin and meet him outside if he was going to wait. He didn't, though. And, it wasn't long before he disappeared into the dark of the night.

"I'm so sorry about that. The kid, he's got some problems. His mother's all messed up. I only keep him around for her.

"But, let me assure you that we welcome all types in Snow Tip Falls. In fact, you know what, your dinners are on the house. Sorry about him again. Really," the cook said before returning his attention to our meals.

Calming down, I returned to the booth and found Quin's eyes.

"Have you ever experienced anything like that before?" I asked him knowing that I hadn't.

"Not like that. But, it's never too long before someone reminds me that I'm not like everyone else."

"You mean that you're hotter? Is that the difference you're talking about?" I asked with a smile trying to rescue the mood.

"No. But I can imagine that's an everyday problem for you," he said smiling at me.

I chuckled. "Maybe. But the only one I care who thinks that is you," I told him meaning it.

"I think it," he said allowing his soul to settle in my eyes.

"Good," I told him barely able to keep my eyes off of him.

It didn't take long after that for the cook to bring over our food and apologize again. The burger hit the spot and it was good. With dinner out of the way, all I could think of was what we were going to do next.

"Have a good night, now. I hope to see you again," the cook said as we got up to go.

"What are you doing?" I whispered as Quin retrieved a twenty from his wallet and left it on the table. "He said the burgers were on the house."

"I know but, we were the only customers there. It's a slow night for him. It's fine, Cage. Let's just go," he said leaving the money and ushering me out.

Back in the truck, I turned to him.

"You really are a great guy, aren't you?"

Quin gave me an adorably bashful smile and I immediately started thinking about all of the things I was going to do to him. I couldn't get back to the B&B fast enough. Luckily the town didn't have any traffic lights or stop signs. And when we were out of the truck and behind the closed door of our room, I stared at the drop-dead gorgeous guy in front of me and finally let myself go.

Staring into his eyes, I sprung across the room to him. With bubbling fury, I wrapped my arms around him gripping the back of his head. Meeting his lips, I became lightheaded. I wanted to kiss him forever and when he parted his lips and our tongues danced, my body sizzled needing his.

Quickly relieving him of his shirt, my lips returned to meet his earlobe. With my tongue tracing the ridges in his ear, he moaned. When it dipped in touching the outside of his canal, he giggled.

Again nibbling his earlobe, I licked the dent where his chin met his neck. I wanted to have all of him. Kissing down his alabaster skin, I had that. I wanted to know every inch of him. And, stopping on his protruding collar bone, I used my crouch to whip him into my arms and carry him to the bed.

I loved holding him. This was the way I would carry him over the threshold when the time came. I never wanted to be apart from him again. So, when I lowered him onto the center of the bed, I climbed on top of him. With my thighs bridging his legs, he reached up and pulled off my shirt.

"Wow!" Quin moaned staring up at me.

His appreciation of my body drove me wild. Gathering his wrists, I pinned them above his head. Leaning forward, I kissed him. It was electric. It made every part of me tingle. I would have stayed there kissing him for the rest of the night if his smooth, lean chest didn't flood my mind.

I wanted to hold every part of him. I wanted to know what it felt like to caress his body with my fingertips. So, ending our knee-wobbling kiss, I sat up and wrapped my large hands around his narrow frame.

Gripping his sides, my thumbs were just inches apart. The feeling made me want to protect him. It made me want to circle my tongue around his areola. He groaned as I did, so I took it further by pulling his protruding nipple with my teeth.

It drove him wild. Teasing him, his chest rose. And, switching to the other nipple, his body danced with pleasure.

Easing my knees further down the side of his legs, I had to extend my chin to kiss the dip that fell beneath his rib cage. My hands were on either side of his hips. Tightening my grip, his jeans pressed against his flesh.

Although I was slowly kissing down Quin's stomach, my thoughts were entirely on my hands. They rounded his curves slowly heading for his zipper. I froze when my left hand touched something poking out past his hip. It was his hard cock. I hadn't been prepared for how big he was. My breath hitched.

Pushing my hand onto him, I explored him unable to do anything else. He was long and thick. I squeezed him. When I did, his cock flinched. He was very hard. That made my cock flinch in unison.

I had to touch his warm flesh. I needed to see him. So, moving my hands to his button, I unsnapped it, unzipped him, and pulled his jeans off of him.

Kneeling at the end of the bed, I looked down at the beautiful guy lying in front of me in his boxer briefs. He looked up yearning for my touch. His chest rose and fell waiting for my return. When he saw me shift my gaze to his underwear, his cock twitched again. That was where he wanted me and I gave him what he wanted.

Pushing my hand over his protruding cock one last time, I grabbed the band of his shorts and pulled them down. His dick was so big that I had to help it out. But when it was free, it sprung erect. It was an impressive sight. And he was large. His length and girth rivaled mine.

With him completely naked, I lost control. Pushing my hands up his thighs, both of my hands wrapped around his cock. There was more than enough of him still exposed to touch the tip of my tongue to the ridge of his head. When they connected, he inhaled.

I didn't give him a chance to relax. Teasing the ridge of his cock, his hands whipped down and grabbed the sheets. As he pulled at them, I flicked my tongue tickling him. He could barely breathe.

When he was ready to climb the walls, I did what I had wanted to do from the first time I pictured his hot body naked. Parting my lips I pushed his head into my mouth. I could taste the tang of his pre-cum. It turned me on as much as it did him. I had Quin's cock in my mouth. It was his most sensitive, secretive part and it was inside of me making us one.

Pushing him as far into my throat as I could, I released one of my hands to push further. To my surprise, my throat swallowed him. My tight muscles gripped the head of his cock squeezing the life out of it.

Quin slapped the bed with pleasure. I was willing to stay like that for as long as I could, but he pulled my hair wanting to be released. Pulling him from out of my throat, he gasped panting for air.

He couldn't take being in my throat anymore, but I wasn't ready to stop increasing his pleasure. I wanted to see my boyfriend cum. So, wetting my mouth as much as I could, I stroked him with one hand while washing the ridges of his head with my mouth.

It didn't take long before his grip on my hair again tightened. He wasn't pulling me off of him. This time he was encouraging me to go deeper. Fucking him with my mouth, I jacked my hand faster. His body shifted lifting his chest. His leg muscles tightened. Then with the force of a firehose, the hottest guy I had ever seen shot his cum in my mouth.

It was like he would never stop cumming. I drank it all. Even when his fluids ceased, his cock continued flinching. Any movement I made sent his body into spasm. I couldn't move and he couldn't lift his arms.

When it felt safe to pull away from him, I released him and crawled up his body. I wanted to hold him. I wanted to cradle him in my arms and feel his warmth against my bare chest. It was incredible to have his naked body in my grasp.

I held him until he helplessly fell asleep. I loved this guy so much. Staring down at him, I couldn't figure out what I had done to be this lucky.

Quin was the love of my life. I was sure of it. And I didn't want to be apart from him again.

Chapter 13

Quin

I had really good dreams after falling asleep in Cage's arms. I hadn't meant to fall asleep. As he was giving me the most incredible sexual experience of my life, I was thinking about how much I wanted to see my boyfriend naked. I wanted to touch another man's penis for the first time. But, more than that, I wanted to feel that closeness with Cage.

That didn't happen, of course, because his blow job was too good. That's unfair to say. The truth was everything he had done was too good. I had never been kissed like that or in any of those places. I was ready to blow so many times as his large hands moved over me. I considered it the achievement of my life that I didn't.

I knew what I wanted next, though. I wanted to give him a fraction of the pleasure he had given me. I wanted him inside of me. I wanted the two of us to become one. I didn't care how. But if getting a blow job could feel that good, the best thing I could do would probably be to give him one back.

The thought of it sent a warm feeling rushing through me. What would it be like to hold his most intimate part in my hands? I wanted to find out.

Feeling more awake by the moment, I made my plan. Maybe I would wake him by wrapping my lips around his morning wood. That was a thing that non-virgins did, right? It had to be.

No longer feeling his arms around me, I was about to open my eyes and go in search of his body when a knock on the door snapped me awake. Remembering where I was, my eyes popped open. I looked left and then found Cage on my right. He had popped his head up as well.

Oh well, so much for waking him with a blow job. And as I thought of a new plan, I heard rustling paper. I looked at the door. The sound was coming from a note being slipped underneath it.

Feeling me move around, Cage looked over at me.

"Morning," I told him with a smile.

His tired eyes crinkled as it formed a smile in reply. "Morning. How did you sleep?"

"Like a rock. How about you?"

"I was a little restless."

"It was because I didn't give you any relief, right? I fell asleep so hard. I was going to give you a blow job to wake you up. I had this whole plan."

Cage chuckled. "That's okay. We have plenty of time for that."

"We have right now," I said with a devilish smile.

"We do. But, aren't you a little curious to find out what someone slipped under our door?"

He wasn't wrong. The intrigue of it screamed from the back of my mind. Never before had I felt more alive than I did unraveling the mystery behind Cage's past. Not only was it drawing on everything I'm good at, but it was something I was doing for Cage. Doing it for him made it ten times more engaging.

I was figuring out something that would change Cage's life forever, something that he had been wondering about for a lifetime. If I could do this for him, it would be the best way to show how much I cared about him. So that meant, yes, I was far beyond "a little curious" about the note that was just slipped under our door.

"I guess," I told him not wanting him to think that I didn't want to put my hands all over him.

"Me too. I would get it but I'm a little limited," he said with a smile.

"Right! I keep forgetting that you broke your leg."

"So do I," he said with a chuckle.

"Doesn't it hurt?" I said about to get the note and then realizing I was naked and still hard as a rock.

"I wasn't kidding when I said that it hurts less when I'm around you."

"Do you think you're doing any more damage to it by walking on it?"

"That's a good question. But, I think my body would tell me if I needed to ease up. Last night when I was kneeling looking at you, I didn't feel it at all. And this morning, it doesn't feel perfect, but I wouldn't say that it hurts."

"Maybe you're running on adrenaline? It can reduce pain," I suggested.

"Maybe. But until my body tells me to pull back, why not keep going?"

"Because you know you should rest?"

"I'll rest on Monday when we get back to school."

"Hopefully we'll be able to figure out something today," I told him.

"Hopefully. Which makes me wonder what's on the note."

"Um, I would get out of bed and get it but I'm naked and really hard," I admitted.

"Is that supposed to be a bad thing?" Cage said with a smile. "I'm looking forward to the show."

Cage knew how to make me feel comfortable with anything. So, pulling off the covers, I scooted out of bed and stopped to give him a good look at my body.

"God damn, you're sexy," he said making me even harder.

When I turned, I bent over giving him a full view of my butt and hole.

"Are you trying to give me ideas?"

I stood up and faced him.

"I was hoping you had the ideas already."

"I can barely think of anything else."

It was good to hear. Without thinking if I should return to bed and collect my prize for the show, I unfolded the note and read it.

"What does it say?"

"It says that Titus is downstairs whenever we're ready for the tour."

"Titus?"

"Dr. Sonya had suggested she get someone named Titus to give us a tour of the town. I guess he's here waiting for us. What time is it?"

We both looked around for a clock. When neither of us found one, I retrieved my phone from my jeans that lay crumpled at the foot of the bed.

"My phone's dead," Cage said looking at his.

"I have a little juice left and it is 11:05 a.m.," I said shocked.

"Damn! I wonder how long he's been waiting?"

"I don't know. But did we confirm with Dr. Sonya that we wanted the tour?"

"Don't we want one, though?"

"Of course. I'm just saying his waiting isn't our fault."

"We should probably get down there, right?"

"Probably," I conceded.

"Could you come here for a second, though?"

I walked to his side of the bed.

"A little closer."

I got close enough for him to take my hand. He didn't.

"Closer," he said with a devilish smile.

I got as close to his head as I could get. That was when he took hold of my hard cock and wrapped his lips around it again. The sensation was coma-inducing.

He wasted no time in working his tongue around my head and stroking me off. I was able to hold back last night but I didn't have the strength this morning. I came in record speed. As I did, I placed my hand on his head to prevent myself from falling over.

"That's all," Cage said rolling off of me with a big smile on his face.

It took a moment for me to regain my bearings.

"I could have done that to you," I told him seeing my wasted opportunity.

"But, I did it to you," he said with a smile. "Staring at you all naked and hot, how was I not supposed to? Anyway, time for our tour," he said rolling out of bed knowing he had won.

I watched him thinking about how unfair it was that he had gotten to blow me twice while I still hadn't gotten to touch him. I had to figure out how to get my hands on him. And as he found his shirt and got dressed, he covered the humongous outline stretched across the front of his sweatpants. It looked like he was even bigger than I was.

"Wow!" I said letting him know what I was thinking.

"See something you like?"

"Yes, very much so."

"Maybe I'll give it to you later."

My erection which was finally shrinking after being sucked off, suddenly changed direction. I never became as hard as I was before he blew me, but I was getting close.

"Are you really getting hard again? Don't make me come over there," he said teasingly.

"Is that supposed to be a threat? Because I... um,"

I really wasn't good at this flirting thing.

"Nevermind. We should go."

Cage chuckled. "Yeah, we should."

After we both got dressed, we took turns in the bathroom and then headed down. A guy was sitting on the couch in the living room. He was tall with shaggy brown hair, a welcoming face, and a big beautiful smile. He looked like he could be twenty-one or twenty-two. Whatever he was, he looked older than I was and like he could have been in Cage's year.

"Hi," he said getting up and approaching us at the bottom of the stairs. His smile was beaming. "Dr. Sonya called me up yesterday saying you two were looking to get a tour of our fair town."

"Yes, we wanted to learn more about it," I told him taking the lead.

"I suppose you want to check out the falls."

"That and other things," I said looking back at Cage.

"Are you guys ready to go, or do you need some time? Dr. Sonya packed us a little brunch since you missed breakfast. I imagine you two were a little busy this morning?" Titus said suggestively. "I'm just kidding. No need to guess what two good-looking guys like yourselves were up to," he said with a knowing laugh. "Anyway, did you two want to head out?"

After all of that, I was stunned speechless. He had basically said that he knew we were having sex. As bad as I was with social things, I really didn't know how I was supposed to respond to that.

"We're ready," Cage replied jumping in. "We're really looking forward to this."

"The falls are beautiful. They are snow-tipped if you pardon the expression. It's what gave the town its name. Actually, a town board gave the town its name. They thought it would be better for tourism. What do you think, did it work? Was it the name that brought you two here?"

"No. We came because we thought I could have family here."

"Well, the population isn't that big. Who are you looking for? Maybe I know them."

"My last name is Rucker. But I don't think my parents would have the same name."

"Yeah, I don't know any Ruckers."

"Dr. Sonya said she'd ask around."

"She's pretty good at that. What do you think, should we go? I have the fixin's right here," he said bending down and picking up a wicker picnic basket.

"Yeah, let's go."

Titus turned and led us outside.

"I hope you don't mind if we take my truck. It seats three pretty comfortably."

"No that's fine."

"What about you… was it Cage or Quin? Which one's which?"

"I'm Cage, and this is Quin."

"What about you, Quin? Do you mind sitting in the back seat? I would suggest that you sit up front with us. It's a bench seat after all. But I figure you'll be more comfortable in the back."

"The back is fine," I said finding my voice.

"Alright then. Let's head on out."

Titus drove us back into town repeating some of the things we had already heard. The school used to be a moonshine warehouse. Glen's general store used to be the chief moonshine runner's main office, and that there used to be a wall surrounding the town. From there he made a U-turn and took us past the bed and breakfast.

"Alcohol prohibition ended in the late 1920s, didn't it?" I asked not having learned about this time in American history at my high school.

"1933," Titus corrected. "Between 1920 and 1933, this town was the richest little town in Tennessee. The amount of concentrated wealth rivaled that of Beverly Hills or downtown New York City."

"Then what happened?" Cage asked.

"The same thing that happens to most ideas when their times have passed. People moved on and moved away. There were a few people who stayed. They kept the community going through the dry times. Not alcohol dry times. Those would probably be the wet times for that.

"But the people here did what they could. At one point someone thought they could turn this place into a processing facility for Tennessee whiskey. But that didn't stick."

"What changed?"

"Eco-tourism," Titus explained. "At least that's what Dr. Sonya calls it. She said she came here because she thought it would be a beautiful place to settle down. We have more waterfalls than any part of Tennessee. And with hiking and rock climbing becoming all the rage, she convinced people to rename the town focusing on that. She had said that the money would just roll in."

"Has it worked?" Cage asked.

"It's tough to say. The population is up. Every so often we get folks like the two of you who show up looking to see the falls. But it's been tough getting us on the map."

"Marketing a place like this must be hard," I considered.

"No. I mean that it's been hard getting us on the map. The literal map. You pull out your phone and you couldn't find us if you wanted to. It has to do with the name change, I think. At least, that's what I've been told. And we're unincorporated. A lot of little things add up.

"But it's a beautiful town. A lot of friendly people. Very welcoming. People just need to hear about us. What I'm saying is, whenever you get back to where you came from, tell people," he said with a broad smile.

"We definitely will," Cage said enthusiastically. "By the way, and you may be too young to know this, but have you ever heard of someone who might have died giving birth? It would have been around the time you were born."

"My memories don't go that far back," Titus said with a quick smile.

"Of course. What about any babies going missing?"

"You mean, like, kidnapped? Or, baby napped I guess it would be in this case."

"Yeah."

"Naw. I've never heard of anything like that around these parts. Is that who you're looking for?"

"We don't know," I said jumping in. "We just suspect it was in a town close to Falls County Hospital."

"Oh, I remember that place. I was born there. Of course, I don't remember being born. But, that was where I had to go for anything medically related before Dr. Tom took up residence. You've met Glen, right? That's what Dr. Sonya was saying."

"We did. Nice guy. He gave us my crutches, which I have once again forgotten," Cage said realizing it for the first time.

"I noticed your bum leg there. What's that, a sporting injury? You look like you've played some ball?"

"Football injury."

"I used to play football back in high school. We have a pretty good football program here. We don't get much of an opportunity to travel for games. Funds in this town are always a little tight. But it has potential. Do you play at East Tennessee?"

"I did. My season's over."

"Sorry to hear that. I've always thought about going there."

"Why don't you?" I asked.

"Money. Time. Motivation. Take your pick. I was thinking I could study something that I could bring back here."

"That's a great idea," I said appreciating his loyalty to the town.

"It is, but then I get stuck on what that should be."

"That's what University is for, to help you figure out what you want to do."

"Yeah, you're right. I need to give it some more thought. Now that I have two friends who attend, it might be worth considering," Titus said with another welcoming smile.

Starting about twenty minutes out of town, we began our tour of the frozen waterfalls. No one had oversold them. They were amazing looking. They all looked like they were frozen mid-stream creating icicles that were as much as twenty feet long.

"My friends and I used to skinny-dip out here when we were kids," Titus said as we stared at one of the falls from our parked truck. "When it wasn't frozen over, of course. Yeah, as beautiful as it is in the winter, they are twice as beautiful in the summer. Maybe more. They're hidden gems."

"You're right. I've never seen anything like it," I said.

"Well, that's not saying much because you're from the city," Cage joked.

"Oh, which city?" Titus asked.

"The big apple," Cage volunteered for me.

"Wow! What was that like?"

I froze unsure how much I should say. My childhood couldn't be compared to anything someone who grew up here could have had. And, did I mention that I had two dads and a mom? He seemed fine with Cage and me, but I couldn't forget how the busboy had reacted the night before.

"It's… different," I told him.

"I bet it is. Are cars the only thing you hear?"

"Depends on where you are."

"I can't even imagine that. Do you hear this? It's the sweet sound of nothing. You can't beat that."

"I grew up a mile away from our closest neighbor," Cage volunteered.

"So, you two are the extremes," Titus said with a smile.

"We definitely had different experiences growing up," Cage said.

"We're not that different," I corrected not liking the distance he was putting between us.

"Come on. I can't even imagine the world you grew up in. Or, what it feels like to be in your situation."

"What situation is that?" Titus asked innocently.

Cage and I looked at each other. It was good to know that he wasn't going to blurt out anything that might make me uncomfortable.

"I grew up with a lot of pressure to do something special," I summarized.

"You never told me that," Cage said searching his thoughts.

"I thought I did when we spoke about… stuff."

"No. I remember that conversation very well. You didn't mention that."

I sighed. "Well, I do. I can't just do anything I want with my life. I feel like everyone is expecting me to do something that changes the world."

"To change the world?" Titus said jovially. "Wow! That's a bit of pressure."

"More than a bit," I clarified.

"So, how are you going to do it? What are your plans to change the world?" Titus replied.

"I have no idea. I thought I could figure it out on my own. Then I thought that I could figure it out if I backpacked through Europe. Nope. I still don't know."

"You backpacked through Europe?" Titus asked mystified.

"Yeah."

"Wow! You too?" He said turning to Cage.

"No. That wasn't really an option for me."

"Cage was too busy sharpening his skills to play in the NFL."

"You're going to play in the NFL?"

"Not anymore. That part of my life is over."

"I'm sorry to hear that. Really!" Titus said sympathetically.

"Don't be. It was never my dream."

"What is your dream?"

"To get married… have a family… raise a couple of kids. Maybe I could teach football somewhere," Cage said looking at me.

As nice as his dream sounded, I had to admit that it didn't fit with what I knew I had to do. For my parents and all of the families at my school, I needed to show the world that we aren't misfits and mistakes. I needed to stand out and change the world making everyone grateful that kids who were born to two dads and a mom exist. I had to justify our existence.

When I didn't respond, Titus broke the tension by mentioning the food Dr. Sonya had packed for us. She had made us fried egg sandwiches with melted cheese and ham between toasted English muffins. The flavor was enhanced with a tart jam that was mixed with honey.

"They're good," Titus said enjoying one of them. "She doesn't cook often, but whenever she would bring something to a fair or school function, hers would always be the first I would check out. She's from the Caribbean, ya know? Jamaica, I think. Her jerk chicken is to die for."

"She's from Jamaica? I'm from the Bahamas," I said happy to hear that someone was from nearby.

"I thought you said you were from New York City?" Titus asked.

"He spent his summers in the Bahamas," Cage explained.

Titus just stared at me in the rearview mirror after that. I couldn't tell what he was thinking, but I felt the road being paved for him to think I was the freak everyone saw me as.

"Have we seen all of the falls?" I said wanting to change the topic.

"Not even close. I've only been taking you to the ones that didn't require much walking."

"You don't have to worry about me. I could walk a bit," Cage clarified.

"You sure?" Titus asked doubtfully.

"I don't think I could do a two-mile hike, but we could go further than we have."

"Alright then. Let's get to it," Titus said restarting his truck.

Titus drove for another twenty minutes and then parked the truck by the side of the road.

"How far is the hike?" I asked him.

"About a half a mile. Maybe a little less."

"Are you sure you're up for this? We don't have to," I said checking in with Cage.

"I'm fine. Really."

I didn't want to tell Cage he couldn't or shouldn't do it if he said he was fine. I had a hard time believing that someone who had an injury like his could hike a half-mile on it. That seemed crazy. But I had to trust Cage. No one knew how he felt except him.

The hike to the river was a snowy wonderland. We got quite a bit of snow in New York and Central Park was always nice in the winter. But I had never seen anything like this.

The deeper we got into the woods, the more snow-covered the trees became. It was beautiful. I hadn't imagined that places like this existed in real life.

The only sound I heard was the crunch of the snow under our feet. Past that, there was a light whirring as the breeze cut through the trees. It had to be one of the most relaxing experiences ever. I didn't know life could be so peaceful.

With Titus leading, I continuously looked back at Cage to see how he was doing. He seemed fine just as he said he would be. I wasn't sure how. I'm sure it helped that there were no hills or uneven areas. But even with that, I was amazed by Cage. I knew that there was no way I could do what he was doing. It made me want to be with him even more.

"This is it," Titus said leading us into a clearing.

I looked at the sight ahead of us. Forty feet away was a frozen lake that was a hundred feet across. At the far end was a thirty-foot high rock face. Stretching from the top to the bottom of it were icicles. It looked like a curtain made of ice. It was incredible.

"Wow!" I said unable to wrap my mind around the beauty of it.

"This is amazing," Cage said as blown away by it as I was.

"Come on. Let me show you something," Titus said ushering us forward.

Titus approached the edge of the frozen lake with us in tow.

"Is this safe?" I asked never having walked on ice before.

"Sure is. This has been frozen for the season. What you have to look out for is grey ice. When it's blue it's solid. When it's snow-covered like this, you have to be careful, but for the most part, you're fine."

It reassured me that Titus knew so much about frozen lakes. It was probably something every kid growing up here knew. I couldn't imagine all of the ways his upbringing was different than mine. Was Cage's upbringing more similar to Titus's?

All I knew about Cage when I met and fell for him, was that he was a football star. Because of my uncle and the parents at my high school, I was very comfortable with professional athletes. But Cage was more than that. He was a guy who grew up in the middle of nowhere surrounded by trees and with a father who treated him like the only thing he was good for was football. That couldn't be further from my experiences.

Of course, whose life could have been similar to mine? I guess the other kids at my school might have experienced something close. But could I only have a happy life with one of a handful of people, most of which were a generation younger than me?

That didn't seem right to me. So, if not them, why not a guy who came from a completely different world, like Cage?

I looked back at Cage seeing if he disagreed with Titus's assessment of the ice. When he didn't react, I took what Titus said as fact. I followed Titus's footsteps onto the ice and within a few feet, he looked back and corrected me.

"You never want to walk in a line on ice. Spread out. It reduces risk," he said.

I didn't see the logic in that, but I listened and stepped out of his cleared path. To me, Titus having walked on it was proof that the spot was strong enough to hold us. But, he grew up here while I spent my winters on a tropical island. What did I know?

The further we got across the lake, the more I realized that the ice curtain in front of us wasn't a wall. It was a group of staggered icicles that appeared from a distance to be one piece. More amazing than that was the cave that was hidden behind it.

"It's a different experience in the summer when all of the water's flowing. But when everything is frozen over like this, I think it's something special," Titus said leading us through a gap in the icicles into the cave.

Standing within and looking around its ten-foot depths, I was awestruck. The sight was hauntingly beautiful.

"It's like we're in one of those survival movies," I said trying to wrap my mind around what we were looking at.

"I could see that," Titus agreed. "Could you imagine Hollywood coming here and shooting a movie? That would be something, wouldn't it? Snow Tip Falls has so much potential. All it needs is someone to recognize it and give us a chance."

"Maybe marketing could be something you study at University," I told him. "You definitely have the personality for it. You're selling us on how great it is here."

"That's something worth considering," Titus said with a smile. "I've never thought about that."

"You should listen to Quin. He's pretty smart," Cage said grabbing my attention.

It felt amazing to have a boyfriend who said nice things about me. How lucky was I? Everything I knew about him told me he was a great guy. I mean, he spent his free time playing flag football in the park with 10-year-olds. Who did stuff like that?

I smiled at Cage and reached for his hand. He took it and smiled back at me. It wasn't a blushing smile. It was one that told me he was content. I liked seeing that. I always had so much running through my mind that it was hard to find peace.

We sat in the cave and enjoyed the scenery for over an hour. Half of it was Titus answering my question about what it was like growing up here. He was a talker. That was fine, though, because he was easy to listen to.

The way he described his childhood sounded a lot like mine without the money and travel. It was attending a tiny school. You got to know your classmates really well when you did. You did everything together.

The big difference between our experiences was that after graduation, the kids in my school could go their separate ways. They could meet new people and explore the world. Here, no one left town. If you didn't like someone in high school, you had to deal with them for the rest of your life.

"It's getting late. You guys must be pretty hungry," Titus said finally running out of things to say.

"We could head back," Cage said checking in with me.

While we were sitting, he had pulled me into his arms. I could have stayed there forever. But, the only thing we had to eat all day was Dr. Sonya's sandwiches.

I was okay with that, but Cage was a much bigger guy than I was.

"Yeah, let's head back," I agreed. "But, this was an incredible tour. The town is breathtaking."

"Thank you! I'm glad you liked it. Remember, tell people," Titus joked as he got up.

"Or, you can tell them yourself when you start at East Tennessee next semester," I reminded him.

Titus laughed. "Right. There's that."

With Titus again taking the lead, I kept hold of Cage's hand and followed the group. I kept wondering what it was like walking in Cage's shoes so I did the next best thing. Finding his footprints in the snow, I matched our steps.

Being nearly 6 inches taller than me, his steps were longer. I had to bounce a bit to keep up. Leaping forward to match his stride, I lost my footing and slid. Slipping out of Cage's hand, the ice came at me fast. I hit the ground with a crack.

In a second, my body froze in shock. The crack I heard was the ice breaking. I was surrounded by cold water and sinking like a rock.

I couldn't breathe. The water was too cold. My face was going under. It was all happening too fast. I started to panic.

Losing which way was up, I waved my arms until my forehead hit something hard. It was the ice sheet. I had swum past where I had fallen in. It was so cold. My heart pounded uncontrollably. I was going to have to calm down. How could I, though? Everything in me screamed for me to take a breath.

Forcing myself to slow down, I heard something. People were yelling. I couldn't understand what they were saying, but looking up, I could see their blurred images. One of them was pointing away from me. Was there something in the water he was warning me about? That was usually what that meant when the person was pointing at something from a boat.

No, that wasn't it. They wanted me to go back to where I fell in. They were pointing me towards the opening.

Turning around, I forced my quickly freezing limbs to push me towards the hole in the ice. The shadows above got larger. Something entered the water in front of me. It was someone's hand, I had to grab for it. I wasn't in control of my angle or anything else, but clutching our palms I was dragged towards the opening.

With my free hand finding the edge of the ice, I pushed it out of the water and into the air. Twisting around, I grabbed onto the ice and pulled my head out. It was Cage who had my hand. He was lying on his belly and he was pulling me out.

Locked in his position, there wasn't much he could do once I got my head above water. So, after a deep breath, I did the rest.

"You have to kick your feet. Kick your feet!" Titus insisted.

Without thinking, I did it. It helped. What helped more was as I pulled on Cage's body and dragged myself up. It was then that I realized that the flatter my body was, the more I ascended when I kicked.

Grabbing Cage's arm, then side, then pants, my body left the freezing water. Settling on the ice next to my rescuer, I was exhausted and traumatized, but I was alive and seemingly safe.

"Cage, crawl back. Quin, you have to roll away from the hole," Titus instructed us from a distance.

We both did what we were told and were eventually on what felt like solid ice. Getting up, I just wanted to get off the lake. Crawling on my hands and knees, this time I looked down at every step.

When we were nearing the edge and my pulse no longer thumped in my ears, I stood up. Moving slowly and steadily I made it back to shore. I was relieved and rattled. I looked around to gain my bearing and found Cage rushing towards me. Looking down at me, he gripped my arms.

"Are you okay? You hurt?"

That was a good question. Was I hurt? The sound of the crack as I hit the ice flashed through my mind. There was an ache in the back of my head where it had made contact.

"I think so," I said touching my head where it hit.

"Let me see. Are you bleeding?"

I removed my hand and looked at it. Cage moved around me to see for himself.

"I don't think so. I think I'm good."

"Jesus, Quin," he said again looking me in the eyes and throwing his arms around me.

"I'm okay," I assured him not convinced that I was.

"Fuck, Titus, what the hell were you doing taking us on thin ice?" Cage yelled turning to him.

"I'm sorry. I didn't think it was thin. It's been frozen all winter. Didn't I tell you not to walk in a line?" He said yelling at me.

"Don't blame him."

"I'm just sayin', if he would have followed my instructions, nothing would have happened."

"I'm okay, Cage. It's not his fault. He's right. He told me not to walk behind people and I did. But, everything ended okay. I just want to go."

"Can we go?" Cage asked Titus angrily.

"Of course. Just follow me."

Titus led the way and we were all quiet on the way back. The further we walked, the more I questioned if I was alright. I stopped to re-center myself.

"What's the matter?"

"My head hurts," I admitted.

Cage looked at the back of my head again.

"You might have a concussion. Your head hit the ice pretty hard."

"I can take you to Dr. Tom and have you checked if you want."

"Yeah, that's probably best," Cage conceded.

"Dr. Tom? That's Glen's husband, right?" I asked.

"Yeah," Titus confirmed.

"We should see him," I said thinking less about me and more about the reason we had come to Snow Tip Falls.

Continuing back to the truck, we got there with my teeth chattering. My wet clothes were freezing quickly.

"Let me turn on the heat. You might want to take off what's wet," Titus said unlocking the truck.

"I can't move my arms. They're so cold," I told them starting to feel numb.

"I'll help you. Here, sit up front next to the vents," Cage said directing me to the front passenger door and taking off my jacket and shirt.

Bareback, I was as cold as I was in my frozen jacket. But when Cage slipped his jacket onto me, I was immediately enveloped in Cage's body heat. It felt so good.

"You're gonna want to take off your pants as well. Just until they dry," Titus said with the truck running.

I looked at Cage for confirmation.

"Yeah, probably," he agreed.

I moved my hand to unbutton them and I couldn't control my fingers enough to do it.

"Let me get that," Cage offered before moving his hand to my pants.

I was too cold and uncomfortable to make much out of it. But having him undress me warmed me up. With my pants, shoes, and socks off, I climbed into the front seat of the truck. I moved to the middle of the bench hoping Cage would join us. It wasn't just that I wanted to be able to snuggle up to him for his body heat. It was that I felt better when I was in his arms. I could use a little of that now.

After he placed my wet clothes in front of a vent, he slid next to me and we were off. His holding me was automatic. I cuddled in his arms grateful for having him there.

I couldn't be sure if I fell asleep on the way back or not. I wasn't feeling perfect after hitting my head, but I didn't feel nauseous. Nausea was the classic sign of a concussion. So, at least I didn't have that.

By the time we were making a right turn past Glen's general store, I was, for the most part, feeling better. I wasn't going to tell either of them that. I wanted an excuse to talk to the town doctor alone.

The place we pulled up to was two-stories with white siding. If I were to picture the home of a small-town doctor, it would have been this. His office was a similarly looking detached building to the left of the main house but set further back.

Putting my pants and shoes back on, the chill from the water quickly returned. Having been blasted by the hot air in the truck, it didn't affect me quite as much. Even with there being a slight breeze, I made it to the office without my dick freezing off. I was happy about that. I had barely started using it for its intended purpose. I didn't want to lose it now.

"Dr. Tom?" Titus called bringing an older Latino man into the waiting room.

He was more serious-looking than his husband. He was also shaped differently. Whereas Glen was built like a teddy bear, Dr. Tom was more barrel-chested. Both looked like they enjoyed a good meal, though. This had to be what years of marital bliss in a small town looked like.

"Titus, what's up? Who's this?" The man said in a slight Spanish accent.

"I was giving them a tour of the falls and Quin fell through the ice. He hit his head on the way down so I thought I would bring him so you could check him out."

Dr. Tom turned to me. "Quin, is it?"

"Yes," I confirmed.

"Why don't you join me in my office," he said leading me back.

Behind the closed door, the doctor pointed me to the metal bed in the middle of the room.

"Have a seat. Let me take a look at you. Are you experiencing any nausea or headaches?" He asked sitting in front of me and shining a light in my eyes.

"No nausea. I had a bit of a headache but it's almost gone now."

"Okay, what about any tingling in your extremities? Fingers? Toes?" He said squeezing my fingers.

"I was in the water for less than a minute. Cage rescued me pretty quickly."

"Cage? Is that your friend outside?"

"Yes."

"You two came to town to check out the frozen falls?"

"No, actually."

"What brought you?"

"We're looking for Cage's parents.

"Oh," the doctor said crossing his arms and leaning back. "What are their names?"

"We don't know. His mother is listed as Jane Doe on his birth certificate."

"That's unusual."

"That's what I thought."

"But, why are you looking for her here?"

"Because Cage's father… or at least, the man who raised him, had an I.D. for Falls County Hospital.

That made me think that he worked there around the time that Cage was born. If he wasn't his biological father, and he worked in the hospital, there is only one way he could get a hold of a baby."

"You're making a serious accusation there. And that still doesn't explain why you would come here."

"We checked the hospital…"

"It's shut down."

"Yes. I figured that if his mother was at that hospital, she probably came from close by. Your husband said that you used to work there."

Dr. Tom shifted uncomfortably.

"I did. It was a few years ago."

"Were you there twenty two years ago?'

The doctor instinctually reached for his speckled grey beard.

"I was."

"Did you hear about any children going missing or any mothers dying during birth? That was the story Cage's father told him. He said that his mother died."

"What was your friend's father's name?"

"The I.D. said, Joe Rucker."

I watched for any response that came from hearing the name. He had none. There was no casual dismissal or confirmation. He was blank. Why didn't he have any reaction at all? If the name meant nothing to him, wouldn't he automatically brush it aside?

"I see."

"Did you know him?"

"I can't say that I did," he said stone-faced.

"Do you know of any situation that could put Cage's birth there?"

"You understand that I couldn't tell you even if I did. There's something called patient/doctor confidentiality."

"Sure. I know. But, if there was a kid that went missing, wouldn't someone be looking for them?"

The doctor just stared at me. Was his reaction supposed to be telling me something? Was I missing something that someone who was better at reading people would pick up on?

"As much as I would like to help you, this isn't a topic I could discuss with someone who just showed up off of the street. Did you really fall into the ice?"

"I did. Why would I lie about that?"

"There are all types in this world."

"Are you suggesting that there's something to what I've been saying?"

"I'm neither saying whether there is or isn't. It's not my place."

I stared at Dr. Tom sure that he was looking for a follow-up question. It took me a moment to figure out what it was.

"Then, whose place is it?"

The doctor unlatched his arms and began paperwork as if I hadn't asked the question.

"Have you gotten the chance to meet many people in town?"

"We've met a few. Is there anyone we should meet?"

"I don't know if there's anyone you should meet, but there are some interesting characters. Nero is someone you might find entertaining. He's a little rough around the edges but he's a good kid."

"Nero?"

"Yes. Is there anything else medical-related that I could help you with," he said ushering me out.

"No. Thank you. Who do I pay for the visit?"

"Don't worry about it. You had nothing wrong. It's on the house," he said looking at me with a forced smile.

I was about to go when I thought of something.

"Actually, there might be one other thing that I'd like to discuss."

"What's that?"

"You're married?"

"Yes."

"To a man?"

"Yes?" The doctor said worried about where I was going with my question.

"I'm here with my boyfriend."

"Okay."

"We might be doing something for the first time later. I'm aware that there are things you can use to make such things a little easier... you know when they slide in."

Dr. Tom turned, grabbed a small tube out of a cabinet, and handed it to me.

"Thanks," I told him. "Nero, right?"

The doctor gave me a tight-lipped smile.

"I'll take that as a yes."

I left his office and joined the two guys.

"Is everything okay?" Cage asked concerned.

"Oh yeah. It's just a bump on the head. I'm fine. Do you think he should take a look at your cast?"

"I don't see why he would," Cage said flatly.

"Because you just walked a mile on it. It was broken, wasn't it?"

"I guess my dad was right. I heal fast."

I didn't want to argue with Cage about how he felt, so I dropped the topic and we all returned to Titus's truck. When we were back at the bed and breakfast, Titus made clear that he wasn't joining us in.

"I'm sorry it ended like that," Titus said genuinely disappointed.

"Honestly, I'm fine. It's just something that happened. By the way, do you know someone by the name of Nero?"

"Yeah, sure. What about him?"

"Where would we find him if we were looking?"

"I think he does a couple of shifts at the diner."

"Wait, as a busboy?"

"Yeah. Why?"

I looked at Cage who was looking at me as curiously as Titus was.

"I was just wondering. Listen, thanks for showing us around."

I pulled out my wallet and handed him two twenties.

"Oh no, you don't have to. Especially after what happened?"

"I'm telling you. It's fine. It was a great tour. We're grateful for it. I insist."

"Well, if you insist," he said flashing his brilliant smile.

"And, if we need a little more history on the town, do you think we can give you a call?"

"Of course. Just let me know."

"Thanks, have a good one," I told him before ushering Cage out of the truck and inside.

"Why were you asking about the busboy from last night," he asked me as we crossed the living room?"

"How was your tour?" Dr. Sonya said crossing from the kitchen. "It was a long one."

"It was… very nice, thank you," Cage said relieving me of having to make polite conversation.

"Did you see many of the falls?"

"We did. They were beautiful."

"Oh good! Glad you liked them."

"On a related note, do you have any way of drying these wet clothes?" Cage asked holding up my shirt and jacket having collected them from Titus's truck.

Dr. Sonya reacted with playful surprise.

"So, I assume the tour was eventful," she joked.

Both of us chuckled.

"It was."

"No one was hurt, right?"

"I'm fine," I told her.

"Good. I can take care of these," she said taking my clothes from Cage.

She next looked down at my pants.

"Do you want to give me those?"

"I'm good, thanks."

"Suit yourself. Cali and I are about to have dinner. Would you like to join us?"

"Thank you, but we have plans," I said interjecting.

Cage looked at me confused. He was probably pretty hungry by now, so I was taking food out of the wolf's mouth.

"Yes, unfortunately, we have plans," Cage confirmed.

"Oh! What are you two up to?"

"Ahhh…" Cage said looking at me.

"Boyfriend stuff," I said.

Dr. Sonya fought a laugh.

"Go to it," she said walking away without another word.

Cage turned to me.

"I appreciate your enthusiasm, but I really need to get something to eat first."

"We are. We're just going to get it at the diner."

I explained to Cage what Dr. Tom had said to me and what I thought it meant.

"So, you think that little homophobe has information that could help us?"

"That's what he implied."

"I'm sure he'll be in the sharing mood after we got him docked a day's pay."

"We didn't do anything to him. He was the one who said something to us."

"And, I'm sure he'll see it that way."

"Sarcasm?" I confirmed.

"Yes, sarcasm. He's not gonna wanna talk to us. And, I'm not sure I'm gonna want to talk to him."

"Then I'll do the talking."

"I don't think he's gonna wanna talk to you either."

"Let's hope he does because I think he might have the answers to what happened to your mother."

Cage didn't fight me after that. Taking a few minutes to rest in our room, we headed to Cage's truck and returned to the diner. Entering, it wasn't as empty as the night before. There was a greying couple at one of the tables, and a balding, creepy-looking man sitting in the corner picking at his food with his fingers.

"I'll be right with you," the stout cook said from the kitchen.

We took our previous booth and sat scanning for signs of the busboy. Neither of us saw any. The cook appeared to be doing everything by himself. And when he handed us our menus he added, "Tonight we're out of everything but the chicken dinner, the burger, hotdogs, and I have some pie left."

"I'll take the chicken dinner," Cage said not looking at the menu.

"Fried or baked."

"Baked."

"Fries or mashed potatoes?"

"Mashed potatoes. And a Coke."

"I'll get the same with fries, thanks," I told him.

The man took our menus and got us our Cokes. After, he went to the kitchen and started preparing everything.

"Why give us the menus if he's out of half of what's on it?" Cage asked me with a smile.

"Habit?" I said wondering the same thing.

"I guess. Although, it looks like this place has been here a while and it's the only option in town. I don't think anyone else here needs the menu to know what they want," Cage pointed out.

"True," I agreed. "I don't know."

"By the way, how are you feeling?" Cage asked squinting his eyes at me.

"I'm okay. But I'm still a little cold."

"Really?" Cage asked reaching across the table.

I grunted my reluctance to hold hands here after what had happened the night before.

"No. I won't let you get self-conscious about us showing affection in public. If I was with a girl, no one would think anything about it. I'm not gonna act differently because you're a guy."

I relaxed my crossed-arms and he took my hands.

"Quin, I'm proud to be with you. I want everyone here to know that I got you and they didn't. If they have a problem with the fact that we're two guys, then they could meet me outside. But I won't let it change us. I'll fight for that," he said lifting my hands to his lips and kissing them."

My heart thumbed hearing his declaration. How could he be so confident being with me? My dads had been together for twenty years and had been best friends for a decade before that, yet even they acted differently when they were together in public compared to when they were with my mom.

When my dads were at events without my mom, they barely did more than put their arms around the other's shoulders. But when either was with my mom, they held hands with her, kissed her, they did whatever. How was Cage, a guy who had only dated women until me, more comfortable showing his affection in public than two men who have been madly in love with each other for twenty years?

Although I couldn't explain it, knowing the difference made Cage that much more irresistible. He was everything I could ever want in a guy. Being with him didn't change my history or what I knew I had to accomplish with my life. But, maybe there was a way to have both.

Was he really only interested in settling down somewhere and raising a family? I mean, that sounded incredible. And the idea of creating a family with him felt wonderful and right.

But, I couldn't have a small private life. It was my responsibility to prove that kids from my type of family could change the world. I couldn't do that living in a place as isolated as Snow Tip Falls.

Pushing that out of my mind, I focused on something more immediate.

"I don't think Nero is here tonight," I told Cage.

"I don't think so either."

"What do we do?"

"What do you mean?"

"Tomorrow's Monday. We have class in the morning," I pointed out.

"Did you want to head back?"

"Shouldn't we? Don't you have to work?"

"I can find someone to cover my shifts."

"Don't you need to work? We could always come back next weekend."

Cage looked away saddened.

"You're right like always. It was just that answers were finally starting to feel so close. What do you think Nero knows?"

"I can't even guess. It could be anything. But he's not here and we don't know if he'll be back tomorrow or ever."

"You're right. We should go. After we eat, of course," he said firmly.

"Of course," I said with a chuckle. "I think I've starved you enough for one day."

I stared into his eyes losing myself. I had to touch him. So, freeing one of my hands, I brushed his cheek with my thumb. He was so gorgeous and perfect. I wanted to be his. I wanted the two of us to be one.

When dinner came, we ate, Cage a little faster than I did. The big guy barely had anything to eat all day.

"Interested in a little pie?" The cook asked when he cleared our plates.

Cage looked at me clearly wanting me to say yes.

"Sure, what type?" I asked.

"It's blueberry. Two slices or one?"

"Just one. I only need a bite," I told Cage.

"Just one, thanks," Cage told the cook.

"You want it warmed up?"

Cage looked at me and I nodded. "Sure."

"Ice cream on the side?"

"Absolutely," Cage said not needing to consult with me.

The cook brought out the steaming hot pie with two forks and we ate it in silence. I wasn't talking because all I could think about was climbing into his arms naked. I had seen the outline of his manhood. He was big. What would that feel like pushing into me?

Dr. Tom had given me lube. It was what I was hinting at. I could only imagine him smearing it between my ass cheeks and massaging my hole with it. Would he push in a finger to open me up first? I got hard thinking about it.

It had to happen at some point, right? Maybe I'll stay over at his place tonight. Maybe he'll walk me to my room when we get back to the university and then follow me in. My skin crackled in anticipation. I felt like I was going crazy waiting for it.

"Should we go?" Cage asked when the pie was gone.

"Okay," I said with a smile still thinking about what could happen next.

I went to the cash register and paid the bill and then joined Cage as he walked towards the door. He reached for my hand and I slipped it in his. It felt so right. We were about to let each other go and climb into the truck when someone drew our attention.

"Guys!"

We turned seeing Titus. He was with a woman who looked like an older, female version of himself. She, however, looked like she took life more seriously than he did.

"Titus," Cage said gripping my hand making sure I didn't shy away from his grasp.

Titus led the woman over and genuinely looked happy to see us.

"Cage, Quin, this is my mom. Mom, these are the two guys I gave a tour to today."

"Nice to meet you," we both said.

"Nice to meet you. Titus hasn't been able to stop talking about you two. He tells me he's going to East Tennessee University now."

We looked at Titus who turned red.

"Come on, Mom. I just mentioned that I gave them a tour and said I was going to look into attending some classes. Quin was telling me how it might be able to help the town."

"The town is perfect just the way it is," his mother said firmly. "I don't know why you think things would be better if we were overrun by tourists." She looked at us. "No offense."

"No offense taken," Cage said politely.

"We're hardly going to be overrun by tourists. I just think the town would do better if we had a little more money flowing through it."

"Your generation and your focus on money."

Titus laughed. "I hardly think wanting to be successful started with my generation. Have you heard of the industrial revolution? Robber barons? I think people have been wanting more for their lives before I came along."

His mother huffed. Titus looked at us and shrugged his shoulders confounded but amused.

"Anyhow, did you two just have dinner?"

Cage replied. "Yeah. We had the chicken."

"It's Sunday, so it's what's on the menu. And another thing, Mom, if we had more people coming through the town, maybe Bill could have more than one option on Sundays."

"I've never heard you complain about his Sunday meals."

"Well, consider this me registering my complaint."

"Noted," his mother said displeased.

"Anyway, you guys headed back to the bed and breakfast?"

"Yeah. And then we're driving back," Cage explained.

"Oh! Because I was going to tell you that I know where to find Nero tomorrow if you're still looking for him."

"You do?" I asked perking up.

"Yeah." Titus looked at his mother who was watching us talk. "He has this thing he hosts on Monday nights. It's just a little social club event. Nothing special. But I was going to say that I could take you if you wanted to go."

"Oh!" Cage said looking at me.

I didn't know what to say to him. I was as interested in talking to Nero as he was, maybe more. But, we both had classes and he had to work.

"Can we text you about it?" I said knowing Cage and I had to consider this.

"Sure," Titus said before we exchanged numbers and went our separate ways.

In the warmth of the truck, we watched Titus go inside and settle at a table with his mother. His mom smiled for the first time when the cook came to the table. They were both smiling. There was clearly something more going on between the two.

"So, what do you think? Do we stick around and try to talk to Nero at his "social club event" tomorrow?" Cage asked turning to me.

"We could also drive home and come back tomorrow after you get off of work?"

"We could. But that's two hours there, two hours back here, and then two more hours getting home. I could think of a few better ways to spend our time," he said with a smile.

I got hard as soon as he said it. He was right. I could think of several better things we could do with our time as well.

"It's up to you, Quin. It's your money. But, if you wanted to stay another night, I might be able to make it worth your while," he said sending tingles whipping through my body.

"Oh, yeah? How?"

Cage slipped his hand behind my neck and pulled my lips to his. I was weak in his grasp. The heat of his lips melted any resistance I had about staying. With his undulating on mine, I parted my lips and invited in his tongue.

As our tongues danced, my head swooned. His kiss was a warm breeze on a cool day. Everything felt so good. And, when he released me from my trance, I was willing to do anything to start it up again.

"I think that would be worth staying over for," I told him doing my best not to climb on top of him right there.

Cage smiled. "Good. I'm glad you think so," he said with a sparkle in his eyes.

I couldn't not touch him as we drove back to the bed and breakfast. I slipped my hand onto his thigh rubbing his muscles. Everything about him was so big. It didn't take me long to move my hand up his leg to his crotch. His cock was the first thing I touched. I couldn't avoid it. The thing was huge.

His sweatpants didn't hide anything. I couldn't wait any longer. I had to see it. I needed to hold him in my hands. So, as he drove, I leaned over into his lap, gripped the band of his pants, and tugged them down.

Cage helped me by shifting up allowing his pants and underwear to slide to his thigh. His cock was so big that it got caught as his pants went down. His thick shaft was the first thing I saw. But, having to slide my hand onto it and help it along, I got a full look at it as it sprung out inches from my lips.

I had never held a dick before and the feeling sent my heart racing. I couldn't encircle it with one hand. The most I could do was hold it still while I lowered my head and slipped the tip of it into my mouth.

He groaned as soon as my hot breath encased him. I had never done this before, but I was a fast learner. I knew what he had done that had driven me wild. And sending my tongue to work on the ridge of his tip, I felt the truck slow down.

Putting the truck in park but not turning it off, he stretched out his legs giving me easier access. As he did, he revealed some of his buried length. Wow!

Wrapping a second hand under the first one, there was still space for a third. Feeling his bulging veins pressing against my palms, I pushed the tip of him as far into my throat as I could. It wasn't very far.

Turned on as much as he was, I twisted my head pulling it back before returning it to the boundaries of my throat. As I did, I stroked him with both hands. His legs squirmed.

When he placed his hand on my head, I knew he was close.

"Ahhh!" he moaned squirming in his seat.

Hearing that, I did more. Slapping my tongue back and forth across his head, I tightened my grip on his cock. Gliding across the curve of it, I finally flicked my tongue against the base of his head causing him to explode.

Not removing it from within me, I caught all of it in my throat. I didn't know if he would want me to or not, but I wanted to know everything about him. I wanted to know what Cage's cum tasted like.

Swallowing all of it, it was tangy. He was silent as it kept coming. When it stopped was when he fought to catch his breath and inhaled.

"Oh my god, you're so good at that. How did you get so good?" He asked inspiring me to sit up and release him.

I didn't want to let go of his sturdy manhood. I could have held onto it forever. It was thicker and more impressive than the truck's gear shifter which was a foot away.

I couldn't get over that I was looking at Cage's cock. It was my boyfriend's dick and it was the most beautiful thing I had ever seen.

He reached over and perched my chin on his finger. Leaning forward he kissed my lips.

"Seriously, how are you so good at that?"

"I guess I was inspired," I told him proud that I had been able to bring him so much joy.

Cage lowered his hand and laid back.

"I don't think I can move. Seriously, I think my legs are paralyzed," he joked. "I may never be able to walk again."

"Oh, no! Your football career!"

Cage laughed.

"That's what I'll do. I'll blame my quitting on my boyfriend's blow jobs. They were so good that I lost the use of my legs. I'm sure sports media would understand that."

"I would," I confirmed with a smile.

We both sat quietly as Cage gathered his strength. We were less than 20 seconds from the B&B coming into view. Finishing the final drive there, we parked out front and slowly made our way inside. I was still wearing Cage's jacket so he crossed his arms trying to escape the cold.

Entering we looked around hoping we wouldn't have to talk to anyone about where we were. No one was there. Instead, we found my clothes folded on the living room coffee table in front of us. Hanging beside it was my jacket. Pinned to it was a note.

'*I didn't know if you were going to stay another night. So, either, it was great meeting you and I hope to see you again. Or, I'll see you for breakfast in the morning.*'

"We should leave a note telling her that we're staying, shouldn't we?" I asked unsure of what was expected.

"Either that or she'll just see my truck."

I looked out the window to see the truck illuminated by the living room lights.

"I guess you're right. And she has my credit card number. There's no need to leave a note."

Grabbing my clothes, we headed upstairs and retreated to our room. The bed had been made. I couldn't wait to mess it up again.

"I think I need a shower," Cage said looking very relaxed.

"Should I join you?" I asked wondering if it was a part of my boyfriend-ly duties.

"No. With this thing it's more work than play," he said referring to his cast.

"Then, I could wash your back for you."

"Thanks, but I got it. Did you want to hit the shower first? I'll probably be a while."

"I guess," I said still wanting to wrap my hands around him. But instead, I grabbed my folded shirt and entered the bathroom, closing the door behind me.

Stripping down, I couldn't stop thinking about how Cage's hard cock felt in my hands. I was starting to think that I would never touch a cock other than mine. And for it to be Cage's, I vibrated with excitement.

There wasn't a moment when I was in the shower that I wasn't completely hard. I was so aroused I felt giddy. After getting out I considered putting my clothes back on, but what was the point? So, I wrapped a towel around my waist and rejoined Cage.

"God, I can't stop looking at you," he said washing his eyes over me. His attention caused my hard dick to twitch. He saw it and smiled.

"I'll be back," he said replacing me behind the bathroom door.

I didn't know what to do with myself waiting. Although it wasn't cold in the room, it wasn't warm enough for me to sit around naked. That was a problem because I didn't want to get dressed.

On top of that, I didn't know how long Cage would take. The best option had to be to get comfortable under the covers. I desperately wanted him to think of sex with me, though. So, what could I do to accomplish that?

What I decided was I would put the tube of lube that Dr. Tom gave me on the bedside nightstand closest to the bathroom, and get into the other side of the bed. To make sure he wouldn't miss it, I turned off all of the other lights except the bedside lamp that featured the lube like a spotlight.

If he still missed it after that, I would say something. I wanted him so badly that I was shivering with anticipation. I slipped my hand under the sheets and pressed my dick when the pressure within it got too much.

The minutes felt like hours waiting for him to come out. I was sure I was about to snap in two from tension when, to my relief, I heard the shower turn off and he returned to the bedroom.

He approached the bed like a man out of the shadows. The way the towel rode his hip looked way better than the way it had rode mine. His tapered naked torso resembled that of superheroes' in movies. I could see every ripple of his bulging muscles. But there was only one bulge I cared about. That one didn't disappoint.

His hard cock stretched across the front of him eventually being buried in the ripples from the towel's tuck. I couldn't wait to feel it again. When he approached the edge of the bed and looked down at the nightstand, he chuckled. I was pretty sure his laugh meant I would see it soon.

"Did you bring this with you?" He asked picking up the lube and examining it.

"No. I got it from the doctor."

"You're always one step ahead of everyone else."

I was curious what he meant by that but didn't want to break the mood.

"Have you ever used lube before?" I asked him knowing that I hadn't.

"Once or twice. Not like how we're going to use it, though. I can't wait to try that."

"Me neither," I told him wanting him to get into bed immediately.

Dropping his towel allowing this hard cock to spring out, Cage returned the little bottle to the nightstand and joined me under the sheets. I pressed my forearms against my chest and slid to him face first. With his arms easing around me, I drank in his body heat.

"How do we do this?" Cage asked.

"However you'd like," I said shaking.

"You're cold," he said pulling me tighter.

I loved being in his arms. The sensation made me drunk. Needing to kiss him, I pulled back my head looking up at him. He had been waiting for that because as soon as I did, he leaned down and met my lips.

Facing him, our hard cocks touched. We both felt it. When he suddenly kissed me harder, I knew that it had turned him on as much as it did me.

Without thinking, I tilted my hips rubbing his cock against my belly and mine against his leg. Quickly he started to do the same. I had never imagined how good doing this could feel. And when he moved his hand to my ass and sunk his fingers between my cheeks to pull my body closer, my hips moved uncontrollably. I wanted him to fuck me. I needed him to know that I did.

Briefly letting go of my ass cheek, Cage reached back retrieving something from behind him. I would have barely noticed if I hadn't heard a snap and a blurping sound that got me excited. And when his hand returned and his fingers tested my hole, I lifted my leg giving him full access.

Cage kissed me as his lube-covered fingers pushed into me. The pressure was almost too much. It caused me to stop kissing and groan. Responding, he pulled his finger away. Quickly returning his fingers to his target, he pulsed the pressure until, like a balloon, my hole popped.

Cage's thick finger was inside of me. Cage was inside of me. With it came a flash of pain that quickly retreated. The sensation became fantastic. Moving to again kiss him, he then slowly fucked me with his finger before adding another one and stretching open my hole.

Cage's fingers felt glorious, but there was something I wanted even more. So, hoping he wouldn't get the wrong impression, I pulled away from his lips. Rolling over, he didn't remove his fingers until I had completely turned around. With them out, I pushed my back onto his chest and found his cock with my ass cheeks.

I knew I couldn't just lie there now that I knew how it felt to have him inside me, so I rubbed my ass against him. When he didn't move, I lifted my hips sending my opening in search of his tip.

With his head between my flesh pushing above my hole, he took over. Moving his tip to my target, he clutched the side of my hip. All I could do was take a breath preparing to receive what I had dreamed about for so long.

Unlike his fingers, the head of his cock was overwhelming. As much as he had stretched me, when he thrust forward, I realized that it hadn't been nearly enough.

He kept testing me, pushing himself harder. Each time I flinched and then quickly relaxed. I could tell he was getting further with every pulse. Finally, when Cage gripped his large hand around my side and locked me into place, he pushed his cock unwilling to relent.

As much as it ached, I didn't want him to stop. Did it hurt or did it feel good? I couldn't tell. What I did know was that I wanted Cage's cock in me and then, as if I had been reborn, he popped in sending a wave of agony that was quickly followed by a sea of pleasure.

"Yes!" I moaned needing more.

As soon as I said it, he pushed harder.

"Ahhh!" I groaned.

He was too much, but I wanted more. I wanted him to keep pushing until the two of us were one. Eventually he hit a point when he couldn't go in any further. That was when he retreated and then thrust back in. His cock was strumming me like a fiddle. As he did, my sight went dark and my legs fell limp.

If I were given a hundred years I would still never have imagined how good Cage's cock felt. My head was spinning. He was fucking me. Cage Rucker's cock was inside of me. And as he thrust into me faster and harder, I felt a knot building on the inside of my thigh that slowly crawled to my balls.

I was coming from his fucking alone. How was this possible? I hadn't touched myself. Neither had Cage. Yet, my balls tingled and I felt a growing ache.

I clenched my jaw hoping I could do something to stop it. I couldn't. So, losing control of myself, my toes clenched, my muscles clamped, and I exploded into orgasm.

I grunted as I did, but that was drowned out as Cage moaned. He moaned louder than I had ever heard anyone in my life. We were cumming together.

I moved my hand on top of his as it dug into my hip. I was growing lightheaded. I wanted to stay with him experiencing every moment, but everything was too much. His cock, the way I felt about him, the events of the day, it was all coming to a head.

As it did, I took a final deep breath. Releasing it, my vision darkened. I was in the throes of the greatest feeling of my life and losing myself in it, I slowly blacked out.

Chapter 14

Cage

Sex with Quin was what I always thought sex was supposed to be like. Sex with Tasha and the other girls was fine. No one had any complaints. But with Quin, I felt like a man on fire.

Being with Quin did something to me. I felt complete when I was with him. Holding him I had thoughts about white picket fences and kids running around in the yard. He was my other half. I was sure of it. There was no question that I was in love with him.

I held onto him all night. After I drifted off to sleep and rolled over losing contact with him, I woke up long enough to reach my hand back in search of his body. It wasn't until I found it that I was able to again fall asleep.

In the morning, I opened my eyes to find him cuddled in my arms. I could smell his hair. There was a hint of strawberry in it. I could have lied there forever and we almost did. We didn't even think about getting up until after 11. By then, we were both hungrier than anything else.

"What should we do today?" I asked him as he reluctantly peeled away from me.

"Get something to eat?"

"And then for the next 10 hours before going to Nero's book club or whatever it is?"

"I don't think it will be a book club," Quin said taking me seriously.

"I'm kidding. Yeah, something tells me that Nero doesn't get his kicks from a well-constructed sentence," I joked.

"Probably not," Quin agreed with a smile.

God, did I love to see that man smile.

The two of us took turns in the bathroom getting ready and then we headed downstairs. Dr. Sonya was hovering.

"Well, good morning," she said blushing.

It was pretty clear that she knew what we had been up to the night before. Staring at her, I tried to remember how loud we were. I hadn't been quiet. I looked around wondering about the thickness of the walls. They probably weren't very thick. Whoops!

"Good morning," I said embarrassed.

Quin seemed to miss her playful ribbing.

"It's closer to good afternoon," he corrected.

"I know. And I figured you two might have built up an appetite."

"We're definitely both hungry," Quin said seeming to miss Dr. Sonya's suggestion.

"Good! Because I went out and got you a selection of pastries. I was hoping they wouldn't go to waste. Let me get them," she said heading back to the kitchen. "Have a seat."

Quin and I sat at the round table in the breakfast nook and got comfortable. Dr. Sonya returned with a selection of croissants, sweet buns, and fruit. The only thing that could have made it better was bacon. But bacon made everything better, so that wasn't saying much.

"What are your plans for today?" She asked hanging around as we tried her treats.

"We're not sure yet," I said pulling a croissant apart and popping it into my mouth. "This is really good."

"They're made locally. We have a budding pastry chef on our hands. I've been doing everything I can to nurture his interests."

"They are very flaky," Quin volunteered.

"They're excellent," Dr. Sonya concluded before changing the topic. "Can I expect your wonderful company another night? Or, will you be heading back today?"

Quin answered. "We're meeting up with Titus tonight. But, we're going to be heading back afterward.

We have classes and he has work," he said deciding for the both of us.

It was what we had discussed, but I thought we were going to play it a little more by ear. This place wasn't cheap, so I could see why he wouldn't want to stay another night. But, the way he said it made me think that us having to get back had more to do with me than him.

The guy was brilliant. Him missing a class or two wouldn't matter on his grades at all. I was the one who had to struggle with everything. I was pretty sure that he wanted to get me back so I wouldn't fall behind.

It's very sweet of him to look after me like that. It is the first time in my life anyone has. But, at the same time, I was liking it here. There was something about it that made me feel like I belonged. I was hoping Quin felt the same way.

"Well, it was my pleasure hosting you two. Hopefully, I'll see you again. Cali's going to be disappointed he missed you. He was quite taken by the two of you. I told him that if he wants to see you, he should apply for East Tennessee University. He's been dragging his feet on it. But meeting you two might have given him the push he needed."

"It's a great school," Quin said. "If he decides he wants a tour, I'd be happy to give him one."

"That would be wonderful. I'll let him know. He would love that."

I couldn't help but get a flash of jealousy listening to Quin offer his tour guide services. Maybe he was attempting to push out of his comfort zone, but I couldn't help but remember how much the kid was crushing on Quin. I had told Quin so he was definitely aware of it. Now it was with him that Quin was choosing to go out of his way?

On second thought, I was probably looking too much into it. Quin was a great guy and great guys did nice things for people. Helping Cali get excited about college was a nice thing. I just didn't want to think about my boyfriend with anyone else. I wanted to be the one to take care of him for the rest of our lives.

"Yeah, let us know. We can give him a tour," I said making sure Cali knew not to be too excited about it.

"Wonderful! I have your number, Quin. I'll pass it along. I have a few errands to run. But here is my card. Feel free to give me a call if you need anything else," she said handing it to Quin.

"So, what are we going to do until tonight?" I asked reaching for a slice of cantaloupe.

"We could drive around."

"I think we've seen everything there is to see. But, we could text Titus to see if he has any suggestions."

"Do you think he'll mind?" Quin said with a smile.

"Why would he mind?" I asked already taking out my phone and texting him.

'Any suggestions for what Quin and I could do today,' I typed and sent.

It took less than ten seconds for my phone to ring.

"It's Titus. Who responds to a text with a call?" I asked surprised. "Hello?"

"Cage! I was hoping to hear from you two! Remember how I said that Snow Tip Falls has a pretty good high school football team?"

"I remember."

"Well, that was me bragging a little because I'm the coach."

"You coach the team?"

"I do. It's just something I do to keep the program going. Coach Thompson, the guy who coached our team, died last year."

"I'm sorry to hear that."

"Thanks. And, not wanting to leave the guys without a coach, I volunteered. But, I was thinking, how great would it be if you with your experience came and gave them a little talk? You know, nothing formal. I think it would be thrilling for them. Maybe you can inspire them to get their asses in gear.

"And, honestly, I don't know what the hell I'm doing. I'm trying but, I could always use the feedback. What do you say? You have any interest in coming over and talking to a few talented kids?"

"I would love to," I said looking at Quin. "I'll have to talk to Quin about it, but I think we can swing by."

"Would you? That would be incredible! I'll text you the address. And if you get here around two, I'll give you a tour of the school. It has a rich history."

"I'll talk to Quin."

"Great! I'll see you soon," Titus said ending the call.

"What did he say?" Quin asked having not taken his eyes off of me.

"He wants me to come by and talk to his high school football team."

"You agreed?"

"It's not like we have anything else to do," I told him.

Quin didn't disagree.

Over the next few hours, we lounged around, made out a little, and took back the crutches Glen had lent me.

"Were they useful?" Glen asked.

"Definitely!" I said having barely used them at all.

"How has your stay been? Make any headway on solving your mystery?"

"Dr. Tom suggested we talk to Nero," Quin replied.

"To Nero?" Glen asked confused.

"Yeah. Do you know why he would?"

"Tom isn't the chattiest person when it comes to what he knows about people. It makes having small talk with him a challenge."

"What do you know about Nero?" Quin asked switching into investigator mode.

"Not much. He grew up here, attended the high school, played on the football team. He's always seemed a little angry. I see him every-so-often working as a busboy at the diner."

"We saw him there," I told him. "He did not like seeing us."

"What do you mean?"

"I was holding Quin's hand and he commented."

"Really? That surprises me."

"Why?" Quin asked.

"I don't know. Tom's been his doctor like he is for everyone in town. And, he's had some anger issues, but he's always been respectful to the two of us. He hasn't even hinted at anything homophobic. At one point I even got the impression that he was looking up to Tom as a father figure."

"What happened to his father?" I asked Glen.

"I don't know. But, I don't think he ever knew him. It's tough growing up without a father."

"It can be tough growing up *with* one," I replied.

"Yeah," Glen agreed. "When parents disappoint you, it has a way of leaving a mark."

"I know a little something about that," I said turning to Quin who grew up with three loving parents. He was staring at us blankly.

Picking up a few snacks, we next headed to the local high school. It looked like a converted warehouse. It was yet another location not on my phone's map.

Pulling into the parking lot, we spotted Titus in his truck waiting for us. When we parked next to him, he got out. His broad smile was as big as ever. He certainly had a way of making people feel welcome.

Titus's tour began in the school's main building. It was where they used to store their moonshine after bottling it. In the 50s, the town got a few more kids and they converted it into a school. The building's square footage has been growing ever since.

I had thought that my high school's locker was lacking. It turns out it was professional grade in comparison to what the Snow Tip Falls team had. The field wasn't much better.

"It's not much, but it's about the grit of the players and not the quality of the field. That's what I always tell them," Titus said showing us around.

"You're right," I said sincerely.

"There are guys on the team who have real potential, too. If we had better equipment… and a better coach," he said with a self-deprecating laugh, "some of these kids could go far. Some might even be good enough to get a scholarship to East Tennessee. You would know something about that, right? Maybe you could talk to them about it."

My heart melted at his request. "I would be happy to. Anything I can do to help, just let me know."

Titus's smile in reply was genuine. He cared about the kids. There was no question about it, he was a good guy.

"Are you Cage Rucker?" One of the kids asked me when he came onto the field for practice.

I looked at Quin. Quin smiled.

"Yeah," I said suddenly liking being recognized.

I had been recognized a hundred times over the years. But this was the first time in a long time that it affected me. I wasn't sure why.

"Cali, you're on the football team?" I asked when he joined us on the field in uniform.

He blushed staring at me.

"Yeah. I'm the kicker."

"He has a golden foot, that one," Titus said encouragingly.

Cali turned red and then peeked over at Quin to see if he had heard it. Quin had. Cali was crushing on my boyfriend hard.

Cali was a smaller guy with a style that hinted at emo. To see him on the team, surprised me.

It made a little more sense to find out he was the kicker. You didn't have to be built like a linebacker to kick a football 80 yards. And, sure to show off for Quin before the beginning of practice, that was exactly what Cali did. He was unquestionably good enough to play for a school like East Tennessee. A few of the kids here were.

To my continued surprise, Titus didn't just have me speak to them, he roped me into running practice. It ended up being fun. Something about it felt right even though I was sure that Quin was bored out of his mind.

"I appreciate you doing this for the kids," Titus said as we headed back to our trucks.

"Seriously, it was my pleasure."

"Cage was in his element," Quin told him.

I didn't think Quin would notice that, but he was right. This was definitely what I wanted to do with my new life.

"Would you guys allow me to take you to dinner to thank you? We could head to Nero's thing afterward."

"That would be cool," I said not giving Quin a chance to weigh in.

The truth was that working with the kids had given me a high and I wasn't yet ready to come down from it. Heading back to the diner, both Quin and I looked around for Nero when we entered.

"He's not here," Titus volunteered. "He helps out with the rush on the weekends," Titus said making fun of how few people it took to be considered a rush in Snow Tip Falls.

"Do you know Nero well?" Quin asked putting back on his investigator's hat.

"We went to school together. He was a year under me but he was in a couple of my classes. We did play on the team together, though."

"Football team?" I asked.

"It's the only team we have in Snow Tip Falls," Titus said self-deprecatingly. "We can only afford one extracurricular activity here. So, I hope no one's interested in women's basketball."

"Oh, that sucks!" I said feeling for the girls.

"I came from a small school too. Sports weren't really a thing there either," Quin volunteered.

"What about the math Olympics, or whatever it's called? A school of geniuses would have to be able to crush at that, right?" I asked wanting Quin to feel a part of the conversation.

"We weren't encouraged to do stuff like that."

"Why not?" I asked surprised.

"We stood out enough. If we did something like that and won — which considering the kids at my school, I assume we would have — it would have increased the resentment people had towards us. We were always told to do our best not to stand out until we had to."

"That's a little sad," I told him imagining what my life would have been like if I was told to hide who I was.

"It's what we had to do," Quin said with a half-smile.

"So, you couldn't stand out in any way, you were crucified in the press whenever someone wrote about you, and you had to always worry about being kidnapped?"

"Yes," Quin confirmed with sadness in his eyes.

I didn't say it, but everything about Quin suddenly made sense. The first time we hung out was because I had promised to teach him how to be more social. Ever since, I've wondered how he hadn't learned the skill. You didn't have to be the life of the party to talk to people at one.

But, if you grow up being taught to fear everyone outside of your circle, how could you turn out any other way than Quin did? And honestly, it was admirable that Quin was as normal as he was.

"You two are gonna have to clue me in on what you're talking about," Titus said struggling to follow our conversation.

I looked a Quin. It didn't seem like he wanted to talk about it.

"Maybe later," I told Titus before changing the topic.

We finished dinner and chatted a little longer before we eventually settled the bill. Even though Titus had offered to pay, Quin insisted. Titus fought him on it until I stepped in.

"Just let him. Trust me."

Titus was hesitant but conceded. I couldn't tell what Titus was thinking, but it was obvious that he was used to being the big man. Perhaps I should have told Quin to let him do it, but the truth was that it felt unfair considering what I knew about Quin's family's wealth. Besides, it was something Quin wanted. I had a hard time not giving my boyfriend what he wants.

"So, what is this thing that Nero's doing?" I asked as we walked to the trucks.

"It would be better if you just saw it," Titus explained.

"Okaaaay," I said looking over at Quin who was holding my hand.

Quin didn't say anything about it until we were alone in the truck following Titus on narrow roads leading through the woods.

"Yeah, this is definitely not a book club," he said watching the trees as they went past the window. "Do you think this is a good idea?"

"Do you think we should go back? I can still turn the truck around."

"Do you?" Quin asked me. "We're only going because we want to talk to Nero. We could easily come back next weekend or the one after that. You heard Titus, Nero works the weekend rushes."

"Do you think we can trust Titus?" I asked Quin wondering if my assessment of Titus was off.

"He doesn't seem to be a bad guy."

"You think he would lead us into the woods to kill us?"

I had meant it to be lighthearted and then remembered Quin's history with kidnapping.

"No. I don't think so. This just *feels* like the beginning of every horror movie ever. I don't think it is one."

"You're probably right." I paused. "So, when we get there, you check the barn and I'll check the tool shed. I'm sure we can find a phone somewhere," I said looking over at Quin for his reaction.

He looked at me blankly. "What?"

"It's a horror movie reference," I explained.

"Oh."

I don't think Quin got it.

"Yeah, this road kind of reminds me of the one leading to my place. I'm guessing it's a little different than the ones leading to where you grew up."

Quin looked around again. "It's not even close."

That made sense. Quin grew up in New York City. I could see why driving on a road like this in the dark might freak him out.

"Quin, if anything happens, I'll keep you safe. I promise you. Okay?"

Quin looked at me. "Okay."

He didn't just say he believed me, he acted like it. Having earned his trust, there was no way I would betray it now. No matter what happened, I was going to protect Quin. I was ready to die trying if I had to.

When we finally pulled up in front of a glowing barn, things didn't feel any safer. There were several trucks parked out front and the light within flickered.

"Are you sure it's okay that we're here?" I asked Titus feeling the aggressive focus I did before a big game.

"You wanted to see him, right? He'll be here."

"That wasn't an answer," I clarified.

"I'm sure you'll be fine. You look like you can handle yourself."

"Why would Cage need to handle himself?" Quin asked bringing up a good point.

"You want to see him or not?" Titus asked staring at us.

I looked over at Quin. I knew that no matter what happened, I could fight my way out. But, what about Quin. Was it worth putting him in danger?

"This is our chance to speak to him," Quin pointed out. "He could have the answers to everything. I say we risk it."

I smiled. I would not have thought less of him if he had said we should go back. But, here he was thinking of me, not himself. I was definitely falling in love with him if I wasn't in love with him already.

"Okay. Let's go in," I said to Quin. "This better not turn bad," I said threatening to tear Titus apart if it did.

I didn't know what to expect, but as soon as we stepped through the barn's doors, everything made sense. There were about 20 people there. All of them were facing a circle drawn on the ground where two guys were beating the shit out of each other.

This was bare-knuckles boxing. Although, to call it that gave it more respectability than it deserved. This was a fight club, pure and simple. People came here to beat the crap out of one another.

Right now, one of the people everyone was cheering on was Nero. He was bleeding from his nose, but his wild eyes said that there was no way he was going to lose.

His eyes didn't lie. His quick movements allowed him to land a left and an uppercut. As we watched, he laid his opponent out flat.

I hadn't given him the credit he deserved when I challenged him at the diner. He wasn't big, but he was fast. I was no longer sure I could take him. He had a killer instinct that I had never felt. That made Nero dangerous.

I considered getting Quin out of this place. I was no longer sure I could protect him here.

"You!" Nero yelled spotting me just inside the doors.

It was too late to go anywhere. We were going to have to play this out. I couldn't get us out of this if I wanted to. And, I didn't want to. What I wanted was to make sure that Quin wasn't hurt.

"You two know each other?" Titus asked leaning into me.

"We've met," I said feeling my blood start to boil.

"Was there something you didn't tell me?" Titus asked concerned.

"Yeah. A lot," I said keeping my eyes locked on the shirtless battered man who marched towards us.

Nero's blonde hair was tussled. His face was dirty. And his rippling, lean torso was bruised from hits. That told me how he fought. He guarded his face at the sacrifice of his body. I would remember that if things went wrong.

"What the fuck are you doing here, fag?" He said coming in hot.

"What did you say?" I asked readying myself to break his ribs for it.

"Woah, Nero! Unnecessary!" Titus said stepping between us.

"You brought them here? Why the fuck did you do that?"

"Nero, I know you're just stepping out of a fight so your adrenaline is flowing or whatever. But you need to calm down!"

"Yeah, Nero, you better listen to your friend and calm your ass down," I told him preferring to knock him down instead.

"You wanna say something to me? You caused me to lose two days' pay."

"It was your dumb ass that did that," I made clear.

"Okay, you two. I think you both need to relax," Titus declared.

"Maybe what we need is to settle this in the ring," Nero said wild-eyed.

"Yeah, we do. Point the fuckin' way," I told him peeling off my jacket and my shirt.

Everything around me faded away replaced by a loud ringing in my ears and the tunnel vision I got at the beginning of a play. Walking to the poorly outlined circle, the guys surrounding it parted.

I entered and immediately remembered my leg. I was beyond feeling pain at this point, but I wouldn't have my full movement. Fighting a guy as quick as Nero would be a problem. I didn't care.

"Fag, huh? You ready for this fag to beat the shit out of you?"

Nero laughed and stared at me with an insane smile. Whatever I was going to do, I was going to have to do it fast because there was no doubt about it, the guy was nuts.

"Stop!" I heard someone yell from behind him.

I recognized the voice. It was Quin, but I couldn't let him distract me. I was in this. I had something to prove to Quin. If not to Quin then myself… or more accurately, my dad.

My first blow landed square in his chest knocking him back. He had probably never been hit so hard in his life. I could tell by the light going out in his eyes.

That's when I went in for the attack. This time he bent over protecting his torso so I caught him on his wrist and the side of his face. He stumbled.

I knew if I gave him a second to breathe, he would wipe me out. I couldn't move fast. I had to rely on my power. So, ready to break my hand across his chin, I pulled back my fist in time to hear,

"You have to stop! He's your brother!"

I froze. "What?"

That was when Nero snuck one past me catching me on my chin. I fell to my knees. It wasn't that he had knocked me down. It was that I didn't want to fight anymore.

Quin had yelled that Nero was my brother. Was that true? I had to know. There was no way I was going to fight family.

"Stop!" Quin said suddenly running into the ring and placing himself between Nero and me.

For a second I thought that Nero was going to go after Quin. If he did, brother or not, I was going to kill him. But he didn't. And, it took a second for him to process Quin's words, but as he did, he dropped his fists and stared at the two of us.

"My brother?" He said quickly calming down. "Titus, who are these people?"

Titus looked at Nero as confused as he was.

"What are you talking about, Quin?" I asked shaking off the cobwebs and standing.

On my feet, Quin led me out of the ring and away from the on-lookers.

"Remember how I knew that you were adopted?"

"You said my dad didn't have any dimples and the chances that one of my parents didn't was near impossible."

"Look at him. The dimples in his cheeks, the ones under his lip, his chin."

I stared at Nero. He did have a dimple in his chin and on the two sides below his lower lip. But, so what? Didn't a lot of people?

"Quin, that's not much to go on."

"But think about it. Why would a doctor, who probably worked at the hospital you were born in, tell us to talk to a guy with the same rare mixture of dimples that you do?"

I looked back a Nero. Could Quin be right? Could Nero be my brother?

"What the fuck is going on?" Nero said staring back at us.

How was I supposed to handle this? How was I going to tell an asshole, homophobe that my boyfriend thinks we could be brothers because he's an expert on dimples? I wasn't sure, but when he and Titus followed us away from the crowd, I knew I was going to have to be honest.

"Seriously, who the fuck are you two, and what the fuck is going on?" Nero said as Titus hovered.

Knowing there was no way around this, I pulled back my shoulders and resigned myself to whatever was going to happen next.

"My name is Cage. This is my boyfriend Quin. A couple of days ago, I learned that the man who raised me might not be my biological father. We believe he might have taken me from the hospital I was born in, Falls County Hospital.

"We've been here the last few days because we believe that my birth mother might have lived in this town. We don't know if she's alive or dead. We don't know anything. It's all just a guess.

"But, Quin is smart, very smart. And he said that you have a rare trait that I do too. And the only way we could both have that trait is if we were brothers."

Nero stared at me calmer than I would have guessed he would be. What I was telling him was insane. Yet, all he did was look at me questioningly.

"What trait is that?" Nero asked.

I took a deep breath before answering.

"It's your dimples."

"My dimples?"

"Yeah. Some dimples are rare."

Nero looked at me strangely.

"Dimples?" He turned to Titus. "Titus has the biggest dimples I have ever seen. Does that make me related to him too? Half the people in this town have dimples."

"It's the combination of them," Quin said defending himself. "Dimples aren't rare. Well, certain ones are like the ones under your lip. But, they aren't rare enough to matter. To have all of them at the same time…? The odds are low."

Nero's eyes bounced between the two of us. "Why'd you come here?"

"I told you. We came here because I thought my birth mother might be from this town."

"No. I mean, why did you come here tonight? You tryin' to say that you just showed up here by accident?"

"We came looking for you," I told him.

"I figured that. Why?"

I looked over at Quin.

"Because after I asked about Cage's mother, Dr. Tom told us that we should talk to you."

"Dr. Tom?" Nero said suddenly rattled.

"Yeah. I saw him yesterday. I asked him because his husband had said that he worked at the hospital during the time that Cage was born. He wouldn't tell me anything, but he suggested that you would be someone in town I might be interested in talking to. I think he said that because he knows you two are related."

Nero stared at Cage intensely. "No. No, this is bullshit. You all are just makin' this up."

"We're not," I told him. "I swear to you, we're not."

I didn't know how to ask what I knew I had to next. I opened my mouth hoping words would come out. It took a moment but they did.

"Tell me, is your mother alive?" I asked, my heart thumping in my chest.

"Yeah," he said hesitantly. "You're not telling her this crap if that's what you're thinking."

Quin spoke up. "Has she ever talked about something like this? Did she mention a child dying after birth or being kidnapped or something?"

Nero backed off. "No. No. Who put you up to this? Is it you Titus? Did you do this shit?"

"I just met these two giving a tour. I had no idea about this."

Nero turned back to us angrily.

"Who have you been talking to? Did you just think it would be funny to fuck with a sick woman's head?"

"Your mother's sick?" I asked suddenly scared to lose her.

"No. I'm not saying a god damn thing more. Prove to me this shit is real. Prove to me you're who you say you are."

"You want to see our I.D.s?" I asked.

"I don't want to see your fuckin' I.D.s. I want you to prove to me that anything you said is real."

"How are we supposed to do that?" I asked him hoping he would be reasonable.

"I know how," Quin said grabbing our attention.

"You do? How?" I asked.

"We could test your DNA. I have an uncle who works in genetics. I was named after him. He would help us figure this out. The test would be able to tell us if the two of you are related even if it's just cousins."

Nero looked at Quin suspiciously.

"No. I'm not doing this. You people are making this up. It's all bullshit."

Titus turned to Nero. "What if it isn't? I've spent the last two days with them, and they're decent guys. What if he is your brother? I know that if I had a brother I would want to know. What if they're telling the truth, Nero? Imagine that."

Nero turned to Titus. "This is a lot, you know. It's a lot."

"I know, but what if? How would you feel if you do have a brother and you pushed him away?" Titus said putting his hand on Nero's shoulder.

Nero softened as his thoughts swirled. He looked tortured before looking resigned.

"Listen, I didn't mean all of that fag stuff. It's just that when I saw you two sitting there looking so happy, I thought, 'what about me?' You know? Why does everyone but me get to be happy? I didn't mean anything against you."

I looked over at Quin for his reaction. I wasn't sure I was willing to forgive him.

"That's okay," Quin said being the good person that he is.

"Yeah. You're forgiven," I confirmed. "But, don't ever say shit like that again. You hear me?" I said meaning it to be a threat though I wasn't in a threatening mood.

"No. I won't. It's not me. Ask Titus."

Titus shrugged not taking a side.

"Anyway, I didn't mean it. You two seem like okay people. But, I can't let you tell my mom any of this. Not until there's proof. She couldn't take it if you're wrong or lying or something. She's not like that, ya know?"

"So, you'll do the test?" Quin asked.

"I'll do your test."

I stared at the disheveled, shirtless guy in front of us. He was no longer the angry, wild man from the ring. He was vulnerable and scared.

Was this who he always was? Was this guy my brother? I couldn't believe that after feeling alone for so long, I could have a real family.

"How do we do this, Quin? Do we have to spit in a tube or something?" I asked suddenly needing answers.

"I mean, we could do that if you wanted to do one of those ancestry tests."

"You mean like in the commercials?" Nero asked.

"Yes. But they take weeks. If we got blood samples, I could ship them to my uncle overnight. I'm sure he would rush it through and we could have the answer in a couple of days."

"Let's do that," I told him.

"Yeah. Days sounds better than weeks," Nero confirmed.

"Okay. The only question is, how do we get the blood samples in Snow Tip Falls?"

"Dr. Tom," Nero suggested.

"Do you think he'll do it?" Quin asked.

"Dr. Tom and I are cool. If I asked him, he might," Nero said.

"When?" Quin asked. "Because we're heading back to school tonight."

"Quin, I think we can stay over one more night if it means getting blood samples."

Nero interrupted. "No. He might do it tonight."

"Really? Then, give him a call," I told him.

"Nah. If I called him, he would tell me to come by in the morning. I have a better idea," Nero said retrieving his clothes and getting dressed.

When we all returned to our trucks, we caravanned out of the middle of nowhere back into town. Things took a while to look familiar. When they did, we were pulling up to the house we had visited the day before. In the back was Dr. Tom's office. In the front was a beautiful two-story home that glowed.

"Someone's still awake," I told Quin. "Do you think this is a good idea?'

"Which part?"

"All of it. Any of it. We don't want to piss off the only person who will be able to do the test."

"We don't know this town or the way it works. Maybe people do this all of the time, here."

"You think people show up at his house in the middle of the night requesting genetic tests all of the time?" I asked with a smile.

"You know what I mean."

"I do. But, that wasn't really what I was asking. Do you think finding out if Nero is my brother is a good idea? I mean, the man hosts fight clubs and throws around homophobic slurs. Could all of this end badly?"

"It might," Quin conceded. "Anything could end badly. We could end badly. But, just because it might end badly isn't a reason not to try to make it end well."

It rattled me that he suggested that things between us might go bad. Did he really think that? I was ready to be all in with Quin. Not only is he the hottest thing ever, but no one has ever done for me what he has in the few months I've known him. Quin was a keeper and I was going to hold onto him with every breath I had.

Parked in front of the house, Quin and I followed Nero and Titus towards the porch. The front door opened before we got there. Glen and Dr. Tom stepped out wearing robes.

"Nero, Titus, is that you?" Dr. Tom asked as we approached. "What's going on?"

They didn't reply. When Dr. Tom saw us, they didn't have to.

"I see you found Nero," he said to Quin stoically.

"I did. But not before the two of them tried to kill each other," Quin told him.

"Huh. And, what are you doing here?"

"We need a blood test," Quin explained.

"Come back in the morning."

"Did you know that I could have a brother?" Nero asked Dr. Tom.

He didn't answer.

"You did," Nero said shocked. "After all of those things I told you were going on, you couldn't tell me that my mom might not be crazy?"

For the first time, Dr. Tom's stone face cracked. Regret washed over him.

"There are a lot of things that a doctor can't disclose to anyone no matter…"

"That's bullshit!" Nero injected. "I was a kid crying to you about all the crap that was going on and not once did you even suggest that this could be a possibility."

"That's not true. I hinted. I told you that sometimes things aren't what they seem."

"And that was supposed to mean something to a ten-year-old? That was just a bunch of adult garbage to me. How was I supposed to know that you were telling me that I had a brother and that my mother wasn't nuts? No. You're a fuckin' asshole."

Dr. Tom regained his composure.

"Fine. I'm a fucking asshole. If that's all, you can all have a good night."

"Wait," I said stopping him from going. "Look, I don't know you. But, I'm getting the sense that you know me, at least a little. I don't know why you wouldn't have told Nero that he might have had a brother. I don't care. All I know is that for 22 years I've been denied having a family, at least one that cares about me. And, if you take 20 minutes of your time, you might be able to cure me of that.

"Isn't that what doctors are supposed to do, cure people of disease? Well, this is my dis ease. Help me. It'll take two minutes."

Dr. Tom's eyes bounced between the four of us yet he didn't budge.

"Just do it, Tom," Glen said moved.

"There are things going on, Glen."

Glen put his hand on his husband's shoulder and spoke to him kindly. "Just do it."

The doctor melted looking into his love's sympathetic eyes.

"Fine. Follow me to my office. But, I don't know where I can get a genetic test done."

"I have a place. My uncle works in genetics and…"

"Quin Toro!" Dr. Tom stopped and whipped back around to look at Quin. "You're Quin Toro. I can't believe it. After you left, I thought it could have been you, but I didn't think there was any way," he said suddenly awestruck.

I've had a lot of people recognize me for football, but none of them looked at me the way Dr. Tom looked a Quin. It was like Dr. Tom was looking at a god.

"You know him, Doc," Nero asked confused.

"Yes, you're looking at a miracle," Tom proclaimed. "I've been following everything I could about your life. You have given Glen and I hope that we could have a family one day," he said with tears forming in his eyes. "The procedure is expensive so we've been saving up. But, you… you're everything to us," he said becoming breathless.

Quin listened politely and then turned to me. There was pain in his eyes. I didn't completely get it. But, I was starting to understand some of the things he had been telling me about his life.

He had said that he felt pressure to do great things. I thought he was talking about the pressure that everyone felt to do well. But, no.

What must it be like for Quin to know that people looked at him like Dr. Tom did? What must it be like for him knowing he had to live up to that?

The pressure I felt to make it to the NFL was nothing in comparison. Quin's life was unlike anything I could imagine. What the hell was someone like him doing with a nobody like me?

"I'm sorry," Dr. Tom said gathering himself. "Come, let me get you what you need," he told Quin.

Drawing a small vile of blood from Nero and me, the doctor labeled them and handed them to Quin.

"This should be more than enough," he said composed.

"Thank you," Quin replied.

"Yes, thank you," I said before looking over at Nero. Nero looked away still pissed at the bearded, Latino man.

Standing in front of our trucks, Quin turned to Nero.

"We'll let you know as soon as we find out anything."

"Okay."

"Can I get your number?" I asked him as nervous as I would be on a first date.

"Yeah. What's your number I'll text you it."

I told Nero and a few seconds later my phone buzzed.

"I got it," I told him.

"Cool."

"So, I guess we're heading back," I told them.

"Okay," Nero said hesitant to say goodbye.

Instead of walking away, Nero threw his arms around me pulling me close. I thought he was hugging me. He was instead pulling my ear to his mouth.

He whispered, "Seriously, I'm really sorry about what I said. It's not me. Alright?"

"Alright," I assured him.

"It's not me," he repeated.

"That's cool, Nero. A fresh start."

Nero pulled away and smiled. "Yeah. A fresh start."

I saw it. He was as covered in dimples as I was. If Dr. Tom hadn't practically confirmed it, I would now have no doubt. I was looking at my brother.

"Quin, it was good to meet you," Nero said offering him his hand.

"Good to meet you, too," Quin said politely before both of us got into my truck and pulled away.

Most of our two-hour drive back to school was in silence. The last three days had been a lot. Not only had things happened between Quin and me, but I might have found my family, and I might have realized that Quin and I weren't meant to be together.

Quin had bigger things he had to accomplish with his life. I saw it now. He wasn't meant to live the life I envisioned for myself.

That didn't mean that I didn't want to be with him. I had fallen for him hard. But, at what point did I become a distraction from him doing something incredible that changed the world?

I drove him to his building and we both sat in the truck with the engine running.

"This weekend was…" Quin said trailing off.

"It was something," I completed.

Quin laughed. "Yes."

"Now that I'm back, I'm probably going to have to make up a few shifts at work. But, I want to see you."

"I want to see you, too," he said with a smile. "After all, you are my boyfriend."

"Yeah, I am," I said having forgotten.

With that, I leaned over, slipped my hand behind his neck, and pulled his lips to mine. The kiss was electric. The heat between us billowed. Having him in my hands again made my body tingle.

"Cage!" I heard someone say.

I pulled away from where I most wanted to be to see Tasha staring into the truck. She looked shocked. Behind her was her best friend Vi, because, of course, she was. With her mouth still hanging open, she ran to the door of their building.

"I take it that she didn't know?" Quin asked.

"She didn't have to know. She broke up with me. Besides, I'm proud to have you as my boyfriend. You're too good for me."

Quin smiled. "Did you want to come up?" He asked with the cutest shy smile.

"Thanks for the invitation, but I should go home. I have class in the morning and it was a long drive."

Quin was disappointed. "Okay. When am I going to see you again?"

I thought about that. There was a part of me that wanted to go to his room with him and never let him out of my sight for the rest of my life.

"When do you think you'll get the results of the test?"

"Oh. I'll call Uncle Quinton first thing tomorrow morning. I'll send it as soon as I can after that. It will get to him by the next day. I'm not sure if he will be able to get to it immediately, but I assume he'll have everything done by Friday?"

"Wow, that's fast. It's good to know people."

"It comes in handy sometimes. So, when do you think I'll see you?"

"How about I send you a text?" I told him.

"Oh! Okay. Yeah, send me a text."

I smiled, kissed him one more time, and then watched him walk away. He was the sexiest person I had ever seen. I couldn't believe that someone like him wanted to be with me.

It wasn't until Quin was out of my sight that pain shot up my broken leg. I flinched. Where had that come from? All weekend I hadn't felt a thing. Suddenly, the ache was overwhelming.

It took everything I had to focus on the road instead of the pain in my leg. 40 minutes of it was enough to wipe me out. So, when I got home and found the house as empty as I had left it, I dragged myself to bed and collapsed.

I had told Quin that I needed to sleep at home because I had an early class. That was true, but the next morning I didn't make it. I was in too much pain. I could barely make it to the bathroom to find my painkillers. They were the strong stuff so they kicked in pretty quickly. But not before I missed my only other class for the day and guaranteed I would be late for work.

'I sent it! Not long now!' Quin texted.

Reading the text was immediately followed by a clench in my chest. Why was I feeling this? Yeah, something was wrong, but what? I mean, I knew what was wrong, but what was I going to do about it?

'He sent it off,' I texted Nero. 'Not long now.'

'Cool,' he texted back a few hours later. 'When do you think you will know?'

'Quin guessed Friday.'

I didn't hear back from him after that. I wasn't sure why. I also didn't know why I didn't text Quin back. I wanted to text him back. I wanted to pull him into my arms and hold him like I had in Snow Tip Falls. Why wasn't I?

As I thought about it, I considered if it was because my life was in limbo. Maybe I had made a mistake to give up on football. I didn't love it but wouldn't me being a starting quarterback in the NFL be something Quin could be proud of? Wouldn't our pairing make more sense like that?

I could never be equal to Quin. No one could. But couldn't my fame help contribute something to a life like his?

As much as that seemed to make sense, there was still the problem that I didn't want to do it. I stepped away from football for a reason. I gave up the money, the lifestyle, even my relationship with my father, or whoever he was, to be rid of it. But, would it be worth the fight to get back to it for Quin?

If anyone, I would do it for him. I would probably have to do it if I wanted to be with him. I absolutely wanted to be with him. Maybe I wasn't texting him back because I wasn't ready to make that commitment. I just wish there was any other way for us to be together forever other than committing to a life I didn't want.

    The week went by without me texting him yet I thought about him every day. I longed to see him, to hold him in my arms. I felt like my skin was being peeled from my body without him. I felt paralyzed without him, yet I couldn't get myself to reach out.

    I was going through the motions of life knowing that I would eventually hear from him again. Finding out whether Nero was my brother would put Quin and me in contact one way or another.

    On Friday when I woke up, I grabbed my crutches and drove to campus. After my classes ended, I headed to the student activity center for my shift at work. Today was a day when the pain from my leg radiated into my thigh and hips. Even sitting didn't relieve the pain.

    Despite how loopy they made me, I was thinking about popping a pill. I had been trying to cut back on how many I had been taking. It felt like I was getting a little dependent on them. They didn't just make the pain in my leg go away. They briefly allowed me to forget how much I needed Quin.

    Deciding I couldn't take the ache anymore, I eased over to my backpack and reached for my prescription. I was fumbling with the cap when I heard the beep of someone scanning their I.D. card to enter.

My eyes flicked up to the computer and saw a face I hadn't seen in a while. It was Lou, Quin's roommate. My heart sank because the last time he had signed in, it had been with…

I looked past the monitor to the entrance. Quin was standing behind Lou with his head down. Seeing him made my heart race. I shot up feeling none of the pain I had felt moments before.

"Quin!"

"Oh, you remember his name now?" Lou said pissed.

"What?"

"You call him your boyfriend, you take his…" Lou lowered his voice. "You take his virginity, and then you don't contact him for 5 days? What type of shit is that? You know, if you just wanted to get your dick wet, you didn't have to play with his emotions to get it. Guys like you think you can treat people however you want…"

"Lou, it's not like that. I've been wanting to contact Quin every day."

"Then why haven't you, huh? Why haven't you?"

"It's complicated."

"It's complicated, huh? It seems pretty simple to me. Either you want to be with an incredible, wonderful, caring guy like Quin, or you don't."

"I do!"

Lou looked at me as confused and frustrated as I felt. "5 days!"

"I know! Lou, can you give us a minute."

"You think I'm gonna leave him here to let you hurt him again. No way! Anything you can say to him, you can say in front of me."

Quin looked up. His eyes looked red like he had been crying. Had I been the cause? Of course, I had. My chest clenched thinking about it. What the hell was I doing? I had to figure it out.

Quin touched Lou's shoulder lightly. "Lou, can you give us a minute?"

Lou looked at Quin and froze. "Are you sure? Because you're gonna need someone to stand up for you if you're not gonna stand up for yourself."

"I'm sure, Lou," Quin said with pain in his eyes.

Lou looked at me still boiling with anger. I couldn't blame him for that. I probably wouldn't have been so nice if the person hurting Quin was anyone other than me.

"I'm going to be right inside, okay? Just say my name and I'll be here."

"Thank you," Quin said genuinely.

Once Lou had disappeared around the corner, Quin and I turned to look at each other. I desperately wanted to hold him.

"How have you been?" Quin asked his voice weak.

"Not good," I told him honestly. "All of the walking I did last weekend caught up to me as soon as you left the truck. I've been popping these things just trying to stop myself from passing out," I said holding up the bottle still in my hand.

"I'm sorry to hear that. I did think you were pushing yourself a little hard."

"You tried to get me to stop. Multiple times. But, it's like, when I'm with you, the pain goes away and I think I can do anything."

"Why haven't you texted me, Cage? Is it just something you don't do? I remember your relationship with Tasha and how you two didn't spend that much time together. Is this just how you do relationships? Because I don't know if I can do this if this is what you're expecting. I want you to be my boyfriend. And, I don't know much about how things like this work, but I don't think it can work like this."

Wow! I had forgotten about Tasha. As I thought about it, this is what I did with her. The difference was that Tasha preferred having her space.

But, I hadn't avoided texting Quin because I didn't care whether or not I was with him. I hadn't texted him because being with him came with a commitment that I was having a hard time making. Looking at him now made the decision a lot easier.

When I was with him, all of my pain was gone. I was sure that he was the one I was meant to be with. I just had to suck it up and do my part to make our relationship work.

"It's not that. How I felt about Tasha doesn't compare to how I feel about you."

"Then what is it, Cage? Help me understand what's going on," he implored, his eyes filling with tears.

"I've had a lot on my mind. A lot is going on, ya know. I might have a brother I didn't know existed. I might have a mother. How do I even wrap my mind around that? And, I've been thinking that…" I lowered my head to gather strength. "I've been thinking that I should go back to football."

"You're thinking about playing football again? I thought you said that you didn't enjoy it."

"I've been thinking that it might be what's best… for us," I said closely watching his reaction.

"For us?" He asked not giving away his feelings about it.

"Yeah. It would be hard, but I could still get to the NFL. This injury won't last forever. And, I might not get drafted as high as I would have before all of this. But with time, I could get myself into a starting position. I'm sure I could."

"If that's what you want," Quin conceded.

"I think it's what's best."

"For us?"

"Yeah."

"Okay. If that's what you want to do, you should do it."

"What do you think, would you want to be the boyfriend of the first out football player in the NFL?" I asked mustering a smile.

"I just want to be your boyfriend. I don't care what you are," Quin said as sweet and caring as ever.

Even though he didn't say it, I knew that my playing football made a difference to him. He needed to be with someone as special as he was. I was willing to be that for him.

"And, I just want to be your boyfriend. I want it more than anything," I told him leaning over the divider and taking his hand.

"I love you, Cage," he said causing my heart to soar.

"Quin, I love you, too," I said before moving to my boyfriend's lips and losing myself in his kiss.

Pulling away I stared at him awash in warmth. I couldn't believe that I had stayed away from him for so long. We had so much to catch up on.

"I heard from my uncle," Quin said suddenly bringing my elation to an end.

"Your uncle with the results?" I said letting go of his hand and pulling away.

"Yes. Do you want to know the verdict?"

Did I want to know the results? Of course, I did… I think. What would knowing them change? Probably everything.

I didn't even know what it would mean to have a family. The man who had raised me and then had disappeared, wasn't what family was supposed to be. I had always known that. What if I could have that other thing with Nero and… my mom?

"I wanna know," I said preparing myself for anything.

Chapter 15

Quin

The days that I hadn't heard from Cage had been the worst days of my life. The only time I didn't think about him was when I slept and even then I dreamed about him. At first, it was because I couldn't wait to hear from him again. Then it was because I needed to figure out why I hadn't.

I was a wreck and poor Lou had to deal with it. He listened to me ask why I hadn't heard from Cage, again and again. It was him who had suggested that we find out when Cage's next shift was and to show up. Lou's superpower was definitely figuring out relationships with guys. I loved him for it.

Although it was Lou's idea to do it, when we did it was up to me. No matter the reason for Cage's disappearance, I knew that I had to get him the results of his genetic test. It was too important to him. I hadn't expected him to say everything he had, but I had liked it.

To be honest, I even liked that he was returning to football. The dream life he was talking about when we were in Snow Tip Falls sounded fantastic. I would love a simple life with him and a family. But, I had responsibilities to others. Hell, I had a responsibility to the kids like me who hadn't even been born yet.

Being the boyfriend to the first out NFL player fit that picture. I wouldn't have to figure out how to change the world if I were that. Cage and I would change the world together just by loving each other.

The problem was that this wasn't the end of the story. There was something I knew that he didn't. There was a part of me that wished that he didn't want to know the results of the test. In that case, we could freeze everything where it was and live like this forever. That wasn't the case, though. And all I could do was tell him that I loved him.

"I wanna know," he said having pulled away.

I swallowed and braced myself.

"You and Nero are brothers," I told him.

"We're brothers?"

Cage looked at me shocked.

"Yes."

"That means I have a mother."

"You do."

"Oh my God," he said falling into a seat. "I can't believe this."

"There's more."

"What?"

"You're not just brothers. You're full brothers. You share the same mother and father."

Cage stared at me stunned. His mouth hung open trying to process it all.

"I need to tell him," he said scrambling for his phone.

Beside himself, Cage found his brother's number and called him.

"Nero, we got back the results… Yeah. We're… brothers," Cage said with tears forming in his eyes.

There was a long pause before Cage spoke again. Tears streamed down his cheeks as he listened. Cage turned to me and mouthed, "He's crying."

"Yeah," he said returning his attention to the call. "I would definitely like to meet our mother… What about tomorrow? I could drive up… Okay. Then I guess I'll see you, and mom, then… I know, right," Cage said with a smile.

Cage ended the call and stared at his phone.

"I'm going up tomorrow."

"Can I come with you? I mean, if you want me to. I can get us a room for the weekend in case you want to stay over," I told him wanting to be a part of what was going to be the most important moment of Cage's life.

"Of course you can! None of this would be happening if it wasn't for you. I want you there," Cage said sincerely.

Relief washed through me knowing that he wanted me there. I was sure that he would hear he had a brother and things would be over between us. I couldn't compete with that.

"Did you want to grab something to eat tonight? My treat. I could maybe stay over at your place and we could head out in the morning," I suggested wanting to be with him as much as he would let me.

"I'd like that," Cage said with a smile.

It was amazing to see his smile again. It was what I had missed the most. Well, maybe it wasn't what I missed the most. What I missed the most I was hoping to get tonight back at his place.

After making plans with Cage, I met up with Lou and watched him climb the rock wall for a bit. I made a half-hearted effort to join in, but I was too excited about meeting up with Cage. There was a pizza place I had been wanting to take Cage to. When I had gone with Lou, we had found it romantic, as awkward as it was to be there with him. But it was the perfect place for a date.

Sitting across the table from Cage felt exactly how it did in Snow Tip Falls. With his face glowing from the candle lighting the table, he reached over and placed his hand on mine. My heart thumped staring into his eyes. God, did I love him. I could barely contain myself I loved him so much.

"Do you still have any of that ice cream at your place?" I asked suggestively.

"I do," he said with a smile. "Did you want to head to my place and see what comes up?"

Cage knew how to make me hard. Just his suggestion made me have to stick my hands in my pockets to stand up. The drive to his place did nothing to dampen the heat bubbling between us. So, arriving at his cabin we didn't even pretend to get ice cream. We just went straight to his room and tore each other's clothes off.

Although, Cage had been the one to initiate things the last time, this time I was the one all over him. Kissing him, my tongue went in search of his. Twirling around his, I pulled him deeper into me. I wanted Cage inside of me and I didn't care which part.

Sinking my fingertips into his naked flesh, I grabbed him. It drove Cage wild. Pushing a hand down onto the front of his pants, he was hard. I hadn't forgotten how incredibly big he was so I was ready this time.

Dropping to my knees, I peeled down his pants. I was eye to eye with his bulging underwear. I rubbed my face against it wanting to smell his manly scent. He smelled like sex. It made my cock ache.

Quickly removing his shorts, I took hold of him with both hands and pushed him into my mouth. So big! He was a mouth full. But I slobbered over every inch of him that I could take. Rounding the rim of his dick I pulled my hands back and forth over his impressive shaft.

"Ahhh!" he groaned as I did.

He could only take it for so long. Cupping the back of my head in his large hands, he pulled me to my feet and moved me onto his bed. It didn't take him much time to finish undressing me. Then with both of us hard and naked Cage climbed on top.

"I want you to fuck me. I want to feel you inside of me," he said to my surprise.

I didn't know why I thought he wouldn't want that, but I was more than happy to give it to him.

Even though I would be penetrating him, it was clear that Cage would still be in control.

"I have something," he said leaning past me and retrieving a bottle from his nightstand drawer.

I recognized it. It was the lube. He placed it beside me as I lay on my back and then bent down taking my dick in his mouth.

God was he good at that. In seconds, my leg started to bounce. He didn't let go of me, though. Seeing how close I was, he instead squeezed a dollop of lube into his palm and smeared it behind him and on my cock.

Even the grip of his stroke brought me closer to cumming. I was helpless to his will. Seeing me struggle, he didn't waste time in moving his hips over my cock. With his hand guiding it, he touched my tip to his hole.

It was then that I felt one of the greatest sensations of my life. Taking his time with it, Cage eased me inside of him.

"Yeah," I moaned losing my mind.

I could barely hold on much longer. With my skin crawling and on fire, I felt him swallow me and sit on my crotch. The sensation was amazing. Looking up, Cage looked down overwhelmed and mesmerized. He could see that I was quickly losing it. And once he started slapping his hips against me, I gave in to my struggle and exploded.

"Ahhhh!" I bellowed tearing into the sheets.

It was like it was what Cage was waiting for because as soon as I released, he grabbed his cock and jerked himself until he came.

Exhausted, Cage collapsed onto my chest. With him panting I thought that this was how we were going to fall asleep. It wasn't, because as soon as I shrunk out of him, he wrapped his arms around me and rolled me over so that I was beside him. That was when he pulled me into his arms. This was the only place I ever wanted to be.

Unlike the last time, this time I laid awake thinking about how great everything had felt. I didn't think I was a top guy. It was one of the reasons I had never seriously thought about dating women. But apparently, I was. It took Cage to bring it out of me. I was so glad he did, too. The sensation was unlike anything I had ever had.

"I didn't know you liked that," I said to him wanting to hear his voice.

"Neither did I. But I've always wanted to try it and you have such a great dick."

I blushed. "Thanks. Yours is pretty great, too."

"You think so?"

"It's amazing."

"Then give me a minute and I'll let you have it."

"Okay," I said feeling myself getting hard again.

"Is the minute up, because I think I am," he said with a laugh.

I reached down and got a handful. He definitely was. Again climbing on top of me, this time he lifted my legs and placed the back of my thighs against his chest. Retrieving the lube, he smeared a generous amount between my cheeks and on his shaft.

This time facing him, he placed his tip on my hole and leaned forward to kiss me. It was as he kissed me that he pushed himself in. Entering didn't take him nearly as long as the first time. Then perching himself on top of me, he balanced himself and fucked me silly.

Having recently cum, our new session went on and on. When he was done with that position, he twisted me into another. I did anything he wanted me to do and I loved it.

We fucked until I no longer had the strength to lift my arms. I was his rag doll. And, when he finally came then reached around and jerked me off, there was nothing left for either of us to do except collapse into each other's arms and fall asleep.

When I woke up the next morning, there was no forgetting that my very large boyfriend had spent the night fucking me. I could barely walk straight. It felt weirdly good. I liked being reminded that I had been with Cage and that he had manhandled me. I wanted a lifetime of that even though I knew my ass couldn't take him again any time soon.

"How are you feeling this morning?" Cage asked me with a smile.

"Sore. But, good," I said blushing.

"I'm a little tired myself. I don't think my dick works anymore. It's worn out."

"Yes, I know the feeling. But it's not my dick."

We both chuckled.

"So are you ready to sit down for an hour and a half drive," he asked teasingly.

"I can't wait!" I said wondering if I could take it.

Mercifully, we didn't immediately head out. He fixed us breakfast while I stood around the kitchen. And we ate as I leaned against a wall. It was only after that that I was ready to go.

Driving to Snow Tip Falls, I could tell that Cage was excited but nervous. I was nervous too. What if his mother didn't like me? What if she was against the idea of her son being with a guy?

Nero had said that his calling us "fags" wasn't him. That had to have come from somewhere, didn't it? What if it came from her?

Nero had suggested that we meet at the diner since nowhere in Snow Tip Falls showed up on a map. Driving past the town's welcome sign brought back a lot of memories. It was hard to believe that it was a week ago that we were here and that we had only been here for three days. It felt like we had built a lifetime of memories in that time.

Coming from New York, I never imagined I would enjoy spending time somewhere with such a slow pace, but I did. It almost felt like this was the speed that you were supposed to live life.

Approaching the diner, I asked him if we should check in with Dr. Sonya and drop off our bags before we met up with Nero. Cage didn't see the point. I agreed, so we headed right over.

"You guys hungry?" Nero asked when we entered.

He looked like a different person than the one we had first met. For one thing, he had a smile on his face. Everything about him looked lighter.

"Are you going to join us?" Cage said as happy to be with Nero as Nero was to be with him.

"Yeah, I'll join you," he said enthusiastically.

"You're not off yet," the cook yelled from the kitchen.

"Is there anyone else in here? I'll get back to work when someone comes in," he said with bravado. "You guys want burgers? I'll ask him to fix us a couple of burgers. Pick a seat," he said before heading back to the kitchen.

"He seems happy to see you," I told Cage.

As nervous as Cage had looked before we arrived, he was now glowing. If this wasn't his brother, I would have guessed that he was in love with him. Maybe Cage was, just in a brotherly way.

I was an only child so I didn't know how the two of them felt. Was this the way it was when you had a sibling? It must be nice to have someone you can count on and have your back. I had always thought that was what a boyfriend was for. But, as I think of it, that is also what family did.

Once Nero rejoined us. I couldn't do much but sit back and listen to the two talk. Every so often Nero would direct a question at the both of us. He even asked me a few questions directly. I tried to keep my answers short, though. I knew why we had come, and I wanted this to be as little about me as possible.

Once we were done with lunch, the look on Nero's face changed. A weight took over him.

"So, did you want to meet our mother?"

"Yeah," Cage said with the innocence of a ten-year-old.

Getting up, I reached for my wallet to pay.

"I got it," Nero said.

"That's fine. I have it," I said not wanting to put him in that situation.

"No, I got it," Nero insisted.

I was about to object when Cage cut me off.

"Nero, says he has it!" he said abruptly.

It startled me. I had clearly upset him. But, at the same time, I couldn't let him pay for me. It would be unfair. Nero might not have known it. And, Cage might not have realized how unfair it would be. But I knew, so I couldn't let it happen.

"Can I at least leave the tip?"

"The tip?" Nero asked confused.

Cage growled. He was not happy.

"For the cook," I clarified.

"If he wants to tip the cook, let him tip the cook," the cook yelled from the kitchen.

I didn't realize that he could hear us.

Nero laughed. "Alright, you can leave the tip."

I pulled out enough to pay for the meal and left it on the table. I tried to do it so Nero didn't know how much I was leaving, but he did. His eyes flicked up at me amused by what I had done. Thankfully he let it go.

"Do you want to leave your truck here and ride with me, or follow?" Nero asked.

Cage looked at me.

"Whatever you want to do," I told him not wanting to upset him any more.

"We'll follow you," Cage said getting into his truck.

The drive to Nero's place turned out to be long. They lived 25 minutes out of town. That was fine because it gave me time to check in with Cage.

"How are you feeling?"

"Nervous. Scared. What if she doesn't like me?"

"Cage, she'll love you. Everyone does. I just hope she likes me."

Cage didn't reply. Didn't that mean that he was worried about the same thing?

I probably shouldn't have come. I could see that now. But it was too late for him to drop me off at the bed and breakfast without making things worse between us. So I instead chose to keep my mouth closed and be as invisible as possible.

Cage was meeting his mother for the first time. I just wanted him to be comfortable. He seemed to be having a hard enough time as is. He didn't need all of the complications that I brought along with what he was already going through.

When Nero's truck pulled over, it was into a sparsely populated trailer park. I didn't know what I was expecting but I wasn't expecting this. I looked over at Cage to judge his reaction. He didn't have one. I could tell that he was on edge, but it probably didn't have to do with where we were.

Following Nero to an aging mobile home that reminded me of the office on a construction site, we parked next to Nero's truck and joined Nero in front of it. Nero looked at Cage with sympathy in his eyes. He looked like he wanted to tell Cage something before he invited him in. He didn't.

"Come," he said nervously before leading us up the wobbly stairs to the front door.

Waiting at the bottom of them, I put my hand on the railing. Paint chips stuck to my palm. Subtly brushing them off, I waited my turn to ascend and enter.

Inside was worn, but tidy. The linoleum floors, floral wallpaper, and wooden kitchen cabinets had all faded to the same shade of beige. It was also very small. To the right of the door was the kitchen. To the left was the TV room and past that was a small hallway with three doors.

I turned to Cage. His eyes were locked on the woman sitting on the couch in front of the TV. With her dark, graying hair, angular features, and face full of dimples, there was only one person she could be. She had clearly been as beautiful as Cage was handsome. But time, and a hard life, had caught up with her.

Not having turned when we had entered, Nero called to her.

"Mama?" Nero said getting her to turn around.

Seeing Nero, Cage's mother next turned examining us. She looked confused.

"Mama, remember I said that I was going to bring some friends by?"

She didn't say anything but her eyes bounced between the three of us.

"This is Cage and his boyfriend Quin," Nero said speaking slowly.

"Nice to meet you," Cage said stepping forward. He lifted his hand to shake hers, but when she didn't move, he abandoned the gesture.

"Nice to meet you," I said questioning if I should be here.

"Mama, I found out something about Cage that you should know."

Her eyes turned to Nero.

"Cage is… my brother."

Her increasingly confused look said that she had understood.

"Your brother?" she said slowly.

"Yeah, Mama. Quin took our blood and everything. He's my brother."

"Your brother?"

"Yeah. Our blood says that we share the same father… and mother."

She looked extremely confused after that. As she fought to wrap her thoughts around what Nero was saying, Cage stepped forward.

"Mama, you know how you say that they took your baby away from you and told you that he had died? Mama, this is your son. He's your baby," Nero said getting emotional. "You were right, Mama. He was alive. This is him."

"Nice to meet you," Cage, said again.

She stared at his face from the couch.

"Augustus?" She said squinting at him.

"My name's Cage," he told her.

"I named you Augustus," she said slowly melting into tears. "They took you from me and told me you had died. I knew you hadn't died. I told them to show you to me. They couldn't. They couldn't," she said reaching up for Cage overwhelmed.

Throwing himself into his mother's arms, both held each other crying. I couldn't imagine what Cage was going through. But it felt good to know that I had helped do this for him. It had to be the most fulfilling thing I had ever done.

Soon, Nero joined them on the couch and embraced the two. The three cried and held each other not saying a word. I couldn't escape the moment. Tears rolled down my cheeks as much as they did theirs.

This was their private moment, though. I shouldn't have been there. Without any of them noticing, I slipped outside and made my way to the truck. Getting in, I bundled up and thought.

This was a different world than anything I could have imagined a short time ago. I had grown up around billionaires and geniuses. I knew people had lives like Nero's and his mom's, but only from movies and TV. It is hard to see something as real if that is your only reference.

But, sitting in the truck looking around it was now all very real. I didn't know what to think about it.

I was in the truck for thirty minutes before Cage came out and joined me.

"You left," he stated.

"I wanted to give you all some privacy."

Cage's eyes dipped down without him responding.

"You did this. You and your big brain found my mother. All I can say is thank you."

"Of course," I responded not knowing what else to say.

"It's not "of course." My entire life I've wondered what she looked like and what it would be like to hear her voice. You gave me that. And, I don't think anyone else in the world could have."

I responded with a tight-lipped smile. I didn't know what I was supposed to say.

Cage's eyes left mine as he measured what he would say next.

"I want to spend some more time with her... with the both of them. But, I don't want you to feel like you have to sit out here. Do you mind if I drop you off at the bed and breakfast? It would probably be more comfortable than sitting in this cold truck. Maybe you could call Titus. I'm sure he'd want to hang out."

I didn't know what I was expecting Cage to say, but it wasn't this. Maybe I thought he would encourage me to come inside. Maybe I thought he would want to bring me into his moment. But, thinking about it, that was probably just a fantasy.

Cage had just met his mother for the first time. He had so many questions for her. What would I do except sit there? He was right, it was better that I go somewhere else instead of being the awkward guy sitting in the car during the most important moments of his life.

"I wouldn't want you to have to drop me."

"This is Snow Tip Falls. You can't exactly call an Uber," he said with a smile. "I'll drop you and come back."

"Okay," I agreed feeling Cage slowly pull away.

Cage headed back to the front door and Nero came out to talk to him. Nero looked back at me as Cage spoke. I hated being the asshole breaking up this amazing moment. I felt awful.

Both Cage and he walked back to the truck. As Cage got in, Nero circled to my door. Withdrawing his hand from his pocket he knocked and stepped back. I took that as a sign that he wanted me to come out. When I did, he threw his arms around me.

"Cage said that you were the one to bring us together," he whispered into my ear. "Thank you. Thank you!" he said before slapping my back and pulling away.

"You're welcome," was the only thing I could reply.

I couldn't truly understand what this moment meant to them. How could I? I had grown up with more love and family than I knew what to do with. But the moment wasn't completely lost on me. Would I ever in my life accomplish anything greater than what I had done for them? I didn't know.

Cage and I didn't speak much on the drive back to town. He was deep in thought. The selfish part of me wished that a few of those thoughts were of me. It was probably too much to ask for, though.

Pulling up to Dr. Sonya's bed and breakfast, Cali quickly came outside to greet us. Standing in front of the door on the porch, he looked at us with a light in his eyes. Before I got out, Dr. Sonya joined him.

"It looks like I'm leaving you in good hands," Cage said staring at the two.

"Don't worry about me. Go. Spend time with your family. You deserve this. I'll be fine," I told him.

"I love you," Cage said leaning over and kissing me.

"I love you, too," I told him before grabbing my bag and leaving the truck.

Walking to the veranda, Cage didn't wait for me to get there before driving away. I turned to watch him go. I got the sense that he didn't look back. I couldn't know that for sure, but it certainly felt like it.

"Welcome back!" Dr. Sonya said enthusiastically. "It's good to see you," she said putting her arm around me and leading me in. "Will Cage be coming back?"

"I don't know," I told her honestly. "We found his mother."

She gasped in delight. "Really? That's amazing!"

"It is. It's quite wonderful."

"Well, we'll have to do something to celebrate," she concluded making me feel at home.

I dropped my bag in my room and lied in bed thinking about everything. I couldn't help but feel uneasy. I wasn't sure why.

Maybe it had to do with him not texting me for a week. That had really hurt me. And the worst part was that I still didn't know what had triggered it. If I didn't know what caused it, how did I know that I wasn't triggering it again right now?

After I had driven myself crazy thinking about it, I decided to head downstairs.

"Did you have dinner plans? Would you like to join us?" Dr. Sonya said from the kitchen.

"I don't think I have plans. I haven't spoken to Cage, though."

"Then how about you join us, and if you have to run off, you do?" She suggested with a smile.

"Sounds great. Thank you," I told her before joining Cali in the living room watching TV.

I could feel Cali's uneasiness as I sat there with him. Always having been the shy one, I knew how he felt.

"How long have you been playing football?" I asked him causing his cheeks to turn bright red.

Cage might have been right. He did seem to have a crush on me.

"Since freshman year," he eventually squeaked.

"That's cool. Are you thinking about attending East Tennessee?"

"I was thinking about it."

"It's a good school. I think you'd like it there. If you ever want a tour, let me know."

Cali didn't respond, but he did turn beet red at my suggestion. I was going to have to be careful with what I said to him. The last thing I wanted to do was hurt him or lead him on.

Bringing up Cage many times, I spent the rest of the night with my two hosts. After dinner, Dr. Sonya suggested a game of Scrabble.

"I have to warn you. I'm pretty good," Dr. Sonya said proudly. "There's a group of us in town that play and I haven't lost a game in two years."

I nodded politely and then beat them by 50 points.

Dr. Sonya stared at the board shocked.

"We need to play that again," she announced.

We did and the results were similar. But, more importantly, it was fun. It took my mind off of Cage. So, when he texted saying that he was going to sleep there, it stung less.

Heading to bed alone and waking up alone, I tried not to let my imagination get away from me. The only reason Cage hadn't returned was because he wanted to spend time with his family. That made complete sense. It had nothing to do with me or how he felt about us. He needed this time and I was going to give it to him.

I didn't hear from him until nearly 11 A.M. when he told me that he would come by around 7 P.M. to pick me up.

'Are you having a good time?' I texted in reply.

It took him 30 minutes to text me back. 'Definitely! I'll tell you all about it later.'

I was trying, but it was getting harder not to take this personally. No matter what I told myself, I couldn't shake my insecurity.

To take my mind off of it, I texted Titus. It took less than a minute for him to call me back.

"Quin! How the hell are you? I was just thinking about you two."

"I was texting you because I'm in town."

"Seriously! Let's get together! When are you two free?"

I explained to him where Cage was and what they were doing, so he instead suggested that we do some ice fishing.

"You already made the hole," Titus joked.

Although I had never gone ice fishing, I had done plenty of shallow water fishing during my summers in the Bahamas. Most days it was the only thing to do.

After a day out on the ice, we didn't end up catching anything. Titus said it was because they weren't biting. My guess was that it was his non-stop talking.

That was fine with me, though. What was I going to do with a fish other than throw it back? And Titus was interesting to talk… I mean, listen to. He had ideas about a lot of things, most of which involved Snow Tip Falls.

"Have you given any more thought to coming to East Tennessee University?" I asked him knowing he would fit right in.

"Yes, I have. I have to say that the two of you have inspired me. I will be filling out an application for next semester," he said with a smile.

"That's awesome!"

"Yeah. And, maybe when I'm there, I'll find myself a great guy like you did," he said with a knowing smile.

I stared at Titus not wanting to express my surprise. I really shouldn't have been. The one thing I should have learned from the people I grew up with was that you didn't have to look or act a certain way to like someone of the same sex.

"So, you're... gay? Bisexual?"

Titus's head bobbed around as he answered.

"Let's say, I'm open," he said with another of his brilliant smiles. "I haven't said that to anyone before."

"Thanks for sharing it with me. If you come to E.T. I'll have to introduce you to my roommate, Lou. I don't know that many people at school like us... I don't know any other people at all, really. But, he'll be able to tell you all of the places to meet guys. That's kind of his specialty."

"He sounds like a great resource."

"He's a great person," I said not able to say enough about Lou.

The rest of our day was spent discussing when we each realized that we were into guys. I also shared my three-parent upbringing. He was fascinated by it.

After he expressed a tremendous interest in meeting them, I promised I would introduce him. I certainly would have preferred to spend the day with Cage. But the day I had with Titus was pretty good.

Overall, the weekend ended up being better than any I would have had if I had stayed at school and allowed Cage to come up by himself. I liked Titus, Dr. Sonya, and Cali. When Cage came to pick me up, I promised that I would come back and hang out with them again.

"You're always welcome," Dr. Sonya told me as I left.

"How was your time with Nero and your mom," I asked Cage as soon as I entered the truck.

"It was pretty amazing," he confirmed.

Cage looked different. The tension that had enveloped him as we drove up was gone. He seemed calmer and more settled.

For the next hour and a half, Cage filled me in on what he learned about the mystery surrounding his birth.

"I couldn't ask all of the questions I wanted to. She's not fully there, mentally," Cage explained. "Dr. Tom thinks she has some type of dementia. She has an unusual set of symptoms, though. And the longer I was there, the better she got. Nero said that he hadn't seen her this clear-minded in years. That's why I decided to sleep over and spend today. The longer I was there, the more she was able to tell me. I didn't want to risk leaving and losing the momentum."

"That makes sense. I'm glad you were able to spend so much time with her."

"Yeah," he said letting the conversation drop.

Though he wasn't saying it, it was clear that there was something else on his mind. Everything about it filled me with dread. I wanted to ask him what he learned about Nero and maybe their father, but I didn't dare bring it up. At this point, I just wanted to get home without a disaster happening. I thought I had made it until Cage parked the truck in front of my place and turned the engine off.

"Did you want to come up?" I asked hoping it was the case.

"Actually, we need to talk."

The blood rushed from my face hearing those words. I was a deer in headlights.

"About what?"

"I told you that the more time I spent with my mom, the better she got, right?"

"Yes."

"I think I'm going to move to Snow Tip Falls and stay there for a while."

My fingers tingled and there was a hollowness in my throat that made me want to throw up.

"What about classes? Are you gonna drive back and forth? That's a long drive."

"I think I'm going to drop out of school for now."

"But you're so close. This is your last semester?"

"My mother needs me. Nero needs me. He's been taking care of her alone all this time. It's been hard for him. He said that she isn't always as in control as she was this weekend. He needs help and they're my family."

My next question caused heat to flash across my face.

"What about us? Will you be coming back to see me?"

Every second Cage didn't answer sucked the life out of me. I thought that was painful until he spoke.

"I'm not sure if we should be together."

"What?" I said starting to sweat. "But, you said you loved me."

"I do. You don't have to question that. I do."

"Then, what?"

"You are an incredible guy, the most amazing guy I've ever met. But I'm not enough for you."

"What do you mean, you're not enough? You're everything I've ever wanted."

"I'm not. I thought I could be. But I can't. I don't want to play football anymore. I know how important that is to you."

"I never said you playing football was important to me. I never said that."

"You didn't have to. Remember when I talked about what my dream was? How all I wanted was to settle down somewhere and raise a family? How what I wanted was a simple life?"

"Yes."

"It's true. And, I don't have it in me to live someone else's life. Even if that other life is for you."

"But, I never asked you to."

"No, but be honest, when I told you that I was going to go back to football, didn't you feel relief? Be honest!"

I thought about it. "It wasn't exactly relief," I explained.

"Okay. Was it that with me as the first out football player, the two of us made sense together?"

I stared at him. He was right. That was exactly how I felt.

"I thought so. We don't make sense together without football. I wish it were different, but that's the truth."

"Cage, I love you," I told him no longer able to hold back my tears.

"Quin, I love you too. I do. And, if you say to me that you can imagine having a simple life with me in Snow Tip Falls instead of you going off to somewhere amazing and changing the world, then I will be all in. Tell me that you don't need that and I will promise to spend the rest of my life with you without hesitation. Just tell me that," he pleaded.

The tears flowed down my cheeks realizing what I had to say.

"Cage, you can't imagine the responsibility that I have. People are depending on me."

"And, with my mother, you can't imagine the responsibility I have. She and Nero are depending on me," he said his eyes filling with tears.

"Is this it?" I asked him desperate for him to say that it wasn't.

"I guess so," he said shattering my heart.

I knew I should have said something after that. Anything. But, I couldn't. The pain I felt disconnected me from my body. I floated somewhere over the two of us looking down. I was sad for the boy crying his eyes out in the passenger seat of Cage's truck. But I couldn't feel him. It would have been too much.

I was grateful when he opened his door and stepped into the cold. Anything was better than watching him suffer. Now, he just needed to make it inside and to his apartment before his legs gave out from under him and he collapsed.

Wishing him forward step-by-step, he ascended the stairs. When he took out his key and attempted to put it into the lock was when I couldn't hold it back anymore. Suddenly drowning in pain, the world around me spun. Luckily I didn't have to open the door. A friendly face opened it and now it was looking back at me.

"Are you okay?" Lou asked. "Quin, are you alright?"

I wanted to say I wasn't. I wanted to tell him that Cage and I had broken up and that we weren't getting back together. I couldn't. All I could do was step to him and fall into Lou's arms.

"He hurt me," was what I said. "I don't know what to do," I explained before spending the rest of the night suffocating on my tears.

As devastated as I was when Cage hadn't texted me back, it was nothing close to what I felt for the next few weeks. One thing became clear to me. I wasn't made for this.

Maybe I was weaker than everyone else. Lou went through guys like popcorn. None of them even left butter on his fingers. Yet, I dated one guy, and breaking up with him left me catatonic. I should have known that I wasn't made for love.

Not in twenty years had I found someone to love me back. Why was that? I thought it was something I could escape at a school in the middle of nowhere. But, the real problem was that no matter where I went, I was there. The thing that no one loved about me… was me.

Lou did his best to get me out of bed and at least attend classes, but I couldn't do that either. Part of me knew that no matter the subject, I could probably cram it a few days before the exam and pass. The other part was that I didn't see the point in school anymore.

What was the point of anything? Why should I leave bed except to eat and go to the bathroom? With all of my genius, I couldn't figure that out. So, instead, I lied there, I cried, and I allowed my thoughts to endlessly spiral around Cage.

One second I loved him. The next second I hated him. But every moment I cursed the fatal flaw in me that had made me unlovable.

"Quin, you have to get out of bed!" Lou said insistently. "If not for you, for me. There is a smell coming from here that's making the guys I bring home think I'm using the room to store dead bodies."

"Sorry," I said not wanting to be the burden I was.

Lou sighed and then crawled into my bed wrapping his arms around me.

"Come on, Lamb Chop, you gotta snap out of this. There are other guys out there. Believe me. And a hot guy like you would have your pick. You just need to go outside. Lamb Chop, how do I get you to leave this room?"

"I don't know," I told him honestly.

"Okay, maybe that was too much to ask for. How do I get you to leave this bed?"

I didn't respond.

Lou popped up and looked around.

"That's it. I was trying to be mister nice guy but you've given me no choice. Where is it?"

"What?"

"Your phone."

"Don't call Cage."

"You think I wanna call Cage, that stinking, rat-bastard? Oh no. He needs to burn in hell for what he did to you."

"He was doing it for his…"

"If you tell me he had to do it for his sick mom, I swear to god I'm gonna lose it. You don't get to defend him until you're capable of standing long enough to take a shower. Do you hear me? I said, do you hear me?"

"Yes."

"Good. Now, where's your phone?"

"In the drawer."

Lou looked at the nightstand and found a charger cord preventing it from closing. I didn't feel like explaining how it got that way and he didn't ask.

Instead, he took it out, grabbed my finger, unlocked it, and searched the contacts.

"Who are you calling?" I asked realizing that I had a few numbers I wouldn't want him to call.

"Hello, Mr. Toro? Hi, you don't know me, but this is Quin's roommate… It's nice to meet you, too."

My head popped up. "You called my dad? Low blow!" He wasn't even on my radar of people I didn't want to face. I turned over and buried my head in my pillow.

"Listen. I'm calling because I'm having a bit of a situation with Quin…"

"You called my dad?" I groaned.

"Yes. I can't get him out of bed," Lou said to my father. "Why is it? It's because some guy broke his heart."

"What? Noooo!" I exclaimed reaching for the phone. Lou jumped out of the way.

"I know! They're the worst, aren't they? …Anyway, I was wondering if you had some way to get him up to at least take a shower or something? …Yeah, it does smell rather rank in here."

"Noooo!" I said mortified.

"Okay. You got it," Lou said lowering the phone. "Quin, I have your dad. He wants to talk to you."

"I hate you!" I told him meaning it.

"But, I love you," he said handing me the phone with a smile and leaving my room.

I looked at the phone and took a deep breath. It wasn't that I didn't want to talk to Daddy Laine about this. It was just that it was humiliating. I wanted him to be proud of me. But now, more than any other time, it was clear that I wasn't someone anyone should be proud of, especially a guy who was strong enough to hold two race cars together like he could.

"Dad?" I said doing my best to sound composed.

"Quin, I'm sorry. I'm so sorry, Quin."

That was when I lost it. Retching pain waft out of me as snot drained down my face.

"It just hurts so much, Dad. Why does it have to hurt so much?"

"Because that's love. Sometimes it hurts."

"But why?"

My father went quiet on the other end.

"Okay, that's it. Get out of bed, get dressed. I'll be there in four hours."

"What?"

"Your roommate caught me on the jet flying back to New York. I'm making a detour to see you. We're gonna go get some dinner and we are going to talk this out."

"What are you talking about?"

"I mean it. Get out of bed. Get dressed. I'm gonna be there in four hours."

"Is mom and dad with you?"

"Nope. They're back in New York. It's just me. We're gonna have a father and son talk about dating guys. This conversation is long overdue."

As much as I didn't want to, after the call, I dragged myself out of bed and into the shower.

"Hallelujah!" Lou yelled from the living room.

"I hate you," I mumbled with the shower droplets drowning me out.

I didn't hate him. Lou was the best friend I'd ever had. I might have starved if it wasn't for him because there was no way I was walking to the front door to get my food deliveries.

He also cared about me in a way that I had hoped that Cage would. Lou deserved more from his college experience than having to take care of me.

Returning to my bedroom clean, I smelled what Lou had talked about. My room smelt like a tomb. I cracked a window. I didn't want my dad to see me like this.

All of my parents, but especially Daddy Laine, imagined great things from me. Yet, here I was unable to feed myself after having my heart broken by a guy. I wasn't as special as he thought I was.

I sat on the edge of my bed in my towel for a long time. It had taken a lot of energy to take a shower. I needed to rest. When I received the text from Dad saying he had landed, I forced myself to get dressed.

"He emerges!" Lou said when I entered the living room.

I gave him a resentful glare. That didn't stop him from running over and throwing his arms around me.

"And you smell good! I had my doubts about calling your dad on you, but look at my Lamb Chop now."

I wasn't resisting his hug. It felt really good, actually. But when the intercom buzzed, he let me go so I could reply.

"Hello?"

"Quin, it's Dad."

"Coming down."

"You're not going to invite him up?"

"Why would I?"

"So, I could meet him. Any tree that you fell from has got to be… yum!"

I gave him an annoyed look and headed for the door. The truth was that my whole life I have had people tell me how good-looking my dads were, but especially Daddy Laine. I didn't need Lou having fantasies about him and then telling me about it. Ewww!

I tried to leave Lou behind, but when I left the room, he did too.

"What are you doing?"

"Just making sure you get downstairs alright," he said with a devilish smirk.

"Whatever," I said not having enough energy to fight him.

Lou followed me downstairs with a smile on his face.

"Dad," I said looking at my father just past the door.

Lou gasped. He didn't need to tell me that I would never live up to Daddy Laine. It was obvious. Daddy Laine went from being so poor that he and his mother couldn't afford heat during Wisconsin winters, to having billions of dollars under management at his investment firm. On top of that, he looked like the guy sailing the yacht in cologne commercials.

No matter what I did, I could never measure up to him. And now Lou knew it too.

"And, who's this?" Dad asked.

"This is my roommate, Lou."

"Nice to meet you, Lou," Dad said with one of his charming smiles. Lou giggled, and then pulled himself together and offered Dad his hand.

"Nice to meet you too, Mr. Toro."

"Thank you for looking after my son. He needs some looking after."

"Dad!"

"Of course. Anything for my Lamb Chop… I mean Quin."

"And thanks for giving me a call. It looks like I came just in time."

I looked at him confused and then looked down at myself. I thought I had done a good job of pulling myself together.

"Shall we go? Again, it was good to meet you, Lou. The next time I'm in town, we'll all have to go out to dinner."

"I look forward to it, Mr. Toro," Lou said blushing.

Yea, I was sure he was.

Walking away, Dad put his arm around me. It felt good to feel him there. Though, he might have done it so that he could fix my hair.

"What are you doing?"

"Did you look in the mirror before you came outside?"

"Not everyone cares about looks as much as you do, Dad."

The truth was that I had forgotten to. And although I had managed to get dressed, it had completely slipped my mind to brush my hair. Baby steps.

As he always did, Dad took me to the best restaurant he could find. Considering we were in East Tennessee it wasn't like the ones in New York and Los Angeles, but it was nice. For some reason, I could barely taste the food, but that probably had more to do with Cage than the chef.

"So, tell me, what's going on, Quin? Who's this guy who broke your heart?"

Despite whatever faults Daddy Laine had, he always listened closely. As he did this time, he seemed to genuinely feel my pain.

"You know, your dad once left me heartbroken."

"That's not the way he tells it. He said that *you* broke *his* heart."

"I guess it's a matter of perspective. It was a crazy time."

"You mean with the hurricane?"

"Yeah. It was insane. You can't imagine it. And I was a kid back then. I hadn't quite figured out what was important. It was your dad who was important… and your mom. What they needed and wanted was what was important."

"What's important to Cage is taking care of his mother," I told him.

"As it should be."

"But, it hurts. I loved him. And he loved me. He told me he did."

"I'm sure that he did and that you do. And, that's wonderful for as long as it lasts. But, loving someone sometimes means letting them go.

"Do you think your parents and I wanted you to move so far away? Don't you think that we would rather you live with us forever? You're our little miracle. Even if you aren't that little anymore," Dad said with a smile.

"You probably didn't. But I needed to get away to find myself," I told him still feeling guilty about leaving.

"And we know that. We want you to be all you can be, not just for us but for everyone. So, you can love this guy, but sometimes loving someone means letting them go."

"It hurts, Dad. It really hurts."

I could see that I had made my dad sad.

"You know you don't have to do any of this, right?"

"What do you mean?"

"I mean school. You're probably already smarter than everyone here."

"I'm not."

"Aren't you, though? And, even if you don't have the information now, couldn't you learn it in a week? Quin, you decided to go to university to help you figure out who you are, which is admirable. But, it's not like you couldn't figure it out on your own. There's no magic formula that universities have discovered that spits out fully formed people by the end.

"Quin, you have a destiny. You are going to change the world. There is no question about it. And, taking a class called 'Introduction to Childhood Education' isn't going to get you there. Quin, come home and join the firm."

"Dad…"

"Everyone knows you're gonna change the world. Wanna know a secret? The secret is that I know how.

"You, Quin, are going to be working with me and you are going to direct your incredible brain power onto a set of business portfolios and you're going to find the one that will end up curing cancer, or recycling plastics or whatever. Then you are going to give them the financial resources that they need to change life as we know it. That's how you're going to change the world.

"Being here doesn't help you do that. In fact, it delays it. You are going to change the world, son. Cage has his responsibilities and you have yours."

"What if I don't want to do any of that? It sounds so selfish to say, but what if I just want to get married and have kids like Daddy Reed did. Can't that be okay, too?"

Dad looked at me like I had two heads.

"Quin, is that what you want?"

"I don't know. Maybe."

I looked up at Dad and couldn't miss the disappointment in his eyes. It took a while for him to be able to hide it.

"Son, I love you. Whatever you choose to do will be just fine with me. But, let me ask you this. Even if that's not what you want, what's keeping you here?

"You can't pretend — and, it hurts me to have to say this but — Cage has made his choice. He could have chosen you. He didn't. So, it doesn't matter if you choose him because he's made clear what he wants. And, believe me, all you can do is respect that."

I didn't want to cry in front of my dad, but I wanted to cry. What hurt so much was knowing that he was right. Cage could have figured out a way. He didn't have to drop out of school. He didn't have to break things off with me.

He should have given us a chance to work things out. Instead, he walked away from us. That told me everything I needed to know about how he felt about me.

"You're right, Dad. I need to let him go. And, every day I spend here is a day wasted when I could be doing the thing I was born to do. There's no point in being here.

"I'll pack up my things. I'm coming home."

Chapter 16

Cage

Sitting at the table eating lunch with Nero and my mother, I again thought about how lucky I was. The man who raised me wasn't a father. He didn't treat me like family. This was what having a family was supposed to feel like.

After a tense conversation with Dr. Tom about what happened, he admitted that there were people at the hospital who knew about my kidnapping. Joe Rucker was a janitor there. The day I disappeared was the last day he showed up for work.

Apparently, my disappearance was immediately covered up. The hospital was already struggling to remain open and the people running the place decided that admitting that they lost a baby would shut the place down. They decided that as the only hospital in the area, more good could be done if they remained open. So, instead of reporting it, they sacrificed me and my mother for "the greater good" and told her I had died.

My mother said she never believed it. She said she kept asking to see my body and they said that she couldn't. Eventually, they told her that it had been accidentally cremated and tried to give her money to go away.

She didn't take the money, but in the end, it didn't matter. My mother was a nobody from the middle of nowhere. No one was going to believe her over a bunch of people with 'Dr.' in front of their name.

I get the sense that that was what broke her. Nero told me that she acted crazy for most of his childhood. Her behavior was that of a tortured woman.

According to Nero, eventually, she stopped her erratic behavior. Nero said he was relieved when it happened, but that was also when her decline began. Each day she became further disconnected from reality until she stopped going to work at all and they were about to be kicked out of their home.

That was when Nero stepped up and took care of both of them. At 13, Nero got his first job. It was a crap job that didn't pay much, but it was enough to keep a roof over their head. And, ever since, he has done whatever he has had to to make ends meet.

I didn't have a job in Snow Tip Falls yet, but I was asking around for one. Nero needed help and I was going to give it to him. Right now I was doing it by watching over our mother while he did what he had to do during the day. But, things were going to change as soon as there was a job opening anywhere in town.

I cleared the table when everyone was done eating. Washing off the dishes and setting them to dry, I could feel Nero staring at me.

"What is it?" I asked knowing that he often had to be prompted to say what was on his mind.

"You think we could go for a walk?"

"Of course," I told him feeling uneasy.

I had only been living here for a few weeks so everything between us was still new. But this was the first time he had suggested we take a walk. It made me think of the last time I had spoken to Quin.

It took everything I had to not think about Quin. Most times I failed. The only thing that prevented me from calling him was that I deleted his phone number. I had to. I wasn't strong enough to simply not call him. I needed to put a mountain of obstacles between us to stop me from running back to him. Deleting his number was just the first.

Finishing up what I was doing, I considered grabbing a jacket. It was getting warmer so neither of us did. Exiting the trailer into the cool early spring air, I followed Nero and the two of us entered the woods.

"There's a place I used to go when everything would get too much for me as a kid. Want to see it?"

"Yeah," I told him feeling a wave of guilt that I wasn't here to take care of my little brother until now.

We walked in silence for almost 45 minutes and stopped when we approached the edge of a valley. The pain in my leg had been off and on since I had moved here. But for the last week, it had been off. I was sure it meant that I could remove my cast soon.

"This is it," Nero said looking out at the waterfall below. After a long winter, it was thawing. I tried to imagine how beautiful it looked when it was warm and flowers covered the valley. Snow Tip Falls really was a breathtaking place.

"It's nice. It's quiet," I told him appreciatively.

"Listen, I wanted to talk to you about you staying here…"

"You have a problem with me staying here?"

"No! Absolutely not. You being here has been the best thing that has ever happened to me."

"Thanks! Me too," I said feeling rewarded for the tough decisions I had made.

"It's just that you're here all the time."

"You want me to find somewhere else to live?"

"No! I'm getting this wrong. What I'm trying to ask is, don't you have classes? When you first got here I thought you were taking a couple of days off. But, it's been weeks. Don't you have to go back soon?"

"Oh! Yeah. I dropped out."

"You dropped out?" Nero asked startled.

"Didn't you say this was your last semester and that you just had three classes left to graduate?"

"Yeah. But, I need to be here with you. I need to help with Mom."

"And I appreciate that. I really do…" Nero stared at me measuring what he would say next. "It's just that, I thought that school was important. I mean, I never used to think that. But after I met you and Quin, I…"

He trailed off.

I wasn't sure what was going on. Nothing Nero had told me about himself had led me to believe that he had valued school. So where was this coming from?

I wouldn't want to push him in any way, but it was clear that if he went to college it would change his life. Nero wasn't the dumb thug I thought he was when we had first met. He was thoughtful, vulnerable, and pretty ingenious. If he was exposed to the outside world, there was no telling who he would become.

"School is important," I told him taking the opening.

"But, you only had three classes left and you dropped out. If it's so important, and you were so close, why did you leave?"

"I left for you and Mom."

"Huh. Okay. And, I appreciate that. It's just that I thought it was really important."

"It is really important! It's just that you two are more important."

Nero didn't respond to that. I obviously didn't clear things up for him. And, honestly, I could see why.

It was a matter of priorities and responsibilities. But, at the same time, I didn't realize that I might be setting an example for my younger brother. I was new at this.

"Why hasn't Quin come to visit?"

"What?" I asked caught off guard. As his question echoed in my mind, I felt a tightening clench around my heart, and waves of pain shot through my healing leg.

"I said, why hasn't Quin come to visit?"

"Oh! It's because…"

As I began to say it, I realized that I hadn't said it aloud before. It took everything in me not to fall to my knees at the thought.

"We broke up."

"What?" Nero asked shocked. "I liked him!"

"I did too," I admitted feeling it for the first time.

"What happened?"

"I have responsibilities now."

"Wait! You broke up with him because of us?"

"I mean…" I didn't want to say it.

"No!" He said turning to me angrily. "Just no!"

"What are you talking about, no?"

"I liked him. He was really good for you, Cage. You two were cute together," he said distressed.

"There's more to being with someone than how you look together."

"I know that. I'm not an idiot. But, didn't you say that he was the one who figured everything out and that he was the reason you found us?"

"He was."

Nero shook his head and shot out his hands as if he had presented his argument on a platter.

"And you broke up with him for it?"

"It was more than that."

Nero looked up and shifted around regretfully.

"It was what I said to you two, wasn't it."

"You mean when you called us fags?"

Nero dropped to a squat and buried his face in his hands. He groaned humiliated.

"No, Nero, it wasn't that. Seriously. It had nothing to do with us breaking up."

Nero looked up at me and dropped to his ass.

"Then what? Why did you break up with him? It couldn't be for us. You couldn't have thrown away everything good in your life because of us," he pleaded.

I sat down next to him.

"I didn't throw away everything."

"You dropped out of school. You broke up with your boyfriend. Didn't you like Quin?"

I thought about it. "I loved him."

"And because you met us, now you have nothing. We're like a disease that ruined your life."

"You and Mom didn't ruin my life."

"Really? It sure doesn't seem that way. This is my fault, isn't it?"

I sat next to Nero.

"It's not your fault."

"It is my fault. When I told you the things I did about the way things were, I was telling you because I needed help. But, I only needed *help*. I didn't need you to give up everything to be here for us. I just needed a little help. I can't let you give up your life for us."

"Nero, it's my choice."

"But, it's not just you you're affecting. You're making choices for all of us."

I didn't understand what he was saying. How was I making choices for him and Mom?

"Listen, you loved him right?"

A lump appeared in my throat.

"Yeah, I loved him."

"Do you still love him?"

I couldn't say the words so I instead shook my head in agreement.

"Then fight for him. That's what I would want someone to do for me."

"It's not that simple."

"It is that simple… isn't it? You fight for the things you love."

"But, his life is so much larger than anything I can offer him."

"You saying he expects you to pay for him, or something?"

"No! He definitely doesn't need that."

"Then what?"

"It's that I just want a simple life here with my family. His life is so much bigger."

"So, there's nothing you can do to work it out? There's no way you can meet in the middle?"

"I don't know."

"Did you try before you two broke up?"

"No," I admitted embarrassed.

"Why not?"

"I… I… Jesus, I don't know. I thought I had to let him go so that he would be happy and I could be here to take care of you all."

"You can't do that, Cage. You can't make me and Mama the reason you gave up on the guy you love. Don't put that on us. Fight for him!"

"I thought I was supposed to be the wiser, older brother," I said trying to be light-hearted. Nero wasn't having it.

"Then act like it, bro. Fight for Quin. Go after the man you love!"

Nero was right. Everything he said was right. There was a middle ground between what Quin needed and what I needed to do. I had been too caught up in the storm of emotions that came with having a new family to see it before now, but there was.

What was I thinking giving up on Quin without a fight? Yes, he needed to change the world. And that might take him away. Or, maybe it wouldn't. Maybe there was a way for him to change everyone's lives from here. Maybe Nero could take care of Mama whenever I needed to visit him.

In either case, I wanted Quin in my life. I wanted to hold him and make love to him. I wanted Quin to be the one I told my secrets to and I wanted to be that person for him.

I didn't need to play football to be that guy. I didn't need to be special in any way. All I had to do was to keep choosing him no matter what. And what I was realizing was that it didn't have to be a choice between my new family and the love of my life.

"Oh God, what have I done?"

"Go after him!" Nero insisted jolting me to get up.

My thoughts swirled. I didn't have his phone number. I had deleted it. I needed to find someone who had it. I needed to get back to my truck.

Jogging back down the path, I slowly hobbled into a run. I felt weighed down. My cast was holding me back. Did I even need it anymore? I was sure I didn't. So, kneeling, I clutched the crumbling cast in my hands and tore it off of me.

Tossing it aside, I felt like I was on the football field again. I hadn't felt this free in months. My strides were long and strong. Jumping over streams and across ravines, I arrived back in a fraction of the time it had taken to get out there.

Sprinting inside, I raced to my pile of stuff on the floor.

"Why are you in such a rush?" my mother asked as I searched for my keys and shoes.

"Mama, I love you, but I made a huge mistake I need to correct."

"Did you finally come to your senses about your boyfriend?"

I looked back at her shocked.

"How did you know?"

"I'm your mother. A mother knows these things," she said with a smile. "Now, go get him."

I smiled unable to love her more.

Hurrying to my truck, I put my foot on the gas racing to town. My first thought was to go to Dr. Sonya's. I knew she had his number. But the closer I got, the more I realized that that couldn't be the plan.

It had been too long. A phone call wouldn't do. I had to see him. I had jerked him around too much already. He had to see that I was serious.

He didn't deserve what I did to him. And, I didn't deserve him. But, deserve him or not, I was going to let him know that I didn't want to live without him. He needed to know that I was going to do whatever I had to do to keep him.

My lead foot got me back to campus in the half the time it usually took. As I approached his place, my heart pounded with fear. What if what I had to say wasn't enough? What would I do then?

Whatever I have to do, I am gonna do it. Quin is my man. He is the love of my life and, no matter the consequences, I'm gonna fight until my last breath to be with him.

Not finding a parking spot, I pulled my truck onto the sidewalk making my own. I didn't care. What I had to tell him couldn't wait another minute. So racing out of my truck with the engine running and the door open, I approached the front door of his building and lunged for the intercom.

The timing of it all couldn't have been worse... or maybe better. Because as I stood there waiting for the intercom to light up in reply, a face appeared on the other side of the glass in the door. It was Tasha. Of all people, why did it have to be her?

"Please, open the door. I know things didn't end well between us, but I have to go see Quin. Please!"

I was half expecting Tasha to turn around and walk off pissed. Instead, she popped open the door. As I stared at her, she smiled. I wasn't sure why until I saw who was standing behind her. It was her best friend, Vi. Vi was smiling too, and I didn't make the connection until I looked down and saw that they were holding hands.

"Go get him," Tasha told me not needing to say anymore.

"Thank you!" I said rushing past her and bounding the stairs three at a time.

Arriving in front of Quin's door, I was exhausted and crackling with excitement. I didn't know how I had managed to stay away from him for so long. I knocked on the door trying to calm myself. As soon as I did, it flung open. A very pissed face stared back at me from within.

"Lou, where is he?"

"Gone! He's gone because of you!"

"What? Where? When?" I asked pushing past him and seeing that half of the living room furniture was missing.

"You hurt him. He decided to leave school because of you."

"What? No! When did he go?"

"An hour ago."

"An hour ago?"

"His family came and packed him up. They're probably flying away right now. I guess you're too late."

"No! This can't be happening."

"What do you care? You just want him so you can have someone you can hurt again."

I looked at Lou devastated that he would think that. But, he was right. All I had done was hurt Quin.

Quin was probably better off without me. ...But maybe "better off" wasn't always better.

"Lou, I know you hate me. And you have every right to. I didn't treat Quin how he deserved to be treated. But, he is the most special person in the world to me. And, even if I have to spend the rest of my life making it up to him, even if I have to follow him around the world to do it. I will.

"I love that man. I love him more than I thought possible. So, if there's anything you can tell me, anything that will allow me to tell him how much of a fool I've been, I will owe you forever. Please, Lou. Please!"

Lou's gaze was ice-cold, until in an instant when his tension melted and tears pooled in his eyes.

"Why can't a guy ever say those things about me?" Lou said overwhelmed. "Okay, let's go."

"Where are we going?"

"To the airport. They might not have left as long ago as I said. But they're taking a private jet so if we don't get there soon, they'll be gone."

Lou didn't have to say any more. Hurrying back to my truck, we climbed in and raced to the airport. It wasn't the one my team flew out from when we traveled for games, it was the one for private planes. I had never been there and knew nothing about it.

Pulling up, I found an open spot next to the entrance of the building. Sprinting out, I entered the terminal and looked around. The place was much smaller than I ever imagined it. I could see everyone in the open space in one sweep. Taking a second scan to be sure, Quin wasn't here.

"There!" Lou said pointing to a door marked 'Exit'.

He didn't have to say anymore. Running to it, someone yelled, "Hey!"

Exiting the terminal, I stepped onto the tarmac. Still, there was no Quin. Had they gone? Was I too late?

No. There was only one place he could be. It was on a plane circling the tarmac and heading to the runway. I ran after it.

"Quin! Wait! Stop! Don't go! I have to talk to you!" I yelled.

It was no use. I could barely hear myself over the roar of the engine. All I could do was sprint towards the runway and hope he saw me.

Racing as if for a touchdown, I leaped everything in my way and spun around the things I couldn't. I was two hundred feet away as the plane raced past me. I couldn't stop it. But as it crossed in front of me, I saw a familiar face in one of the windows. It was Quin. Our eyes met.

It wasn't enough, though. Nothing I had done had been enough. With the force of a rocket, the plane approached the end of the runway and took off. He was flying away. Quin was gone. I had waited too long. It was over.

Watching his plane disappear into the air, I slowed down giving up. The second I did, I was taken down by a linebacker. Maybe he wasn't that big. Maybe it was just that I hadn't seen the hit coming.

Whatever it was, my face was now pressed against the ground. A man was kneeling on my back. All hope was lost.

"Do you realize how illegal it is to run onto a tarmac? It's a federal crime? You're going to jail for a long time," a large, angry, out of breath man yelled into my ear.

If I wasn't going to be with Quin, what did it matter if I was in jail? I was realizing that, without Quin, nothing mattered. He was gone and it had all been my fault. I didn't care what happened to me now because I had let the best thing in my life slip away. From here on out, I deserved everything I got.

When another man joined us, they grabbed my arms and pulled me to my feet. I didn't resist. I was going to let them do their job. My fight was gone. My will to go on was gone… until I heard something I hadn't expected.

The plane that had taken off with Quin in it was circling and heading back down.

"Wait, look," I told the guys turning their attention to the landing plane.

The three of us watched it. As soon as it touched down and came to a stop, the door opened. Someone raced out. It was Quin Toro, the love of my life, and he was running towards me.

Two freight trains couldn't keep me from him after that. Pulling from my captors and running to Quin, I didn't stop until I was right in front of him. He leaped into my arms.

"You're here! I didn't want to leave without saying goodbye," Quin declared.

"Why are you going? Please don't go."

"Why shouldn't I? I have nothing to stay for."

"What are you talking about? You have Lou and school. But, more than that, you have me. I love you, Quin. I was crazy not to do everything I could to be with you."

"But you were right, Cage. We both have responsibilities. We can't deny that."

"No, we can't. But I'm willing to do whatever I have to to have you in my life. I'll go wherever you need me to go and do whatever you need me to do. All I ask is for you to love me."

"I would never want to take you from your family, Cage. I can't do that to you."

"But, I want you to be my family. You're just as important to me as Nero and my Mom are. It's because of you that I have them. I love you, Quin Toro. I want to love you for the rest of my life. Please, be with me," I said with a smile.

"I don't know, Cage. I want to. I want to more than anything in the world, but…"

"Quin, what are you doing?" A voice said from behind him.

We turned to see the most James Bond-looking guy I had ever seen in my life. He was standing with a very attractive couple. They could only be Quin's parents.

"The man's telling you he loves you and that he's willing to figure things out. Quin, you have to know when you've won."

"But, what about my responsibilities? You said I have to change the world."

"You told our son that he has to change the world?" The light-haired guy said to James Bond shocked.

"I say a lot of things, Quin. You should know that about me by now. And I might not always be right. But, what I'm sure about is that when you find someone who you love and who loves you enough to risk being run over by a plane to be with you, you figure it out. Quin, you're a smart guy. Figure out a way."

I turned to Quin who looked back at me.

"What do you say, Quin. You want to figure out a way?"

His smile lit up my heart.

"Yes, Cage. We'll figure out a way. I love you. I want to be with you no matter what it takes."

That was when I leaned in and kissed him. His lips had never tasted sweeter. Lost in the wonder of his touch, I knew that Quin and I were about to live the rest of our lives happily ever after.

Epilogue

Quin

Unpacking the plane turned out to be a lot easier than packing it. It was probably because Cage was there doing it with me. It gave him a chance to meet my parents and for them to meet him. They liked him as I knew they would.

Moving back into the apartment with Lou, my parents agreed that I should finish up the semester and then said goodbye. I had a lot of classwork to catch up on, but I did it in no time. What took longer was helping Cage catch up with his. It required a lot of late nights together, but there was no complaining about that.

I did have to make a deal with Daddy Laine for all of the back and forth I put him through, however. Next semester, along with all of my classes, I had to start work with him at the firm. For the most part, I would be evaluating prospectuses and doing deep dives into the companies. I had more than enough band with for that.

I also decided to tie the industries of the companies I was evaluating into the classes I chose. It was a win-win for everyone. More than that, it would leave my weekends free to spend time with Cage and his family in Snow Tip Falls. My time with them became an adventure. There were still many things we didn't know about their past.

Who was Cage and Nero's father? Even as their mother became more coherent, she wouldn't say.

"You have no idea?" I asked Nero as we sat together at Cage's graduation.

"I'm not sure," he responded in hushed tones.

"Wait. That's not what you said to Cage. You told him that your mother forbid you from asking about him."

"That's true. She did forbid me. But that hasn't stopped me from looking into stuff."

"So, you think you know?"

"I might. And, since you were able to find us in a town that wasn't even on the map, I was thinking maybe you could help. I don't know how much time I'm gonna have while taking classes next semester, but…"

"Wait, are you going to be taking classes here next year?" I asked shocked.

Nero looked at me and blushed.

"I was thinking that with Cage helping out and my mom doing so much better, I might give it a shot. I might even try out for the football team. I was pretty good in high school."

"Pretty good?" Titus said leaning over from the seat next to Nero. "This guy set the record for most yards run in a season. This one is lightning on the field."

Nero blushed.

"I might have run a few yards," Nero said humbly.

"Trust me, Quin, this school won't know what hit them," Titus said with his usual salesmanship.

"Hey Quin, do you know who that is?" Nero said staring at someone standing under the oak trees past the chairs.

I turned to look. It was a guy with shaggy dark hair, a thin frame, and round glasses. He was cute.

"No. I've never seen him before. Why do you ask?"

"It's just that I thought I saw him look at me."

"Oh."

I turned back to the guy. As I did, he looked at us. I couldn't tell who he was looking at. But as the three of us stared at him, he smiled. I looked back at Nero. Nero couldn't take his eyes off of him.

Wait. What was going on? Was Nero into guys? My mouth dropped open.

"Cage Augustus Rucker," a man said over the P.A. system.

I turned to see Cage step onto the stage to collect his diploma.

"Oh, he's getting it," I said tearing Nero's attention from the guy.

Once the scroll of paper was in Cage's hand, everyone in our little group, which included Lou and Cage's mother, stood up and cheered. The love of my life was graduating from university. I loved him more than I had ever loved anyone and I couldn't be happier for him.

The next chapter of our lives was about to begin. Would it include Nero and the guy he still couldn't take his eyes off of? Would it include finding out who their father is and solving the mystery behind Cage's birth?

I didn't know. But, whatever it included, I was all in. So was Cage. And as long as we had each other, I knew that anything would be possible.

The end.

Want to read the steamy romance that created Quin? Check out 'Hurricane Laine' the first book in the 'Taming the Beast' series.

Thinking about rereading this book? Consider reading it as a male/female story in, the sexy sports romance 'My Tutor', a steamy wolf shifter romance in 'Son of a Beast', or a wholesome romance in 'Going Long'.

*****
Sneak Peek:
Enjoy this Sneak Peek of 'Hurricane Laine':

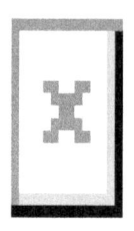

Hurricane Laine
(MMF Bisexual Romance)
By
Alex McAnders

Copyright 2020 McAnders Publishing
All Rights Reserved

A cocky billionaire, his selfless best friend, and the curvy woman neither can resist, fall into a sizzling MMF bisexual romance. Fake boyfriends, first time gay experiences, and heart-aching love follow.

JULES
Jules just got a job offer and it could not have come at a better time. Days away from ending up on the streets, she has a chance encounter with Laine, a forgotten college classmate who offers her a weird proposal. If she

pretends to be his girlfriend for a few weeks, she and her mother can keep their home.

But, why would Laine, who has become richer than god, need someone to pretend to be his girlfriend? And why would he reach into the past and ask her?

LAINE
Laine breaks things. Companies, markets, hearts, nothing is safe once he sets his sights on them. That's what made him a billionaire and why everyone worships the ground this cocky ass walks on.... That is, everyone except for one man. And for Laine, that one man is the only person who matters.

REED
Unlike Laine, his long-time best friend, Reed couldn't care less about money. In fact, after college, while Laine was becoming a corporate raider, Reed moved to a small island in the Bahamas to run an after school program for less privileged kids.

His is a quiet life... that is, except for when Laine comes to visit. So, when Laine invites Reed to stay with him on Laine's private island telling him that he will be bringing a guest, Reed braces himself for what could follow. But, as much as he prepares himself, he could never guess what Laine would do next, and how much it would change their feelings for each other.

'Hurricane Laine' is a steamy bisexual romance with as many laughs as twists and turns. Loaded with enough MM, MFM, and MMF scenes to make your toes curl, it will leave you satisfied with its not-to-be-missed HEA ending.

*****

Hurricane Laine

It was as the tears made their way to my eyes that I looked around and saw someone I truly never expected to see. It was a guy I knew from college. At least I think it was. That was approaching ten years ago. And it wasn't anyone I was friends with, but I certainly saw him around campus.

We had both gone to a small, mid-western college. The school wasn't big enough to not at least recognize everyone's face. What were the odds of running into him in a coffee shop in the middle of the day in Calabasas?

Now, here's the tricky part. I recognize him, but I don't remember his name. Here's the other thing. I have put on a few pounds since college. I was never really a thin girl, so those few pounds have tipped the scales for me.

Back then I could have considered myself to be "solid". Now, I'm… how would I say this so that I'm not being horrible to myself? Now I'm pleasantly plump.

So, with all of that in mind, do I even bother striking up a conversation? What would be the point? It wasn't like we were friends.

On the other hand, I don't remember him being this good looking. It wasn't like he was a part of the sweatsuit brigade in college, but the tailored shirt he was wearing was hanging on him like a bad habit. He's the type of guy who, if I were in a better state of mind, would make me think of sex. That's worth fumbling through a forgotten name.

As to the extra 50 pounds, couldn't I tell him that it wasn't mine and I was just holding it for a friend? Sure I could. He'd believe that, right? Besides, it's not like my life could get any worse.

"I'm sorry," I said grabbing the good looking guy's attention. When he looked at me, he had this steely look in his eyes that, if I were in a better state of mind, might have made my down-below quiver. "Do I know you?"

The good looking man flashed a good looking smile. "I don't know. Do you know me?"

He said that like he was famous or something. Wait, did I actually go to school with him or do I just recognize him from TV? Freakin' Calabasas!

"No, we went to school together, didn't we? Beloit College?"

The man's face dropped recognizing the name. He stared at me trying to figure out what was going on. It took him a second, but soon his smile returned.

"Wait, yes. Yes, I know you. You used to live in… What was that dorm closest to the gym? It was our senior year," he said excitedly.

"Haven. Yeah, it was Haven. It was our senior year. You got it," I said feeling a glimmer of hope remembering a time when my life was so full of possibilities.

"That's right, Haven," he agreed with a smile. "Laine," he said offering me a wave from two tables away."

"Jules."

"That's right, Jules," he said as if he recognized my name.

Laine stared at me for a moment with a pleasant smile on his face and gestured for permission to come over.

"Please," I told him welcoming the company.

"So, Jules, what have you been up to? What are you doing in Calabasas? Do you live here?"

Here was the tricky part. What was I supposed to tell him? In these types of situations, aren't you supposed to humblebrag about the great things going on in your life? So, what was that for me? I could tell him that I recently found $10 in a pants pocket, but I didn't want to make him feel *that* jealous.

"Honestly, not much," I told him instead. "I was up in Seattle for a while. But a family situation brought me back here."

"Are you from here?" Laine asked getting better looking by the second.

"Yeah. Not Calabasas, but Southern California."

"And, where do you work? What do you do?"

He had to ask me that, didn't he? It was such an L. A. thing to ask. I didn't have the energy to blow smoke up his ass. It had already been a long day, so I told him the truth.

"I don't work anywhere, actually."

"Oh, are you married?"

I laughed. I hadn't even dated anyone since moving back here. My lady bits have already twice filed for unemployment.

"No. It's just that I've been looking for something temporary because I don't know how long my "family situation" will last, and the agency I was working through can't seem to get their act together," I said deciding it was better to blame my situation on corporate.

"Oh, okay," he replied with quickly diminishing interest. Freakin' L. A.!

"But, how about you? What have you been up to? You look like you've done well for yourself."

This was what got his focus back on me. Who would have guessed that a guy would want to talk about himself?

"Actually, I'm doing very well. I own an investment firm."

"Really?" I asked suddenly understanding what he meant by "very well".

"Yeah. After college I moved to New York to work for one of the big banks. I shorted a couple of stocks right before the great recession and then took home a fortune," he said with a million-dollar smile.

"So, when the economy was crashing?" I asked him.

"I was raking it in."

"Huh," I said as I began to consider the morality of how he made his money.

"But, don't mistake me for those asshole bankers packaging those toxic mortgages. That wasn't me."

"No, you just made money by betting on those banks to fail."

"Actually, it was by betting on them being too big to fail," he said with another smile.

It had been a long time since I had thought about back then. We were just recent graduates entering an about to be devastated job market. It wasn't something I had the energy to think about now.

"So, are you married?" I asked him trying to cut to the good bits.

"No. Not married," he told me flatly.

"Special someone?"

"Nope. Nothing."

"How?" I asked sounding like I was flirting… because I was.

"Who knows," he said with a charming smile.

Yeah, that told me everything I needed to know. He wasn't married because he didn't want to be. Clearly, he was the type that liked to keep his options open. If today was going to end in sex, I would have to remember that. Not that it was…

"I see," I said returning his smile.

"It's funny that you asked me about that," he said seeming like he wanted me to probe.

"Why?"

Laine leaned back in his seat and looked away. "You ever get yourself in a weird situation, that you don't know how you ended up in?"

"Laine, you don't know how often. I live in that state."

Laine chuckled. "Then maybe you can relate. I'm heading down to the Bahamas in about a week…"

"Nope, can't relate," I said cutting him off. He chuckled again.

"I'm heading down in about a week and I'm going to be hanging out with a friend."

"Sounds nice."

"Yeah, but I might have told the friend a bit of an exaggeration."

"What's that?"

"I told him that I was dating someone and that I would be bringing them."

"Why would you tell him that?" I asked confused.

"I don't know. He's just a guy that makes me feel… There are some people who always make you feel bad about yourself no matter how well you're doing. That's him."

Damn, how rich does his friend have to be to make a successful investment banker feel bad about himself?

"I think I know something about how that feels," I told him genuinely relating.

"Yeah, well, that's him. And, in order to not look like a total loser, I have to find someone to go with me and pretend to be my fiancé."

"Your fiancé?"

"Yeah, I know," he said lowering his head and rubbing his eyebrows in frustration.

"I gotta say, Laine, you've gotten yourself into quite a dilemma. So, are you gonna tell him the truth?"

"Oh, god no. I can't do that."

"Why not?"

Laine paused for a moment as something flashed through his mind. "I just can't do that."

"So, what are you gonna do?"

"I have to find somebody."

"You have to find someone to go to the Bahamas with you. Yeah, good luck with that," I joked.

"It's not as easy as you think," he protested.

"Really? You can't find somebody to go to the Bahamas with you?"

"No. I can't."

"I find that hard to believe."

"I can prove it," Laine said confidently.

"How?"

"Like this. Jules, would you like to go to the Bahamas with me and pretend to be my fiancé?"

"Oh, I would love to but can't. I have to work."

"See!" He said triumphant.

"Okay, I see what you mean. But the only reason I can't do it is because I have to work. Believe me, if I didn't, I would absolutely do it. I can't tell you how much I need a trip to the Bahamas right now."

"What, the family thing?" He asked becoming more serious.

"It's a money thing. I really need to work right now. I mean, I'm not gonna get into it, but I really need the money."

So you know that feeling when a suuupper rich, suuupper handsome guy is staring at you with a twinkle in his eye that makes you want to throw yourself at him like a rug? Well, that might be what's going on now.

"Why are you staring at me like that?" I asked him.

"The only thing stopping you from helping me out is money?"

"Yeah. I don't know what world you live in. But, in my world, it's a big thing."

"I'm sure. But it's something I have," he said starting to beam with confidence.

I wasn't sure how I felt about where he was going with this. "What are you suggesting?"

"How much would get you out of your "family situation"?"

"How much? Geez, I don't know. Probably more than you have."

Laine twisted his head in doubt. God was this guy cocky. How much money did he have? My family situation could have been in the millions.

"Give me a number," he said making me question what the hell was happening.

Steadying myself I looked at Laine again. How much did I remember about him from college? Not much. I think I do remember him being a little full of himself back then, too. I really didn't interact with him, but I was starting to remember female friends who did. If I remembered correctly, he was a bit of a man whore.

And, didn't I have a girlfriend who came crying to me about him? Was that about Laine or someone else? It was such a long time ago. It's hard to remember.

Whoever it was about, it had been ten years. People change. Situations change. More importantly than all of that, *my* situation had changed. And here was a guy asking me how much money I needed to get out of the hole I'm in. What do I tell him?

If his offer was real, I certainly didn't want to scare him off by saying a number that was too high. At the same time, he was bragging about having a lot of money. Why shouldn't I at least be honest?

"$200,000."

"$200,000?" He asked with a broad smile.

"Yeah. There are medical expenses involved and a student loan that…"

"Deal," he said cutting me off.

"What?" I asked sure that I had misunderstood him.

"I said it's a deal. I'll do it. If you come with me to the Bahamas and pretend to be my fiancé, I'll pay you $200,000."

I was stunned.
Read more now

Sneak Peek:
Enjoy this Sneak Peek of 'Until Your Toes Curl':

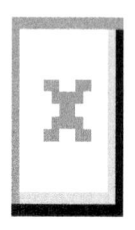

Until Your Toes Curl
(MMF Bisexual Romance)
By
A. Anders

Copyright McAnders Publishing
All Rights Reserved

8 steamy must-have MMF romances about bad boys, billionaires and boyfriends who know how to treat their curvy girls. Closeted guys will have their first loves. Wiser couples will have their second chance at love. Friends will become lovers. And, enemies will become lovers in romances filled with lust, love, endless twists and turns and HEA endings.

Her Best Bad Decision
A cocky baseball player falls for, the off-limits billionaire who owns his team, and the sassy curvy girl

who moves in with him uninvited. Laughter follows in this feel-good romance that will have you tearfully cheering for the sexy threesome by the end.

Island Candy (Complete Series)
A billionaire bad boy and a brilliant artist meet their match when they fall for the same untamable girl. Friends become lovers having mind-blowing sex. But it's the emotional connection between the three which leads to a closeted guy's first love. Humor and tears makes this story a tasty treat. (Includes the all new story 'Island Candy: Baby News')

The Muse (Complete Series)
A billionaire businessman and a brilliant artist meet a wild, curvy girl and get their lives turned upside down. A sassy heroine is seduced by a billionaire, while an angsty artist tackles his past. Expect humor, mind-blowing sex, and emotional-fulfillment in this perfect escapist romance.

In The Moonlight (Complete Series)
A genius billionaire, a sexy rocket engineer, and an introverted curvy girl, go on a wild ride towards love. Dating the boss leads to humor, out of this world sex, and a few tears in this heartwarming romance.

'Until Your Toes Curl' contains very steamy, ultra high heat bisexual menage romance series with explicit MF, MM, MFM and MMF scenes. With lots of humor and twists and turns, each series has a not-to-be-missed HEA ending!

*****

Until Your Toes Curl

Read more now

*****

Subscribe to my YouTube channel 'Bisexual Real Talk' where I create bisexual empowerment videos:

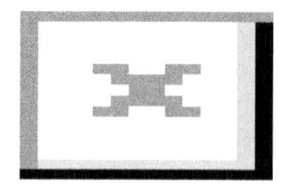

Printed in Great Britain
by Amazon